THE TOWN I CALL HOME
Published by SAPELO PUBLISHING

Printed in the USA.

Cover Design & Interior Format
© THE KILLION GROUP, INC.

THE TOWN I CALL HOME

VERONICA MIXON

For Joy O Mixon, my amazing sister-in-law who lived her life with a giving heart and faced the end of her life with dignity and grace. Caring for you was one of the greatest honors of my life.

CHAPTER ONE

MY DARLING JACKSON,

I'm not going to lie. I'm mad as hell about dying at thirty-six. For the last six years, I've tried pushing my mad away. I failed miserably. Some days my mad was so intense it mushroomed into paralyzing fear. Not at dying. Dying for me is peaceful. No more cancer. No more weakness. No more nausea. No more pain. No, I'm devastated at the realization I'll not see your high school graduation. I won't dance at your wedding. I won't hold my grandchildren.

I'm telling you this because I want you to know I've experienced enough mad to fill an ocean. This is my last gift to you.

I've lived the mad.

Jackson, you don't have to. And for this gift, I have only one request.

I don't have to ask you to look after your dad, because I know you will. I don't have to ask you to be the kind of friend you want to have, because that's already who you are. I don't have to explain the necessity of guiding your life with a steady moral compass. At sixteen, those traits are already woven into your character.

But there is a promise I need, Jackson.

You see my death as unjust. And nothing makes you more furious than witnessing injustice. Because of this, I'm asking you to accept my death as a gift. A gift you and I might not understand, but I promise you, my death is a gift.

To be truly happy and at peace, you cannot harbor anger. I'm asking that you bury your fury along with me.

This is my last request.

My one dying wish.

Always remember, I loved you from the depth of my soul,

Mom

Senator Sandra Benton handed me this letter a week after Mom's funeral. I'd carried it like a talisman, a guiding star for my life since I was sixteen. Now, fourteen years later, my father was ill and needed me, and Mom's best friend, Sandra Benton, and her son Ethan, my childhood friend, required my legal expertise. As unbelievable as it is for me to imagine, Ethan faces arson and murder charges. It was as if Mom had prepared me for this day. As if she knew it would arrive, and I needed to be ready.

I carefully folded the worn paper and slipped it into my wallet, then pulled my suitcase from the top shelf of my bedroom closet.

After twelve years in Atlanta, I was going home.

Home to Loblolly.

CHAPTER TWO

JUDGE AND SENATOR Benton had the finest home in Pine County. A sprawling, four-story antebellum with stately white columns and crepe myrtle trees flanking the front steps. The house sat on high ground, with a looming two-hundred-acre pine forest to the front and the Chattahoochee River to the back. A discreet plaque hung beside the door: JOSIAH BENTON HOUSE C.1839. A NATIONAL REGISTER OF HISTORIC PLACES.

I rang the doorbell.

Jasmine, the Benton housekeeper, answered.

"Hello, beautiful," I said. The smile in my heart slipped into my voice.

She enveloped me in a hug, then sized me up, instantly transporting me back to my teen years.

Jasmine was a tall, elegant woman in her mid-fifties, and had the kind of beauty that increased with age. Her eyes, a soft, rich, dark brown with hints of green, were framed in thick jet-black lashes. I happened to know, when riled, those eyes turned as dark as charcoal.

Even as teens, the thought of disappointing Jasmine had kept the Loblolly musketeers, Ethan Benton, me, and Jasmine's oldest son Benjamin, in line more than we cared to admit.

She waved me into the expansive foyer. "I've missed you, and so glad you're here."

I stepped over the threshold and glanced up at the stunning rotunda's glass dome. The creation, credited to an architect named Ferret, was an explosion of blue, red, rose, and amber, nestled into a cage of black wrought iron. My heart pinged with a prick of sadness at the memory of Mom standing in this foyer gazing up at the ceiling. She claimed the narrow wrought iron cone stretched its colors like a morning glory's petals in the early morning sun.

I resettled my gaze on Jasmine, and asked, "What do you hear from Ben?"

"He's on maneuvers." Worry laced her voice. "Haven't heard a word in over two months."

Two months without a word from Ben, a captain in the Navy serving on an attack submarine must mean he and his crew were on a mission. I said a mental prayer for his safety.

Jasmine squinted, sized me up. "You look a little on the thin side."

I slung my arm around her shoulders. "Maybe you'll rectify that problem."

"I expect so. I was sure relieved when the senator said you were coming. We're in a mess, Jackson. A pure-d mess."

I hadn't heard anyone use that euphemism for *pure damned* since leaving for college. And, I wasn't sure a pure damned mess was strong enough to describe the horror of Ethan being arrested for murdering his girlfriend, Grace Underwood, then burning his office building to cover his tracks,

"I'm planning to drive the senator to the courthouse, but right now, I need a few minutes with the judge."

Jasmine led me down the hall to the kitchen. "The senator's nibbling on a piece of toast. She pointed up. "Judge is in his study."

The Benton main house was close to 8,000 square feet.

The flooring, like the ceiling, was heart pine felled on Benton land and sawed to size in a small family mill.

We passed the formal living room, dining room, and library. Everything looked the same, ornate and stuffy. My dad referred to the Benton residence as "the museum".

In the kitchen, Sandra Benton, in an all black suit, looked dressed for a funeral. She sat at the breakfast table with a cup of coffee and two untouched pieces of toast. Even though her hair was neat and she wore her trademark pearls, she seemed off. Maybe it was her complexion. She looked pale, and her eyes were watery as if she were fighting back tears.

Jasmine slid the toast plate closer to Sandra. "I see you poured another cup of coffee, and you haven't eaten a thing."

Sandra jumped out of her chair and wrapped me in the same hug she'd given me at sixteen when Mom died. Only this time, I ran a soothing hand down Sandra's back, whispering, "Shhh. It's going to be all right. We'll figure this out."

She placed a palm against my cheek. "Thank you for coming."

I checked my watch. "I'd like a few minutes with the judge, and then we'll need to head to the courthouse."

"Vernon's upstairs." Sandra turned to Jasmine. "Let's send up a fresh coffee. Do you still take your coffee black with one sugar?"

"I do."

I jostled my briefcase and accepted two mugs of coffee from Jasmine.

"Will I be able to see Ethan before the hearing?" Sandra's pain was etched into her tightened cheeks and the corners of her eyes.

"I've never tried a case in Blakeley County, but generally, only the attorney has access to the accused."

Sandra kneaded the space over her breastbone as if

attempting to soothe a broken heart. "I'd worry a lot less if the trial were here in Pine County."

In an effort to shove away the fear rolling off Sandra, I sat the coffee cups on the kitchen table and ran a soothing hand over her shoulders. "I think the State Attorney moving the case to Blakeley will work in our favor. Vernon would've had to have to recuse himself as judge, and with Ethan's brother being a deputy sheriff, it just makes more sense to transfer the case to Blakeley County."

Tears overflowed Sandra's eyes, and my heart marshmallowed. In my thirty-six years, I'd never witnessed this powerful, stoic woman lose her temper or raise her voice, and the only time I'd seen her shed a tear was at Mom's funeral.

I found Sandra's hand and squeezed.

Her sad eyes pulled me under, and I wanted to promise her anything to take the pain away. "I'll see what I can do about getting you a few minutes with Ethan before the hearing."

She clutched my hand to her chest. "Thank you. I'll pull myself together and be ready to go in fifteen minutes."

I found Vernon in his study, sitting on a sofa, staring through the window at the river. I rapped my knuckles on the doorframe.

He turned and a flash of confusion passed over his face as if he'd forgotten why I would appear at his door. He slowly rose. The act of standing appeared to use the last of his strength. His mouth curved into a smile and then fell away.

I handed him his coffee. "Sandra thought you could use a fresh cup."

He accepted the cup and gripped my free hand, pumped. "I appreciate you agreeing to take Ethan's case. Murder isn't the sort Mathew Finn handles, and I wouldn't trust anyone else."

Six months ago, after five years juggling a grueling schedule as a prosecutor, I'd joined a private firm specializing in divorce law. The money, plush working conditions, weekends free, all perks of jumping to the other side of law and order had been great in the beginning. But when Sandra called two days ago and asked if I'd consider taking Ethan's case, I didn't hesitate. The Bentons were like family, and Ethan charged with murder impossible to swallow.

Vernon looked like hell. His voice quivered and the pronounced strain in his eyes gave the appearance of defeat. Small towns thrived on gossip, and more than a few believed Vernon Benton saw himself more a king of Loblolly than just a judge. Some said it with humor, others with resentment, but I knew Loblolly would close ranks and protect their own. Before the trial began, I counted on Vernon bouncing back and adopting his usual confident, take-charge demeanor.

I sat in a navy leather wingback and waited for him to return to the adjacent sofa.

"Do you think I should clear my court calendar and accompany you and Sandra today?" His usual assertive voice was tentative and unsure.

"No need. Today is a simple bail hearing. Having the senator there will be enough."

He appeared to accept my answer. "Have you talked to your dad?"

"Not yet. I'll have time with him after the hearing."

Six months ago, Dad was diagnosed with Alzheimer's and resigned as the Pine County Sheriff. He and Vernon had been friends for over thirty years, and while they often disagreed on town business, they had a mutual respect for one another.

Vernon sipped his coffee, then set it aside. "I'm sure Judge Larson will agree to reasonable bail. I can't believe they arrested Ethan." His voice cracked, and he inhaled a shaky breath fighting for control.

My heart filled with empathy, but I couldn't afford to lose focus. "I don't believe bail will be a problem. Might be pricey, though."

He laced his fingers together and leaned forward. "What's your guess?"

Vernon was a judge. He knew better than me what bail to expect. I attributed his unsureness to stress.

"A half-million, maybe higher," I said.

"I've called Jerry and set up a credit line." Jerry Sutton was the president of Pine County Bank and also Vernon's second cousin. The beauty—or some believed the curse—of small-town living: everyone in town was either a friend, a neighbor, a relative, or occasionally, an enemy.

I took out my phone and opened the notes app. "Any news from Alfred on Ethan's arson charge?" Alfred Davidson had been Loblolly's fire chief for over twenty years.

He seemed to sink into the sofa, his towering form shrinking by six inches. His gaze didn't leave my face.

A shiver of trepidation ran up my spine. Whatever Vernon was about to say would not be favorable to Ethan's case. "I called Alfred last night for an update. They found evidence of an accelerant and have definitely ruled arson. That's going to be a problem since Ethan and Grace had a public altercation on Thursday night."

I sat with this news. Ethan argued with his murdered girlfriend only hours before her death. "Where and when did they argue?"

Vernon rose from the sofa and walked to the pine desk he once told me his great-grandfather had built. He pushed his desk chair back and stood flipping through papers on his desk. "Witnesses estimate seven o'clock, Thursday night, give or take ten minutes." Vernon must have a copy of the police report.

"Where was the argument?"

"The diner."

Jesus. It couldn't get more public than Loblolly's only downtown restaurant. "Define the altercation. Verbal or physical?"

"From Caleb's reports, a verbal argument inside the diner." Caleb might be a sheriff's deputy, but he was Ethan's brother and Vernon's son. No surprise he'd shared the police report with his dad, even if it was against protocol.

Vernon flipped another page. "After they left the diner, Ethan and Grace continued their argument on the sidewalk. Ethan shoved Grace, held her shoulders against the building. Things got even more physical when she tried to move away." Vernon read the report as if it were the evening news. Someone else's son manhandling a woman on the street. Compartmentalization—perhaps that was the only way Vernon could see his way through this nightmare.

My only contact with Ethan in the last ten years was the occasional beer when I came into town to visit Dad. I'd never known my friend to strong-arm girls in high school. But truthfully, I had no idea how adult Ethan treated women. Although, no matter how I turned the facts over, bludgeoning a person to death didn't square up with the man I knew.

I didn't bother taking notes, not likely to forget details this damaging. "Did Ethan and Grace leave together after the fight?"

"No. Grace's sister showed up, and Grace left with her. Ethan left several minutes later in his car."

Vernon slid into his desk chair "There's more. Caleb called an hour ago. As you know, the State Attorney transferred the case to Blakeley County. Blakeley PD searched Ethan's house yesterday."

Dread filled my spine. "They find anything?"

"Caleb didn't have access to the formal police report, but he has a friend on the Blakeley force. Word is, they found an empty container of the same accelerant used in the fire. Caleb also said the baseball bat, believed to be the murder weapon, turned up in a dumpster four blocks from Ethan's business."

The news sent my heart racing. "Ethan's bat?"

"I doubt it. Ethan never played baseball. Why would he have a bat?" Vernon's voice sounded confident, but his sagging shoulders and worried expression were evidence he was no longer sure about anything.

"What's the accelerant?"

"Coleman's Fuel."

"That should work in our favor." The first good news out of Vernon's lips. "Every hunter and camper in Pine County has Coleman's fuel in their garage."

"You ever known Ethan to go camping or hunting? "Frustration laced his tone.

He pulled himself to standing and walked to the window, keeping his back to me. "Problem is, they didn't find the Coleman's fuel in Ethan's garage. They found it in the trunk of his car along with Grace's purse. And she had one of those home pregnancy tests."

"Positive?"

Vernon turned in my direction, his face now a blank slate. "Yes, the test was positive."

No need to say more. We both knew the odds of Ethan getting out on bail had shifted to fifty-fifty.

I had a memory caught in my mind. A conversation with Ethan a few years back. We were having a beer at Big Al's, and I asked after several high school classmates. Ethan said most were married with a couple of kids. Ethan claimed he didn't plan on having kids, ever.

My cell rang, and I recognized Dad's number, I answered. "Morning. I'm with the judge. Can I call you back?"

"What time is the hearing?" Dad's question caught me off-guard. I'd called not two hours ago to give him my schedule. "Hearing is at ten-thirty."

"Make my house your first stop after court." Not like Dad to bark orders. "Anything wrong?"

"There are things you need to know." Dad's friends in law enforcement sat higher on the ladder than Caleb's. Maybe Dad had finagled a copy of the search report. "See you after court. I'll bring lunch." I disconnected.

"Judge." Jasmine's panicked voice rang through the house intercom. "The senator fainted. I called 9-1-1."

CHAPTER THREE

VERNON AND I found Sandra and Jasmine on the kitchen floor with Sandra's head in Jasmine's lap.

Jasmine motioned toward a set of drawers by the sink. "Dishcloth. Wet one with cold water."

I did as she asked.

"I'm fine, Jasmine." Sandra pushed Jasmin's hand away.

"You didn't look fine sprawled out on the floor." Jasmine laid her hand over Sandra's shoulder and kept her from rising.

Vernon knelt. "Sandra, what happened?"

"I don't know." Sandra pressed her fingertips to her forehead. "I got dizzy, and the next thing I remember is waking up on the floor." Her voice came across a little shaky.

"She hit her head when she fell out of her chair." Jasmine folded the wet dishcloth and laid it across an angry welt on Sandra's forehead. "She's flushed, and her pulse is running sky-high."

Vernon took the wet cloth from Jasmine, blotted Sandra's face. "How long before the ambulance?"

"The dispatcher said ten minutes."

Sandra raised on one elbow. "I don't need an ambulance."

"Unconscious people don't get to make decisions." Vernon helped Sandra to her feet. "Let's go wait in the front room.

Jasmine and I followed them into the hall. "Did you take your blood pressure pill this morning?" Jasmine asked.

Sandra looked over her shoulder. "I can't remember." She wobbled.

I grabbed her arm, and Vernon and I walked her into the living room.

A siren wailed in the distance.

We settled Sandra on the gold velvet sofa. Jasmine fussed with the pillows and placed a throw over Sandra's legs.

I checked the time and motioned Vernon to the side. "If you think Sandra's okay, I need to leave. I want to talk to Ethan before he goes before the judge."

"I think she'll be okay." Vernon's gaze drifted to his wife. "This nightmare has taken a toll on all of us." The worry in his eyes crept into his voice. "The Atlanta press is relentless. Sandra can't go into her office without wading through a sea of reporters."

"Wish I could say it'll get better, but I don't see it."

"I made a formal statement yesterday. Hopefully, it'll feed the beast for a few days."

"Until the trial is over, I doubt you or Sandra will catch a break from the press."

The piercing ring of the siren grew louder.

"I'll meet the paramedics at the door." Jasmine rushed past.

Satisfied Sandra was in good hands, I agreed to check back after the hearing and slipped out the kitchen door.

I backed out of the driveway and called Caleb. "I'm at your parents' house. Your mom fainted and the paramedics are here checking her out. I have to leave, but—"

"I'm on my way."

"Okay, good. But I need your help. I didn't get a chance to get a copy of the police report from your dad." Figuring Hank okayed Vernon being in the loop, I didn't acknowledge the breach of protocol. "I want to review the witness interview notes." I turned onto Highway 80 and headed towards Blakeley.

"Yeah, okay." A car door slammed. "I'll have someone text the report to you, thanks but there were no witnesses to the fire."

"Send everything you have."

After my call to Caleb, I made a call to my distant cousin Sheila, who worked as a court reporter in Blakeley.

After spending thirty seconds catching up, she said, "I'd love to chat some more, but I'm due in court in twenty minutes."

"Any chance you're working Judge Larson's court this morning?"

Her laugh ended in a groan. "I wish. I drew family court this month. I'm craving chocolate and wine and seriously considering Xanax."

Family court, also known as divorce court, had that effect on a lot of people. "I'm going before Judge Larson this morning. What can you tell me?"

"Larson? Well, she's the daughter of a three-star general. Has a low tolerance for courtroom grandstanding and runs her court with military precision. Personally, I like her."

Military precision suited me. "What do you know about the prosecutor Abigail Morgan?"

"You're going up against the Cougar?"

It was my turn to groan. "The Cougar?"

"It's Morgan's nickname."

I coasted into Blakeley and turned right onto Main Street. "What can you tell me about her?"

"A couple of times, I worked depositions in her office. I remember seeing a Duke Law School diploma on her wall. I know she wins most of her cases, and her paralegals rarely stick around for more than a month."

"Thanks, Sheila. I owe you."

"You babysit?"

No one ever labeled Sheila as shy. "Maybe. How many kids you up to?"

"Four. All boys, ranging from twelve to seven."

She'd been busy. "I'm game as long as I can keep them at Dad's. He has a list of yard projects, and I'd welcome the free labor."

"I might just take you up on your offer."

We said our goodbyes, and I wheeled into the visitor parking lot of the Blakeley County Municipal Complex, a flat-roofed, stucco building, that looked more like a small grocery store than a county municipal complex.

I skimmed the police report and the notes Caleb had forwarded to my inbox.

The killer bludgeoned Grace Underwood to death, then burned the office building. The report stated that Ethan's home and office keys were beside Grace Underwood's charred body.

I walked across the parking lot reviewing my bail argument in my head. The keys could be explained as a spare set Ethan had given Grace. The accelerant found in the trunk of Ethan's car, easily justified as camping supplies purchased for the family hunting cabin. Both reasonable explanations for circumstantial evidence.

My biggest obstacle was Grace's purse in the trunk of Ethan's car with a positive pregnancy test inside. The test alone wasn't enough for Judge Larson to reject bail. One logical explanation for the purse could be Grace left it in the trunk of Ethan's car the night they had dinner. But what woman does that?

Did she have her purse inside the diner? I didn't know, and it didn't appear to be a question the police had asked witnesses.

I set aside the problem and focused on the overall hearing. Seemed too many holes in the prosecutorial case to warrant a conviction. Which led me to believe the district attorney had something more.

Just as important, how would Judge Larson handle the press? I planned to float the idea of a gag order. Otherwise, Ethan would be tried in the public opinion arena before I had a chance to seat a jury.

I entered the courthouse, but not knowing my way around, I suffered a few wrong turns. I finally ended up in a small ten-by-ten room with four chairs and a square wooden table. Iron bars covered the only window.

A uniformed police officer with the name tag Deputy Johnson escorted Ethan into the room. Ethan's orange jumpsuit would've fit a man twice his size.

It'd been almost a year since I'd seen Ethan, and the amount of weight he'd lost since our one-beer-meetup stunned me almost as much as his wild-animal-backed-into-a-corner expression.

I pointed to Ethan's wrists. "Please remove his cuffs."

Deputy Johnson slipped a knife from his pocket and cut the black plastic strap, the new substitute for stainless steel cuffs. "Shackles stay on," Johnson said. "And you've got fifteen minutes."

I waited until the door closed, then offered Ethan a man hug.

He stood with his arms at his side like a shell-shocked soldier, so I backed off and he slid into a chair.

I sat across from him.

He braced his elbows on the table and cradled his head. "You've got to get me out."

"That's the plan. But first, you need to clear up a few things."

"Where are my parents?" He looked around as if just realizing we were alone.

"Your mom had a minor medical issue this morning, and since today is only the bail hearing, we don't really need them here."

"Is she okay?" Of course, he'd be concerned.

"She was better when I left, but your dad insisted the paramedics check her out. I'll drive you over when you're released." I pushed *record* on my phone. Faster than taking notes. With less than fifteen minutes, I dug in. "Where were you when your office building burned?"

"In bed," he said, confirming his original statement to the police which seemed reasonable since the emergency operator logged the 911 call at two fifty-three, Friday morning.

"When was the last time you saw Grace?"

"At the diner Thursday for dinner." He rubbed his right wrist. Rolled, then stretched his neck.

Before law school, when I planned to follow Dad into law enforcement, I'd studied the science behind kinesics—the interpretation of nonverbal communication.

During my six years as a prosecutor and seven months as a private attorney, I'd honed and used the skill to select jurors, interview potential clients and their spouses, and detect lying witnesses.

Ethan's knee bumped against the table, sweat popped on his forehead and upper lip, and his butt shifting in his seat worse than a meth addict jonesing for a fix kept me from ascertaining his baseline level of nerves.

"You've got to get me released today," he whispered as if we weren't sitting in an empty room.

"According to the police report, you and Grace had a heated argument Thursday night."

His gaze flicked in my direction but didn't hold. Silence loomed and filled the room like a wet cloud. Silence, I'd learned, bothered the guilty much more than the innocent.

Ethan pulled at his collar as if the jumpsuit was too small and not hanging cape-like on his shoulders. His knee jiggled again.

"Did you argue or not?" My tone left no room for evasion.

He scrubbed his hand over his face. "Yes, we argued."

"About what?"

"Grace got pissed at something I said." He wouldn't look me in the eye.

"Heard once you two got outside the diner, your verbal fight turned physical."

If Ethan lifted his chin any higher, he'd risk a nosebleed. I'd seen the look of defiance many times, just never aimed in my direction.

"Don't bother denying it—too many witnesses." I checked Caleb's notes. "Seven witnesses claimed you shoved Grace against the wall, called her a bitch, then told her to shut the hell up." I scanned the next page of notes. "But Grace didn't shut up, did she?" I challenged.

"Grace said she was through with you." I continued reading. "Subject, that's you Ethan, answered by squeezing Grace Underwood's cheeks until her mouth puckered."

Ethan used his forearm to wipe sweat off his forehead.

I kept up the informal interrogation. "According to several-witnesses, you said, '*You don't decide when we're through. I decide when I've had enough.*'"

Ethan's gaze darted from the window to the floor. He shifted in his seat. His jaw set as if he resented the reminder of his abusive behavior.

"That's when Chet came outside, pulled you off Grace and pushed you away. Must have been quite a spectacle if Chet left the kitchen to tell you to walk it off." I closed my phone.

Another thin sheen of sweat covered Ethan's face and neck. "Sure, we argued. But I didn't kill her. I loved her." Agitation rolled off him in waves. "You've got to believe me. I loved Grace."

"Loving someone is not a murder defense. Prisons are full of men who killed women they swore they loved and couldn't live without."

"I know it looks bad." Ethan rubbed his wrist, then

pulled at his jumpsuit. His gaze, like his fingers, darted from one spot to another.

I opened my briefcase, removed a comb, a baggie holding a wet cloth, and a trial-sized bottle of mouthwash. Two nights in county lockup was enough to make anyone look like a criminal. "While you clean up, I'll run through what to expect this morning. First, you say nothing. Not one word. I do the talking."

"Just get me out of here." He buried a plea inside his demand.

"You're charged with arson and murder, which will mean a high bail. No matter the amount, do not respond. No talking. No frowning. No muttering under your breath."

He unfolded the cloth and scrubbed his face. "What kind of bail am I looking at?"

"Half a million, maybe more."

His face faded three shades lighter.

"Your father's prepared to cosign for bail."

His color returned. He swept the comb through his hair. "I didn't kill Grace."

"Do you have any idea why she would be at your office in the middle of the night?"

His hands stilled. "No." His eyes turned glassy as if his mind had wandered away, as if he were remembering something.

"Ethan, do you know why Grace went to your office?"

He refocused as if his brain rebooted. "I can't figure out what she was doing there. And I have no idea how she got past the alarm."

"Keys to your house, car, and office were found next to her body."

"I never gave Grace a set of keys." His furrowed forehead and squinted eyes were classic signs of confusion and hard to fake convincingly. I mentally filed that away for later and gave him the spiel every defense attorney dishes out before bail hearings. "If there's anything I need to know, anything the prosecutor can use against us, now's the time to confess."

He met my gaze but said nothing.

"Whatever you tell me is protected under attorney–client privilege. You need to play straight."

"Grace was pregnant." His voice cracked.

Not mentioning the found pregnancy test was to gauge Ethan's honesty. Pleased we'd surpassed the first hurdle, I pushed for more. "Was the pregnancy why you argued at the diner?"

"No."

"Did the pregnancy come up in the conversation?"

"No." He rubbed the back of his neck with the wet cloth. "Maybe. I don't remember, but that wasn't the reason we argued."

"What was the reason?"

"She called me a selfish prick."

"Well, hell, Ethan. Everyone knows the truth behind that statement."

I hadn't expected his lip tremble or the tears rimming his eyes.

He pushed his hand against his mouth as if to shove back an onslaught of tears. "I can't believe she's dead," his voice cracked.

If his tears were an act, he deserved a golden statue.

"I loved her. I wasn't thrilled about the baby, but she'd already told me she was pregnant. I knew before Thursday night. I didn't kill Grace. I loved her."

Some people confuse love with ownership, a maniacal possessiveness. I wondered if that was the kind of love Ethan had for Grace? In high school, he'd been a player. Although, I never knew him to mistreat anyone. But I had no clue how adult Ethan would treat a partner.

Was Grace also a player? Take pleasure in making Ethan jealous? "Was this the first time a fight between you and

Grace turned physical?"

Ethan gargled the mouthwash, then spit in the trash can. "I told you, I didn't hit her."

"You over-powered her. That's physical abuse." I waited until his eyes met mine. He had the decency to appear ashamed. "Have you ever hit her?"

"No." His voice turned gruff, as if the idea were unbelievable.

"Have you ever hit any woman?"

"No." His jaw clenched.

I studied him. If Ethan had a history of physically abusing women, even one claim the prosecution managed to dig up, defending him would be a tricky defense hill to climb.

Had Vernon, or Caleb or even Dad buried a complaint? Maybe that was behind the news Dad said I needed to know if I planned to defend Ethan.

A knock on the door, and Deputy Johnson walked in. "Time to go."

I redirected my thoughts. This morning, my only job was to get Ethan released and convince the judge to issue a gag order on the case.

CHAPTER FOUR

THE COURTROOM WAS near empty, and I was able to hijack a seat on the first row. I used my prime location to study the judge. Larson reminded me of Sandra Benton, tall, regal, cropped hair. Except Larson's hair was blonde, not jet black, and her eyes were hazel, not ocean blue like Sandra's. And, I noted Larson's eyes spoke with the quiet conviction of *I've seen it all, so save your breath.*

My kind of judge.

A male clerk rose and faced the courtroom. "The state versus Ethan Phillip Benton."

I walked forward. Ethan fell out of a short line of prisoners and shuffled to my side. Under the fluorescent lights, his skin looked sallow and waxy, and his Adam's apple jumped like he had a rabbit lodged in his throat.

The clerk turned to Ethan. "Please identify yourself for the record."

Three seconds of silence.

I glanced at Ethan. He stared straight ahead. It dawned on me his silence came from my order not to speak. I leaned close and whispered, "State your name."

His eyes widened. He looked from me to the judge, to the bailiff, everywhere but at the clerk. "Ethan Benton." His voice landed as a preteen puberty squeak.

The usually self-assured Ethan Benton looked and sounded terrified. Good. I liked my clients off-balance and scared. They tended to follow my advice without question. I only hoped the judge accepted Ethan's demeanor as humble.

"Ethan Phillip Benton, you are charged with count one—arson." The clerk's voice echoed off the ceiling. "Count two—first-degree murder."

Ethan's knees buckled at the word murder. I placed a steadying hand on his shoulder, waited for a beat, then said, "Good morning, Your Honor. I'm Jackson Taylor, Mr. Benton's attorney."

"First time before me, Mr. Taylor?"

"Yes, Your Honor."

"So you don't practice in Blakeley County?"

"No, Your Honor. Atlanta. But I was raised in Pine County and have personally known the defendant for over thirty years."

Judge Larson slid on a pair of black-framed glasses and looked me over. "Jackson Taylor. Any chance you're related to Sheriff Zachary Taylor?"

"Sheriff Taylor's my father."

She beamed a wide smile. "Your father and I are old friends. Give him my best."

A smiling judge who knew my father. This was better than I'd hoped. I could push for nominal or even no bail, and a gag order looked promising. My precourt nerves quieted into a steady hum.

Larson's gaze moved to Ethan. Her flat expression provided no clue of her impression.

To my right, a dark-suited woman, whom I assumed to be "the Cougar," stepped into view. Abigail Morgan's body tilted slightly forward. She rested on her toes and looked ready to spring.

The Cougar glanced in my direction. Her hungry-to-win eyes zapped any hope I had of minimum bail or a sail-to-winning verdict. Suddenly, I understood the nickname assigned to Prosecutor Morgan. As a prosecutor in

Atlanta, I'd seen the same look in defense attorneys' eyes. I called them starving wildcats hungry to make a name for themselves. I didn't often lose in court, but when I did, it was almost always to a starving wildcat.

She pulled her gaze from me and back to the judge. "The State recognizes the insidious and unpalatable nature of this crime and deems Mr. Benton a flight risk." Morgan's voice was as sleek as her navy suit. "Therefore, we respectfully request the defendant remain in state custody."

"Your Honor, that's preposterous." Genuine surprise echoed through my voice. I hadn't expected to defend Ethan against absurdity. "My client is a productive member of society with deep roots in the community. He owns a business. His father's a judge. Mr. Benton's mother is a state senator, for goodness sake. He's not a flight risk."

Morgan strode towards the bench. Her expression determined and ruthless. Her next point would be her kill shot. "The woman who burned to death in the defendant's office building, the fire the defendant is charged with starting, was his girlfriend, Grace Underwood. Grace was nine weeks pregnant." She pivoted and faced me. "Technically, this is a double-homicide."

My mind reeled—Morgan's statement was nothing more than a gut-punch tactic. A double homicide was a significant stretch on a first-trimester fetus. And since the charges against Ethan were for a single murder, the State didn't seriously consider pursuing the charge. But in a bail argument, a double-homicide claim made a decent ploy. No one walked on bail in South Georgia with a double homicide hanging over their head.

"Your Honor." My voice mimicked the disbelief screaming in my head. "Grace Underwood's first-trimester pregnancy adds credibility to my client's innocence. He is devastated with the loss of not only his fiancée but his only child."

Morgan's flashing black eyes registered, 'gotcha. "I have multiple witnesses who will testify Mr. Benton has plans to purchase a residence outside the United States."

My gut said Morgan wouldn't make a claim unless she could back it up. Judge Larson's face resembled a chalkboard without a single mark.

I hoped my blank expression hid the fact I flew blind. "Your Honor, whatever rumors the prosecution believes they've unearthed are just that—faceless rumors. Ethan Benton is not a flight risk. But if the State has qualms over him fleeing, we'll agree to a monitor."

"Your Honor, this man has connections—"

Judge Larson rapped her gavel. "Bail is set at one million dollars. I'm remanding Mr. Benton to one hundred yards of his home."

"And the monitor?" Morgan asked.

The judge locked eyes with me. "The prisoner will wear a monitor."

I stepped forward. "Your Honor, a million-dollar bond seems excessive when coupled with monitoring."

"My ruling stands, Mr. Taylor." She turned to her clerk. "First available?"

The clerk typed on his laptop. "Week of October fifth is open."

Were they setting a trial date?

Judge Larson raised a brow. "Counselors?"

Setting a trial date at the bail hearing was unheard of in Atlanta. But in rural counties with court dockets one-tenth the size of the big cities, judges took a right to a speedy trial very seriously.

Secretly pleased, I made a production out of checking my calendar. "October fifth works for my schedule, Your Honor."

A speedy trial fit my strategy—the quicker we sat a jury, the fewer days Morgan had to prepare, and the less time the press had to dig up every secret the Benton family had buried over the past fifty years.

Morgan tapped the screen on her phone. "No problem here, Your Honor." I didn't miss the look of satisfaction on her face.

I stepped forward. "One more thing, Your Honor. As you know, my client's parents are well-known community leaders. Without a suppression order, sitting an unbiased jury will be next to impossible."

Judge Larson removed her reading glasses. "A media gag order must meet a heavy burden. The rules to demonstrate need are stringent. I'm more inclined to listen to arguments regarding change of venue or rigorous voir dire. And of course, jury sequestration and trial postponement until public attention fades are available options."

She slipped her glasses back on. "If you choose to go down that road, Counselor, you'll need to schedule a time with my clerk. I have a full docket today."

Judge Larson rapped her gavel. "Next case."

Deputy Johnson walked toward us.

Ethan held up a wait-a-minute finger and pulled me aside. "You have to get some kind of special disposition. I can't stay at my house."

My head was still reeling with the realization Morgan wasn't some part-time local attorney who handled wills and divorces and the occasional child custody suit. It took me a moment to catch up. "We'll give the court your parents' address."

"No. I can't stay there either."

"What? Why?"

"I just can't." He shifted from one foot to the other as if his shoes pinched, which was impossible since he wore a pair of tan crocs that were at least two sizes too big.

"I need to hide," his voice hissed more than whispered.

"Hide?" I scanned the courtroom, and my gaze landed on the Cougar. Her satisfied smile chilled every ounce of blood in my veins.

What didn't I know?

CHAPTER FIVE

BEFORE THE COURT would release Ethan into my custody, he was required to provide an address. He refused to list his or his parents' residence, offering instead the family hunting lodge—a cabin located on the Chattahoochee River, in the middle of a five-hundred-acre pine forest, with no physical address.

I solved the issue by locating the property on Google Earth and provided the GPS coordinates. After some back and forth, the community control officer finally agreed the coordinates met the address requirements for the judge's remand order.

I hadn't spoken to Vernon, but he arranged bail and knew of Ethan's release. He'd left a message on my voicemail requesting an update. I shot him a text.

Leaving courthouse. How's the senator?

Better. Resting.

Judge Larson ordered a tether—hundred-yard radius.

Use our address. Sandra wants him here.

I sent the judge a thumbs-up emoji and drop-kicked the problem back to his son. Let Ethan explain why he chose the hunting cabin ten miles from the nearest convenience store in lieu of his parents' southern mansion on the hill.

I pulled my truck to the side door marked prisoner pick-up. A few minutes later, Ethan emerged in jeans, a faded black t-shirt, and butt-ugly bright blue sandals. He slid into the passenger seat.

"Nice flops."

He glanced down, then deadpanned, "Thanks."

I shifted my truck into gear. "Why did you say you needed to hide?"

By the look on his face, you'd think I'd just suggested we rob a bank. "Are you serious? I'm accused of murdering my girlfriend and burning down my business. The press has to be all over my parents. It'll be a thousand times worse if I stay with them. The only chance I have of escaping the press is to stay at the cabin."

"Maybe, but cell service will suck. No WiFi. Not to mention, the cabin is forty minutes from Dad's house." Which was where I planned to stay throughout the trial.

He offered a half-shrug and kept his face turned toward the side window.

I turned left onto Highway 27 and headed for Loblolly. "We have ninety minutes to sync your monitor. Enough time to swing by your house and pack a bag."

"Go straight to the cabin."

Fine with me. The sooner we got to the cabin, the sooner we had the requisite attorney–client-spill-your-guts consult.

"Use the firebreak by the River House Inn," he said.

"Why would I go ten miles out of my way? Goosehead Bridge is closer."

"Too much traffic."

"On Goosehead?" Was he kidding? "No one uses Goosehead—"

"Dude, just do it." He kneaded the three-inch space between his eyebrows.

"There's aspirin in the glove box and a bottle of water on the backseat."

He found the aspirin and dry-swallowed three.

Figuring he needed a few minutes to acclimate to his new tethered life, I opted for no conversation. I added the Goosehead mystery to my list of questions for our upcoming tell-all.

Five miles after the bridge turn-off, we rolled down the firebreak leading to the Benton cabin playing dodge the potholes.

"Walking would be quicker."

Ethan grunted his reply.

We made it to the river, and I turned right for another eight miles and arrived at a cabin that was approximately three miles from Goosehead Bridge. I parked by the back door, and we exited the truck.

Ethan found the spare key for the back door under a rock by the pump house. A blast of stale air hit me as soon as I walked over the threshold.

I stopped in the kitchen and checked out the contents of the refrigerator. Smartwaters lined the top shelf, a selection of beers—Sam Adams, Becks, Michelob—filled the second and third. A quick perusal of the pantry netted three additional cases of Smartwater, several cases of beer, and enough high-end liquor to stock a commercial bar.

Fifths of fifteen-year-old single-malt scotch and Anty gin were nestled beside bottles of top-shelf Russian vodka and eighty-dollar bourbons. Bags of pretzels and nuts, jars of olives and small onions, the kind used in martinis, were lined across the top shelf. "Looks like you'll have plenty of snacks and booze."

Ethan opened the refrigerator and twisted the top off a Samuel Adams, guzzling half.

The furniture in the cabin hadn't changed since we were in high school. Same brown leather reclining sofa, same scarred pine dining table, same god-awful ceramic duck lamps. All the furniture had been shoved to one corner of the living room. Four round tables, the kind used for outdoor weddings and parties, leaned against the back wall, along with a stack of padded white folding chairs.

The Bentons must use the place for entertaining, probably a fundraising event for Sandra's last campaign.

"I need to check in with my dad," I said. "But afterward, I'll do a grocery run, and if you make a list, I'll stop by your house and pick up a few supplies. In the meantime, you need to call your parents and explain why you're staying here."

"Don't have my cell."

"Where is it?"

"I guess it's still at my house. Not something I worried about when the cops dragged me out in handcuffs."

I handed him my phone.

He typed a short text, returned my phone.

"Your dad's expecting a phone call."

He plopped on the sofa. "I'll call when you bring my cell."

"Your parents just shelled out ten percent of your million-dollar bond—roughly a hundred grand and change—and you can't be bothered with a phone call to explain why you're staying here instead of with them?"

He reclined on the sofa and didn't bother with an answer.

I had dropped everything and rushed back to Loblolly to handle Ethan's case. Since arriving, he'd spoken fewer than ten complete sentences. And not one of those offered a *thank you* or an *I owe you, man.*

The firecracker of anger exploding in my chest must've transcended my thoughts because Ethan looked up with the face of innocence. "What?"

Wouldn't do any good to let him get under my skin this early. We had a long way to go before this case wrapped. But for now, I'd had enough of him. "I'm heading out for a few hours." I tapped the note app on my phone. "What do you want from your house."

"My cell. Jeans, a few t-shirts, a toothbrush. And bring

the black notebook in—" He clamped his mouth.

I looked up, waved him on. "Where's the notebook?"

"Never mind."

His head shake was a little too fast. We were definitely having the gut-spilling conversation tonight. "I need your house key."

"I don't have my keys."

"Is your house locked?"

He nodded. "I turned on the alarm before leaving."

"How do you expect me to get inside?"

He opened a drawer in the side table, scribbled something on a pad, and handed me the sheet. "Access my alarm company's website and use this ID and password to turn off my alarm and unlock the back door."

I had a similar setup for my house in Atlanta. My mind circled back to Ethan not having his keys and the set found next to Grace's body. "When you arrived home Friday night, did you turn on your alarm?"

"I always set my alarm."

"But do you remember setting the alarm on Friday night?"

"I was shit-faced. After the fight with Grace, I stopped in at Big Al's, had a few drinks. Don't remember much after that. But when the cops were banging on my door, I remember turning off the alarm before opening the door."

I tapped the paper with his alarm code. "Did Grace know this information?"

"No."

Do you have the same security setup at your office?"

"Yeah."

"Any of your employees have your company alarm password?"

"Grace's sister Naomi is the receptionist. She has the code and a key to the office. She opens the office in the mornings. But I've never given Naomi a key to my house or my house alarm code."

"So the keys found at the scene couldn't have been Naomi's."

"Not if they had my car and house key. They had to be mine."

"And you don't know where you left your keys?"

"I drove home. Usually leave them in the car." He downed the last of his beer, lumbered to his feet, and went into the kitchen.

I followed him. "How long have you been dating Grace?"

He opened the fridge, brought out another Samuel Adams. "Six months or so."

"And you've never given her a key to your house?"

"No." He twisted the top off his beer. "I don't like people snooping around. Women tend to be nosy."

"Did you have an extra set of keys stored anywhere else?"

"At work." He took a long pull from his drink. "I keep them in the bottom drawer of my desk. It's always locked."

Grace ended up with a set of Ethan's keys. I needed to know how she got them and why she went to his office in the middle of the night.

"Have you bought property outside the country?"

"Not yet. I made an offer on a place in the Abacos, but we're still negotiating."

The Bahamas had great fishing, but Ethan had never shown an interest.

"What's the draw to the Abacos?"

He shrugged. "I like the beach. Don't forget my phone," he walked back into the living area. "Should be on the charger on my nightstand."

I pocketed the paper. "I'll be a couple of hours."

He sat on the sofa, leaned his head against the back, and closed his eyes. "Don't use the bridge to come and go."

"Yeah, we're going to have that conversation when I

get back."

"In the morning. I haven't slept in two days."

I started to disagree, but I wanted to spend time with my dad. "I'll be here bright and early. Eight o'clock. Be ready to talk."

Ethan offered a two-finger salute and didn't bother opening his eyes.

CHAPTER SIX

MY CHILDHOOD HOME was a traditional log and stone house that better suited mountain land than the flatlands of South Georgia. It sat in the middle of a sixty-acre tract that faced River Road. As a kid, I loved playing in the surrounding pine forest, but Dad's Alzheimer's diagnosis had turned my old playground into my greatest fear.

In commercially planted pine forests, each tree and firebreak looked identical. Alzheimer's patients often wandered away. With winter approaching, if Dad wandered away from his house, finding his way out of the forest could be difficult. I planned to broach the subject of wearing a monitor alert and didn't look forward to our conversation.

I found the front door unlocked and followed the noise down the hall and into the den. The TV blared an old Jimmy Stewart western, but Dad's faded blue recliner sat empty. I stepped back into the hall and checked the bathroom. Vacant. His bedroom. Same.

"Dad, it's Jackson. Where are you?"

I peeked into my old bedroom, then the guest room, the second bathroom. Nothing.

"Dad?" My heart squeezed.

The dining room drapes were open. My gaze strayed beyond the window to the freestanding shop in the backyard—the one with the open door. My heart settled, and something inside me loosened.

I hurried through the kitchen and out the back door.

Dad stepped out of his shop, saw me, and his eyes widened in surprise. I had the unsettling realization he didn't remember our earlier conversation, only four hours old.

I pulled him into a hug. His once-massive arms hung limp at his side as if unsure of what I expected. Then he slowly raised his hands and wrapped me in a loose embrace.

It was the kind of hug embarrassed boys give their grandparents, but I didn't care. His hug felt like home. Warm and comforting, and for just a minute, I was a little boy again, safe in my dad's orbit. "It's good to see you." I held on a second longer.

I couldn't keep banging against this wall. Every time Dad wasn't where I thought he should be, or he didn't answer his home phone, or he let his cell battery die, my mind careened to the worst possible scenario—Dad wandering, lost and confused.

He extracted himself, gave an absent pat to my shoulder. "Glad you're here." He pointed to the side of the house. "My lawnmower quit this morning. I need help loading it onto my truck."

I scanned the yard and spotted a push mower, not much younger than me, sitting on a half-mowed strip of grass. "I'm on my way into town. I'll drop it at Bubba's," Loblolly's only small engine repair shop.

"Tell Bubba to call as soon as it's ready. I want to get the rest of this grass mowed before the first frost."

"Sorry, Ethan's bail hearing took longer than I expected."

Dad removed a handkerchief from his back pocket and wiped his brow. "Come on inside and have a glass of tea. I'll make us a bologna sandwich."

My stomach rumbled, reminding me I'd skipped lunch. I hated bologna. Stacked it beside liverwurst as the worst luncheon meat on the planet. "Sounds great."

I wanted to warn him not to leave his front door open when he was in the backyard. But I knew he'd wave off my concern. Remind me he lived in Loblolly, not Atlanta. Like most of the locals, Dad freely admitted there was evil in the world, just not here. Not in Pine County. Not in Loblolly.

It was true, in Loblolly, people felt comfortable leaving their homes unlocked, and it was common to see keys dangling from the ignition as you walked by a vehicle. And so far, most of the citizens of Pine County remained impervious to theft and murder. Even if Dad appeared in denial, there was no rebuttal; the evil creeping across the rest of the world had found its way into this sleepy town.

Dad poked through the refrigerator for sandwich makings, and I shoveled ice and poured glasses of sweet tea. I grabbed a bag of potato chips out of the pantry and sat at the bar.

Never one to waste words, Dad seemed unusually quiet.

Since his diagnosis, I'd scoured the internet, searching medical journals in an attempt to understand his disease and what to expect in the coming years. No one knew how long Dad and I had together, but the books said six years was average. No matter how hard I tried, I couldn't wrap my head around not having Dad in my life in six years.

I opened the bag of chips and poured them onto a paper plate. "What did you want me to know about Ethan's case?"

He kept his back turned and continued knifing mayo onto a piece of white bread. White bread, another southern staple I hadn't eaten in years. After a few more swipes of mayo, he said, "According to Hank, an anonymous caller spotted the fire."

"The caller didn't give their name?"

"Right."

Odd. In Loblolly, unlike more prominent cities, people rarely felt the need to remain at arms' length. Being the first to report a fire would award the caller bragging rights for months to come. "An anonymous caller is interesting, but—"

"And they used a drop phone."

His point hit its mark. Drop phone. Anonymous caller. Too convenient. Too purposeful. "You thinking Ethan's involved?"

He slapped two pieces of bologna on top of the mayonaised bread, then added a slice of American cheese. "Could be. Or the fire could be payback. That boy's in with some rough characters." Dad's less than stellar opinion of Ethan swam through his tone.

"Describe rough."

He cut his eyes in my direction but said nothing more.

A disturbing thought crossed my mind. "Is there an active case against Ethan?" Maybe that's why Dad was so tight-lipped.

"No." Dad's tendency to never use two words if one would suffice made conversations feel like peeling an onion, one layer at a time.

"The 911 call could have come from anyone," I said. "Kids use phones off the rack."

"Not many kids loitering in Loblolly at three AM."

I popped a chip in my mouth. "It *was* Friday night."

Dad grunted his reply.

I ate a few more chips, waited for an explanation. When none appeared forthcoming, I prompted, "Something else you're not telling me?"

"You set on taking Ethan's case?"

"I am."

He placed a paper plate in front of me, and we locked eyes. "I don't ask for much."

Where the heck was this going? "You don't ask for

anything."

"I'm asking now. Don't take Ethan's case."

His asking had the ring of a demand and strained the air between us. "Can I ask why?"

"No."

I studied him, trying to read between his cryptic words. In the space of five minutes, he looked twenty years older. Maybe it was the light or my imagination, but I got the impression Dad asking me to give up Ethan's case cost him pride. And for no reason I could explain, a sense of loss filtered through me.

I took a bite of my sandwich, slow chewed, and used eating as a delay tactic. In thirty-two years, Dad never asked me for anything. He'd supported every decision I had ever made. Even when I decided against law enforcement in favor of practicing law. Even when I chose to live in Atlanta instead of practicing law in Loblolly.

Even when Mom was sick, Dad shouldered her illness, never once heaping guilt on my shoulders for my selfish teen behavior. Choosing football practice or a baseball game over sitting by Mom's side during dozens of hospital stays or her four bouts of chemo.

Dad appeared to have no intention of sharing his reasoning, but whatever caused the sudden sadness in his eyes and the slump in his shoulders had to be significant. If he wanted me to drop Ethan's case, I would. End of story.

"I'll withdraw from the case if it's that important to you."

The lines of tension framing his eyes softened, and his entire body seemed to sag with relief.

I'd need to visit Vernon and Sandra and give them the news, help them find a defense lawyer to take my place.

Then I'd have to figure out where to go from here. Taking Ethan's case had given me the final excuse I needed to walk away from my partnership in Taylor and

Vine after only six months. A month after joining the firm, Dad called with the news of his illness. For the last five months I'd wrestled with the realization he needed me physically closer. Ethan's case had been the perfect catalyst to jump ship.

If I were honest, after seven years as a prosecutor, I'd found divorce law, Taylor and Vine's specialty, less than stimulating. Don't get me wrong, I liked the money, but the longer I stayed, the less I could imagine building a life in Atlanta. Looked like I'd have to find a way to make a living in Loblolly sooner rather than later.

Dad and I ate our sandwiches and drank iced tea without saying anything more. By the time we cleaned the kitchen, the silence had grown so thick it could be stabbed with a knife. Dad had never interfered in my adult life, and we'd crossed into untraveled territory.

But the most disturbing part of my visit came during our stilted goodbye. After loading Dad's mower onto the bed of my truck, I moved in close for our typical goodbye embrace. Dad stepped sideways and offered his hand instead. His reaction hit me as peculiar, but even more strange, was his refusal to look me in the eye.

I tried to pass it off as a side effect of his Alzheimer's, but somehow Dad's withdrawal felt personal, more akin to anger. Or maybe anger's cousin—shame. But that seemed far-fetched.

My father was the most stalwart, upstanding person I knew. Why would Dad be ashamed? It had to be Alzheimer's confusion—one of the brief personality changes the medical books described.

I tried shaking off my worry, but an underlying fear of loss, the dread that penetrated my chest and buried into my heart the day I learned my father would one day look into my eyes and not recognize me, exploded.

Nothing else mattered, not Ethan or his case, not me backing out of my promise to the Bentons, not selling my Atlanta law practice without a clear career direction. Nothing mattered but cherishing the time I had left with Dad.

CHAPTER SEVEN

MY PROMISE TO withdraw from Ethan's case played havoc with my conscience. I needed a few hours to finesse my reasons for bailing before facing Sandra and Vernon, so I dropped Dad's antique lawnmower at Bubba's, and since I'd offered to pick up supplies, I headed to Ethan's.

Dad wasn't the only person in my life who'd showered me with love and acceptance and never asked for anything in return. Sandra Benton had been my mother's best friend and all but adopted me during Mom's six-year battle with cancer.

In the summers, before Mom got too sick, my family and the Bentons vacationed together. Vernon and Dad were casual friends, but Mom and Sandra were like sisters—two peas from the same shell, Mom used to say.

After Mom's funeral, I cried on Sandra's shoulder, and it was Sandra who encouraged me to go to law school. She'd called my plan to return to Loblolly and work alongside Dad in law enforcement misguided guilt. "We live in a big, interesting world, and you're not a homing pigeon! Go fly with a few eagles before you plant yourself in Pine County, Georgia."

The only thing she'd ever asked of me was to defend Ethan, and going back on my word didn't go down easy. The ever-present knots in my stomach twisted a little tighter at the thought of causing her added worry.

My phone buzzed with a call. I recognized the number: Kendra, my soon-to-be-ex-law partner. I considered not answering but knew from experience she'd continue calling until I picked up.

"Hi." I kept my voice light and friendly.

"Caldwell's trial begins tomorrow morning at ten-thirty." Kendra dead-panned.

"I transferred the case file notes yesterday."

"This is a three-day trial. A case with millions of dollars at stake. You've deserted our client to represent Ethan Benton." Kendra's talent for laying on guilt rivaled a Baptist preacher on Sunday morning.

I inhaled a breath, counted to five.

"You cannot be a no-show in court." Kendra's tone hit two rungs above incredulous.

"You're the co-counsel. You can take over as lead."

"John Caldwell is your client. He deserves his primary to represent him. I need—strike that—the firm needs you to crush his wife's case."

Divorce court was Kendra's dream, not mine. Jumping into private practice after a gut-wrenching case had been a knee-jerk decision. But the lure of shorter hours, more money, and no dead bodies, had been enticing. But it didn't take long to face an overriding factor—I didn't spend three years in law school to debate who gets the bone china or custody of the dog.

"You'll score a great settlement." I said, and I meant it. Kendra was a terrific negotiator.

"If you hated handling divorces, why'd you partner with me?" Her half-guilt half-confused tone hit a nerve. She'd asked the same question every day for the last month. I understood her anger and disappointment. My decision to sell my interest in our firm after only six months landed as a shock.

But a month after buying into the firm, I learned Dad had Alzheimer's. Sympathetic, Kendra suggested a well-known care facility that would allow me to continue living and working in Atlanta. Realistically, a care facility might be in Dad's future, but we had years left before making that decision, and I intended to cherish every day I had left with Dad.

"Come back to Atlanta. I could really use your help on this."

I'd promised Dad I'd withdraw from Ethan's case. I could meet with Vernon and Sandra tonight and give them the news, then leave for Atlanta early in the morning.

But Ethan's case wasn't the only reason I was in Loblolly. I had over fifty cases in various stages, and going back for Caldwell's would open the door of staying in Atlanta until they were litigated, or, I found my replacement. And even though that seemed a reasonable request, it would take at least two years and I didn't have the luxury. Dad needed me now.

"I'm in the middle of something. Can I call you back?"

Silence.

"Kendra? I'll call you back tonight. We can walk through Caldwell's case and strategize." After, if she was still uncomfortable taking the lead, I'd relent and head back to Atlanta for this one case.

She muttered a few favorite four-letter words, then, "Fine. I'll be home *working* by seven." She disconnected.

The sooner Kendra found a new partner, the better for everyone. I'd reached out to a few of my cohorts working eighty-hour weeks as prosecutors. Three had expressed an interest in working in the slower paced family law arena and requested our firm's financials. With any luck, one of them would reach out in the next few days.

Five minutes later, I turned into Twin Pines Estates, Ethan's neighborhood. The current condition of the homes versus when I'd left for college shocked and saddened me. This sub-division offered a clear picture of what happened when the primary source of income dried up in a small town.

Before the mill closed, this subdivision was considered the ritziest real estate in Loblolly. The once pristine homes now appeared tired and unkempt. Peeling paint, overgrown hedges, and yards with more sand than grass appeared the new norm.

The only exception was Ethan's mini-villa, a home rivaling properties overlooking the Italian Rivera. The sprawling Mediterranean had an impressive central square tower and offset eaves. In Atlanta, even with simulated stone, the house would command well over a million dollars.

In Ethan's circular drive, a boy I guessed to be around twelve performed an impressive skateboard kick-flip. I parked on the street and stopped to collect Ethan's mail. The kid was so intent on his next trick, a clean 180 Ollie, he didn't notice me until he landed twenty feet away.

I stuck Ethan's mail under my arm and clapped. "Impressive frontside."

His eyes lit up like a Fourth of July sparkler. "Thanks."

"You live around here?"

He threw a thumb over his shoulder. "Three houses down." And then, as if he realized I might have an ulterior reason for asking, he added, "I have permission to use Mr. Benton's driveway."

"No worry. You're a good skater. Are you training for a competition?"

He grinned. "The Boardr Am in Atlanta." He studied me and must've decided I was too old to be in the loop. "It's an open competition. Purse is twenty grand."

"This your first time entering?"

"Second. Last year I didn't make it into the semi-finals." He glanced at the front door. "Do you know when Mr. Benton will get home? I wanted to ask if my friend Jason and I could practice here tomorrow. Sometimes he has company, and they park in the driveway."

Ethan wouldn't be home anytime soon, but Dad's warning of him mixing with questionable characters made me cautious of giving the kid the okay. "I'm not sure if Mr. Benton's expecting visitors tomorrow. Probably best if you make other arrangements."

The kid nodded, then laid his board on the ground and rolled away.

I peeked through the black wrought-iron fence encasing a small courtyard that showcased concrete benches scattered among trimmed flower beds. One of the beds looked suspiciously like an herb garden. Since Ethan disliked yard work almost as much as he disliked participating in sports requiring a player to sweat, I was reasonably sure he employed a gardener.

A twelve-foot hedge surrounded the house, but I located an opening near the pool and slipped into the backyard. I accessed the security company's website on my phone, turned off the alarm, and opened the back door.

A small mudroom opened into a good-sized kitchen. Stainless-steel appliances sparkled against dark wood cabinetry. There wasn't a stain or a crumb on the white quartz countertops, and I got the impression the kitchen received very little use.

I checked his fridge, found beer, three bottles of Chardonnay, and a six-pack of Coke. Other than a quart of Vavoom Vodka, the freezer was empty. I grabbed a Coke, popped the top, and went in search of aspirin to beat back a headache brewing behind my eyes.

Walking down the hall, I scanned the rooms as I passed. The entire house looked like something out of *Architectural Digest*—cold, unfriendly, a model home for show not living. A lot like my house in Atlanta, thanks to Kendra's touch.

In the master bathroom, I poked in the medicine cabinet, found the aspirin bottle, and swallowed three. After stuffing the essentials in Ethan's toiletry bag, I went in search of his walk-in closet, which was roughly the size of a small living room.

I yanked down a brown leather suitcase from the top shelf and tossed in jeans, t-shirts, and underwear. The charging station on his nightstand stood empty. Drunks rarely remembered details like where they left the contents in their pockets. I scanned the top of the dresser and a chest: no keys, no phone, no wallet. I remembered seeing a home office and rolled the suitcase down the hall.

His phone lay on the corner of his desk, along with a stack of unopened mail. No keys. No wallet. I grabbed the phone and mail, opened the drawer, and searched for something to secure the envelopes. Except for a box of ballpoint pens and a couple of paperclips, the desk was empty.

I checked the credenza behind the desk and located a box of large manila envelopes. I grabbed one, stuffed the mail inside, and then spotted a black ledger peeking from under the box.

"*Bring the black notebook in—*" Ethan had clamped his mouth shut, refusing to say more.

Lawyers are a curious bunch by nature. Some even say we have suspicious minds. Either way, I experienced no qualms flipping through the neatly printed ledger of names, dates, and sums of money—all north of five figures. My first inclination—a bookie's accounting. Horses? Sports?

I ran my finger down the column of names and looked for any I might recognize. Nothing jumped out on the first or second page, but on the third page, three-quarters of the way down, a name shot off the paper like flashing neon.

Zachary Taylor. My dad?

Why would the name of the sheriff of Pine County

be listed in a ledger kept in Ethan's desk drawer? The entry, dated three months ago, had a hefty dollar notation beside Dad's name—fifty-four thousand, two hundred forty dollars.

Could this have anything to do with Dad demanding I drop Ethan's case?

I checked, then rechecked the pages for other familiar names. Found none. Who were these people? And why was Dad's name among them? Even if Ethan was into illegal betting, Dad never bet on sports, and he'd never shown an interest in playing the horses.

A thought flickered through my mind—payoff. The age-old South Georgia lawman turns his head to illegal gambling by friends or running moonshine, or fixing speeding tickets. Just as quickly as the idea flickered, I stamped it out. Not Zachary Taylor!

My dad was the most upstanding and honest man I knew. He took pride in never using his power. He never granted favors or exceptions for his friends. Never fixed a speeding ticket. Never turned a blind eye when a friend's kid sowed wild oats. The law was the law—the great equalizer. No exceptions.

Dad would never take a payoff from Ethan.

A simmering rage crackled in my bones. Dad's voice rang in my ear—get the full story before going off half-cocked. I reined in my growing fury.

Ethan's ledger held columns for dates, names, and a dollar amount. The dollar amounts appeared to be color-coded in green, blue, or red.

I flipped the pages, determined the earliest date was close to a year ago. The date listed for Dad was June of this year. Dad went on medical leave in May. In June, Dad was no longer sheriff of Pine County.

Despite my best efforts at keeping a cool head, my blood turned hot, spreading through my veins until every inch of my body sizzled.

Dad's Alzheimer's diagnosis might not be common knowledge, but he'd made a point to tell those close to him. Sandra and Vernon knew. And Ethan's younger brother, Caleb, a sheriff's deputy, damn sure knew. I had no doubt Ethan knew of my father's illness as well.

I flipped through Ethan's mail, found his Morgan Stanley bank statement, and checked the balance. He had over a hundred grand in a checking account, and he owned over a million dollars in stock. That kind of money went a long way in disproving the charge of arson due to a failing business.

But it opened the door to a boatload of other questions. Foremost, how did a used car dealer manage to acquire a million dollars in liquid assets?

CHAPTER EIGHT

BEFORE LEAVING ETHAN'S House, I checked his black Cadillac Escalade for his missing keys. He'd parked, slightly askew in the middle of his three-bay garage, but no keys dangled in his ignition. I looked in the storage compartment, under the floor mat, and above the visor. No cigar.

Finding Ethan's keys beside Grace's body gave the Cougar another piece of circumstantial evidence. And the thing about circumstantial evidence—at some point, the jury considered the sheer volume as guilt.

His office had made it through the fire with very little damage. Checking his locked desk drawer and finding the spare set gone would be the quickest way to muddy the water.

The problem—his office building was a crime scene. No one, not even Ethan, would be granted access without a Blakeley sheriff deputy escort. I let it go, reminded myself Ethan's case was no longer my problem.

I left Ethan's house the same way I entered, locked the back door, and reset the alarm. I found the kid still practicing tricks in the driveway. If, as I suspected, Ethan walked on the wrong side of legal, I should warn the kid away.

He has visitors sometimes, the kid had said. Maybe he knew more than he realized. I waved to get his attention, then beamed my best let's-be-friends smile. "Mind if I take a look at your board?"

He rolled over and passed it to me.

"An Element, huh?" I ran my hand down the sugar maple veneer. "Sweet."

"If I place in the Boardr, I'm going to buy a Midnight Glow. Those babies can glide." He made a sweeping gesture with his hand.

"You lived in Loblolly long?"

"No, we just moved here last month."

Still too new to be on the gossip grapevine. But the weekly edition of the *Loblolly Gazette* was released today, and I suspected this would be the last time the kid skateboarded at Ethan's.

"The person you mentioned visiting Mr. Benton during the day, is it his girlfriend?"

"Maybe." He shrugged. "But whoever she is, she drives a sick red MX-5 convertible."

A woman who drove a red convertible. Easy enough to check if the description fit Grace's vehicle. I handed the kid his board. "Good luck in Atlanta."

I tossed Ethan's suitcase behind my seat, placed the black ledger on the passenger seat, and set off for the cabin. Only Ethan could answer my growing litany of questions. Number one on the list, why was Dad's name in the journal? One way or another, I'd get a straight answer. In my present state of mind, beating the truth out of Ethan wasn't off the table.

My phone beeped with a notification that Sandra Benton called while I was inside Ethan's house. I returned her call and it went straight to voicemail. I left a message, promising to call again within the hour.

I placed a preemptive call to Judge Benton's chambers, intending to ask for a quick meeting after my tell-all with Ethan. I caught him on a break.

"Ethan living in the cabin is absurd," he said, dispensing with a formal greeting. "No one has used the place in years. I'm not even sure there's propane in the tank."

Obviously, Vernon hadn't been involved with stocking the cabin with liquor and snack foods. Must be Ethan's party central. And since the pantry was loaded with high-priced liquors, I doubted propane had been overlooked. "I'm on my way to the cabin to deliver supplies. If it's okay, I'd like to stop by your place later tonight."

The news I planned to withdraw from Ethan's case should be delivered quick and fast, much like a Band-aid ripped from the skin

"Come for dinner," Vernon said. In the background, a woman said something I didn't catch. "Gotta run. I'm due back in court. Dinner's at seven-thirty."

Five seconds after my call to Vernon ended, the Bentons' home number popped on my screen. "Hi, Sandra."

"It's Jasmine."

"Sorry. Sandra called, and I just assumed—"

"Don't mention this call to the senator." Jasmine's whispering demand set off a warning flare.

"What's wrong?"

"We got another threat in the mail today. I can't reach Caleb and Judge Benton's in court—"

Threat? I tapped my brakes.

"Can you stop by and—"

"What kind of threat?"

"Same kind as always. I recognized the handwriting and pulled the letter from the mail before Ms. Benton could find it."

"Whose handwriting?" I tried slowing my words and hopefully keeping my growing impatience out of my voice.

"I don't know. No one knows." Her voice no longer whispering. "Can you come by now, before the senator finishes her conference call? You can take the letter to the precinct."

Not like Jasmine to get ruffled. "What kind of threat

did Sandra receive?"

"The kind yellow-livered cowards send." She spat the words as if they were rancid. "They cut letters from magazines and glue them on plain white paper. If I ever get my hands on—"

"What do the messages say?"

"Same thing every time—an eye for an eye, a tooth for a tooth. But this time, they added a third line—a son for a son." Her voice cracked. "You've got to come and take the letter to the precinct. If the senator reads this, her blood pressure will go sky high."

"How are the letters addressed?"

"To the Bentons. Judge and Senator Benton." Jasmine's voice just shy of screeching level.

I held the phone away from my ear to protect my hearing. "How many messages have the Bentons received?"

"This is number four." Her voice hardened and the volume returned closer to normal. "Caleb has the other three at the station. Today is his day off. He's gone fishing and isn't answering his cell. But it's probably just as well. If Caleb came to the house in the middle of the afternoon, his mama would wonder why." She exhaled a weary sigh. "And you know, that boy could never tell a fib."

Her inference didn't go unnoticed. Jasmine had caught Ethan and me in more than one attempt to fib our way out of trouble.

My gaze cut to the passenger seat and the mysterious black ledger. Was Ethan's book at the root of these threats?

I could head straight to the courthouse, find Vernon and get to the bottom of both bombshells, the ledger and the threats. But according to Jasmine, no one knew who sent the letters, and the ledger belonged to Ethan, not his dad. And unlike Vernon, Ethan was alone and only ten minutes away.

I hit the gas. "Do you have a pocket?"

"What?" Jasmine's voice indicated I'd lost my mind.

"A pocket. Do your pants have a pocket?"

"Yes."

"Fold the envelope and put it in your pocket. That way, you can keep it safe, but away from Sandra. I'm on my way to see Ethan. The judge invited me to dinner, so I'll be at the house in a couple of hours."

"I'll put the letter in a plastic baggie to protect the fingerprints."

"Good idea." I didn't bother explaining general mail delivery compromised any hope of lifting a clear fingerprint from the envelope. But if Jasmine hadn't over-handled the letter, we might get lucky and lift a print off the inside sheet. And if our luck held, maybe the perp licked the flap, and we could scrape enough DNA to make a positive ID.

Strike that. If Caleb processed the first three messages and hadn't identified the sender, the culprit likely wore surgical gloves and used a sponge to seal the envelope.

If the Bentons had received three threatening letters, why hadn't Vernon mentioned them before the bail hearing? Maybe he intended to fill me in before Sandra fainted and sent us all scurrying.

A son for a son.

Which of the Benton sons was the intended target—Ethan or Caleb? Caleb was a cop, and cops made enemies, even in small towns. But Ethan was the son framed for murder.

Perhaps one of Vernon's rulings or one of Sandra's casting votes had adversely affected one of the crazies in the world.

Of all the unanswered questions swirling in my head, one still loomed over the rest—why was Dad's name listed in Ethan's book? And why was there a hefty sum of money by his name? I had no clue, but before I left the cabin, I'd have the answer.

Just as the sun began its slow descent below the horizon, I rounded the last curve and skidded to a stop. SUVs and sedans of every make and model filled the backyard. I parked, exited my car. A quick perusal confirmed none of the vehicles had a Pine County registration.

Blazing lights offered a clear view of the inside of the cabin. Someone had pushed the dining room table against the wall and piled it high with bottles of high-end booze and bowls of chips and nuts. Each of the round tables, three in all, hosted six men playing a game of cards. Ethan stood to one side as if overseeing the action.

It didn't take a crystal ball to recognize a game of high-stakes poker. I strode up the back stairs and into the cabin.

Ethan glanced up, and his face drained a shade lighter than Sheetrock.

I raised the black ledger and pointed towards the bedrooms.

He gave a quick glance around the room, then walked down the hall with me a half-step behind.

CHAPTER NINE

ETHAN LED THE way down the hall and into the cabin's first bedroom. I shut the door and blocked his exit. I was six inches taller, and judging by his scarecrow frame, had a good fifty pounds on him. No way he'd leave this room until I had answers.

He'd changed his jeans and flops for a gray pinstripe suit and blood-red tie. All he needed was black and white wingtips and a fedora over his slicked-back hair, and he'd be a shoo-in for a fifties gangster movie. I glanced toward the closet. With no phone at his disposal, the kitchen pantry must not be the only stocked closet in the cabin.

"Care to explain your party?"

A kaleidoscope of emotions swam across his face—anger, embarrassment, frustration, indecision. He shifted in place. The room, so small it could only accommodate a queen bed and a three-drawer chest, offered him no relief from my penetrating gaze.

"What happened to us meeting tomorrow morning?" He actually appeared irritated I hadn't followed his instructions.

I clenched my fist to keep from grabbing his scrawny neck and squeezing the arrogance out of him.

"You lied," I didn't temper my voice. "You aren't afraid to go home. And you don't need to hide. Giving the court this address enabled you to continue running a high-stakes poker game."

Ethan seemed to think a staring contest would back me down. I'd never kowtowed to Ethan and wasn't about to start now. I held up his black ledger. "Any of these names belong to the men playing cards in the next room?"

His eyes served as a gateway to the debate playing in his head. I'd witnessed this particular look in the past, usually right before he tried lying his way out of trouble.

I held my index finger in the air and wagged a *no*. "Truth time."

He gave the stare-down tactic one more try, then raised his hands in a palms-up surrender. "What do you want me to say?"

I tapped the black book. "Do the amounts in this book represent money owed, won, or lost?"

"All of the above."

"What does the color of ink represent?"

"Green is winnings. Red is losses. Blue is the amount I'm carrying."

I let that sink in. The Morgan Stanley file depicting a hundred grand in cash and a little over a million in stocks made more sense. "You're banking this operation?"

He lifted his chin. "Wouldn't consider it a bad risk."

"That's not an answer."

He shrugged.

I suspected Ethan only ran the game and got a cut of the winnings. If he was the power player and banked the game, he couldn't help but brag.

I opened the ledger, flipped the pages until I found Dad's name. "So you're telling me someone is carrying a fifty-four-thousand, two-hundred-forty–dollar debt on my father?"

"Not exactly." He studied his shiny wingtips.

I stepped closer. "Define not exactly."

He glanced up, looked at the closed bedroom door. "Look, I've got to get back out there. If you hold off until tomorrow, I'll explain everything."

"I'll take my explanation now."

He cut his eyes to the door once more, then sighed. "Look, it's just insurance. A few months ago, your old man followed a couple of my players out here." He lowered his voice. "I had two very recognizable high-rollers at the tables that night.

I ran the idea around and couldn't make it work. "If Dad busted you, how are you still running the tables?"

"That's the thing—your old man didn't bust me." No doubt he saw the distrust in my expression because he rushed on. "I know it sounds crazy—"

"I'm listening." Believing would be another matter.

"Naomi was here that night. She took over the game, and I coerced your dad outside. I knew offering a cut of the action wouldn't fly and figured I was screwed. But as soon as we got outside, your dad wandered off towards the river."

I searched Ethan's face for lying tells, found none.

"I don't think your dad knew where he was. He acted weird—mumbled, walked in a circle. When I tried explaining the poker game was just good fun, he seemed to get even more confused."

I recalled the date in Ethan's journal. "This confrontation happened after Dad took his leave of absence."

"Yeah. I don't think your old man knew who I was."

In the early stages of dementia, memory problems and confusion come and go. The periods are usually accompanied by more extended periods of entirely normal behavior. What Ethan described could be true.

Ethan lifted his shoulder. "When I realized he wasn't himself and probably shouldn't drive, I asked Naomi to drop him off at home. I had someone drive his truck home the next day."

"None of this explains his name in your book."

"It's just insurance." I didn't detect an ounce of shame in Ethan's tone.

My blood heated. "Insurance?" My field of vision narrowed. A red haze crept in.

"I haven't—" He backed up a step.

I stalked forward. "Are you telling me that you're blackmailing my father?"

"No. Your old man doesn't know anything about the ledger. It's my insurance just in case—"

I stepped around the bed and backed him into the corner. "In case of what?"

"In case I'm busted." He pressed his back against the wall. "It was my partner's idea. I wouldn't have used it."

"Really?"

"Calm down." His voice now close to a whine.

"I'm withdrawing from your case."

His eyes widened. "You can't do that."

"I can, and I will."

"Jackson, I swear to you, I didn't kill Grace." He wiped his hand over his mouth. "And I didn't burn my business."

"Now, why don't I believe you?"

He scanned the room as if searching for the excuse he needed on the pine paneling. He inhaled a breath, and it was as if the air filled his spine. He looked me in the eye. "Okay, I get you're pissed and want to quit. But right now, at this moment, you're still my attorney, and anything I say is protected, right?"

I wanted to say no. Wanted to walk away and leave Ethan to dig himself out of this hole. I tried ignoring the sweat popping on his brow, the shake of his hand when he wiped his upper lip. Ethan had always been slick underneath his bravado, but in the last ten years, he'd skated into slimy.

"Think about it." His Adam's apple tap-danced in his throat. "I'd be stupid to burn my business. My take on these games is twenty percent. My dealership is my honey hole—"

"You wash your winnings through your business." Of course, it made sense. Explained how a used car dealer could have a million-dollar portfolio.

"I can't risk going to trial, but you can't risk me going to jail either."

"What do you mean?"

He jerked back as if he expected to be on the receiving end of my right hook. "A couple of people around town know about these weekly games. If it comes out, even if acquitted of murder and arson—"

"The police will delve into your business accounts. And if they dig a little, they'll add illegal gambling to your rap sheet." Which would open a Pandora's box of trouble. "Is this the only copy of the ledger?"

He shook his head. "My partner has a digital copy."

The Georgia Bureau of Investigation would oversee an illegal gambling charge, smearing my dad's good name. Looking at Ethan made my skin crawl.

"Look, I'd never lie about your dad's involvement, but my partner—"

"What's his name?"

"He saw your dad on the security tape. Jesus, your old man is an ex-sheriff. I had to tell him."

"Your partner's name?"

"Lou. Louis DeMarco."

"Is he made?"

"No." Ethan hesitated just long enough for me to doubt his response. He shifted, glanced towards the front room.

If DeMarco ran a gambling racket for the syndicate and I turned them in, they wouldn't hesitate to ruin my father.

And Vernon and Sandra held public office. They'd take a hit if Ethan's mob activity made it into the papers. No public official could survive this kind of fallout.

"I didn't kill Grace." Ethan lifted his right hand. "I swear to God."

"You'll understand if I don't take you at your word."

"I loved her." He laid his hand over his heart. "I can't eat. I can't sleep. I'm dying inside. Forget about saving me. You've got to find out who killed Grace."

I turned away.

"I don't have anyone else." His tone pleaded his case. "The Blakeley cops believe I'm the killer. They aren't searching for the real murderer. Caleb believes me, but he's a rookie cop. He's never worked a murder case." His sincere tone turned my stomach.

"Please." His lips quivered. One of the many visceral emotions hard to credibly fake.

No matter how disgusted I was, my gut said Ethan didn't kill Grace. Ethan was right. It made no financial sense for him to destroy the business that washed his dirty money.

The thought of Dad's fake poker loss buzzed in my head, but I forced myself to step back and doused the raging fire burning in the pit of my stomach.

Someday, I'd make Ethan pay for his betrayal. For deceiving Dad and forsaking our friendship—but not today. Today, I needed to focus all my energy on switching from defense lawyer to crime investigator.

The quickest and surest way to protect my dad's good name and Vernon and Sandra's reputation was to prevent Ethan's trial from moving forward. The realization that I couldn't withdraw from his case hit me like an anvil between the eyes.

To protect the people I loved, I had no choice but to solve Grace's murder.

The sound of distant thunder rolled through the air, and I walked to the window. Clouds had rolled in, dark and threatening. A bolt of lightning ripped across the sky, then another.

I turned my attention back to Ethan. "I'm going to ask you again: How did Grace get the key to your office?"

"I don't know. But if the set found beside her body had the key to my car and my house, they couldn't have been Naomi's."

Chances were high Grace either followed the killer inside the building, or she unwittingly let them in. And whoever killed Grace hated Ethan enough to frame him for murder. "Who had access to your car long enough to place the accelerant and Grace's purse in your trunk?"

"No one."

"After you and Grace argued, how long did you stay at Big Al's drinking?"

"Couple of hours."

"Was your car in the parking lot?"

"Yes."

"Did you leave your keys in the ignition?"

"Sure. No car thieves in Loblolly."

Just murderers and arsonists. But Ethan left Big Al's before Grace was murdered. "After leaving Big Al's, did you park your car in your garage Thursday night?"

"Yes." A rumbling of voices drifted from under the door. "Can we talk about this tomorrow? I need to get back to the game."

"When your car's in the garage, do you leave your keys in the ignition?"

"Almost always."

"I noticed a keypad locking system on the garage side door. Is there a security alarm sensor on that door?"

"No." He shifted in place, antsy as a kid waiting for a school bell.

"So someone could come into your garage even if your alarm is activated and not set off the alarm?"

"If they know the door's passcode, but they can't get into the house or raise the garage door and steal my car without setting off the alarm."

But they could wander around the garage, steal the keys out of the ignition, and leave evidence in the trunk.

"Who knows the passcode for the garage side door?"

"Me and my gardener."

"Your gardener?"

"Gardening tools and fertilizer, crap like that, I keep in my garage."

"How about a housekeeper? Or Grace or Naomi?"

"Just the gardener and me."

"Do you keep a list of your passwords?" A risky practice, but not uncommon in our digital environment.

"Yeah, I have a list."

"Where do you store it?"

"On my phone."

"Grace taught technology at Blakeley High School?"

"Yes."

"She has hacking skills?"

Laughter sounded from the front room, then two heated voices. Ethan started for the door. "I have to get back in there."

I side-stepped and blocked his path. "I need to know if Grace had hacking skills."

"She taught a bunch of high school kids and rarely talked about her work."

More like Ethan wasn't interested in a world he didn't share. "I'll be back in the morning." I rammed a finger toward the front room. "This will be your last poker game."

He looked at me like he did in high school when he wanted to apologize but couldn't bring himself to say the actual words.

I felt an odd rush of brotherly love for the fun-loving boy I used to know, but I pulled myself together before he noticed. "I'll leave your suitcase on the back porch. You'll find a drop phone along with your cell. Use your cell for all personal calls. The drop phone is for our communication."

"You think my phone's tapped?"

"No idea. Consider it an abundance of caution to insure a private consultation."

"Okay."

"And if you want to stay out of jail, don't make the mistake of ignoring my advice again. The next time you screw up, I'm gone."

I walked out of the room and didn't bother waiting for his answer.

CHAPTER TEN

AS SOON AS I pulled away from the cabin, I called my friend Howie Cramer, an old law school buddy and an agent with the GBI, Georgia's premier investigative bureau. I asked Howie if he knew of Louis DeMarco. He didn't but agreed to run him through the system and see what popped.

I flipped on my brights, dodged a pothole the size of a small bathtub, and set my speed to crawl. Even with high beams, I couldn't escape the mud puddles.

I mulled over the information I'd learned today, ran it through my internal bullshit meter as truths, maybes, or lies.

Ethan's teary claim of love for Grace resonated as mostly true, with the caveat—each person's definition of love is subjective.

Grace pregnant, and Ethan, the father of her child. No reason to doubt this statement as truth, especially since the Cougar confirmed the pregnancy in court. She'd have the pregnancy test tagged as evidence.

The subtle claim Ethan ran an illegal gambling ring for Louis DeMarco, possibly a made man in organized crime. A made man would give DeMarco protected and untouchable status—that truth was a definite maybe with verification pending.

Regardless if DeMarco had earned a made status in a crime family or not, players dropping the kind of cash logged in Ethan's ledger fell into a top-tier of gamblers who had Vegas–Atlantic City–Monte Carlo–Macau connections. Connections I didn't see Ethan having without a frontman.

DeMarco aside, most of what I'd learned from Ethan today, except for his need to hide at the cabin, appeared to be true.

Sidetracked by the high-rolling poker game and the fake smear campaign against Dad, I left the cabin without discussing the threats aimed at Ethan's parents. Now I had to add the possibility the dangers had a connection to illegal gambling.

My front tires sank into a pothole the size of a small pond. I'd be lucky not to knock my front end out of alignment. I dodged muddy holes another three minutes and finally made it to River Road.

If I turned left, Dad's house was three miles down. To the right and within my sight sat the entrance to River House Inn, the only hotel in Loblolly. Five miles past the inn lay downtown Loblolly.

If I stopped by the house and checked on Dad, I'd be late for dinner with the Bentons. Anyway, chances were good Dad wasn't home. Five nights out of seven, he ate his evening meal at the Loblolly Diner on Main Street.

Chet made a mean pot roast, but I suspected food wasn't behind Dad's trek into town. The honor belonged to a red-headed sprite named Sue Ellen who had worked at the diner for as long as I could remember. Her name seemed to pop up more and more in my conversations with Dad, and I had a hunch he might be a little sweet on her.

A bolt of lightning split the sky in two. A couple of seconds later, cracking thunder shot through the cab of my truck. A slash of yellow exploded against the black sky. No way I'd make it to the Bentons' before this downpour.

I called the house to make sure Dad wasn't waiting on me. No answer. I tried his cell. After six rings, a male voice informed me his mailbox was full. Dad's phone most likely sat on the kitchen counter in the charging station. I made a mental note to clear off his messages and remind him, once again, to carry his phone when he left the house.

I turned towards town and instructed my phone's digital assistant to call the Loblolly Diner.

Two rings, then, "Soup of the day is vegetable, and the pie is lemon meringue." I recognized Sue Ellen's slow drawl.

"How's my favorite girl?"

"Who's this?"

"I'm hurt that you have to ask."

"Darlin', you'll have to give me a hint. I have the body of a God—I'm everyone's favorite girl."

I laughed with a lightheartedness I hadn't felt in weeks. "You're breaking my heart. I've only been gone a couple of years, and you've already moved on."

"Jackson Taylor, your daddy said you were in town. It's been too long since I've laid eyes on you. I expect to see your face this time before you hightail back to Atlanta."

"How's tomorrow for breakfast?"

"Sounds just fine."

"Hey, is Dad there?"

"Corner booth, like always. You need him?"

"No. Just tell him I'm headed to the Bentons' and should be home in a couple of hours."

"Will do. See you in the morning, handsome. And if you're planning to get on my good side, it'll take one of those Dolly Parton roses from Zachary's garden."

"Of course. I wouldn't dream of showing up empty-handed." I searched my memory—almost certain the Dolly rose was the orange-red bush on the far right corner of the garden. I'd have to be up before sunup to sneak by Dad and snip a bud. He allowed no one in his garden armed with clippers.

With my dad-problem solved, I focused on the Bentons and the inevitable conversation we'd have over dinner. I couldn't share anything I'd learned from Ethan with Sandra and Vernon. Ethan was my client, and his admissions, even the one about Dad's fake gambling debts, were confidential.

As a judge, Vernon would respect the client–-attorney relationship and wouldn't push for anything more than general information. Sandra was a different matter.

A huff of wind slammed my truck, and my back tires slid across wet pavement. I white-knuckled the wheel and edged back between the lines. The soft, swollen drops of an early fall downpour had shifted into a full-out surge, and my wipers couldn't keep up.

I leaned over the steering wheel and searched the angry black clouds billowing overhead. Suddenly, it was as if a hundred clinking champagne flutes echoed through the cab. Ball-bearing-sized hail, mixed with the rain, splattered against the windshield. Every few seconds, the kerplunk of ice the size of a golf ball splattered against the glass.

I turned right on Oak Street, then another right on Elm. By the time I reached the end of the Bentons' long drive, the hail had stopped, replaced with sheeting rain.

I pulled next to Caleb's dark blue Ford SUV, the official vehicle of the Pine County Sheriff Department, and sprinted to the back door.

Jasmine met me, towel in hand. "Raining the devil and pitchforks out there," she said.

"Worst gully-washer I've seen in a while." I stepped through the back door and into the mudroom. Sniffed the air. "Is that fried fish?"

"Sure is. Caleb brought a mess home."

I towel dried my hair and arms, then blotted my shirt.

My jeans were relatively dry, so I wiped down my well-worn ankle jackboots and handed her the damp towel.

She hung the towel on a hook by the door. "I gave Caleb the letter. He's in the den with his mamma and daddy. Twenty minutes until dinner."

My stomach growled in anticipation. "You cooking grits with that fish?"

"Of course."

"Cheese or Charleston?" I asked.

"Best way to ruin a good pot of grits is to dump in cheese."

I followed her into the kitchen and eyed a bowl of homemade sweet pickles and another of coleslaw. I remembered Jasmine made hers with a sweet vinegar dressing. A metal mixing bowl filled with jalapeño hush puppy batter sat by a deep fryer.

She handed me a wood board with crackers, summer sausage, and two types of soft fancy cheese. "Take this tray into the den. I need to start on the hush puppies."

The room the Bentons called their den was more of a sitting area with a wall of windows overlooking the river. Sandra's collection of plants rivaled my mom's years ago. Ferns, orchids, and violets filled low glass shelving along the outside wall. Nothing appeared to have changed in the last ten years. Two oversized red chairs flanked a floral print sofa. Other than the kitchen, this was the only inviting and comfortable room in the house.

Sandra sat on the sofa sipping a martini. Her unkempt hair and sad eyes gave her a mournful expression. Vernon and Caleb claimed the two chairs. Vernon lived up to his upper-class gentlemen's reputation in a button-down cardigan and leather slippers. A full martini sat on the small side table next to his chair.

I placed the platter on the coffee table. "Jasmine says dinner is in twenty minutes."

Caleb stood, offered his hand. "Good to see you, Jackson."

I hadn't seen Caleb more than three times in the last eight years. Each time we met, I relived the shock he was no longer the tall, gangly boy with a kind face. Dad mentioned Caleb played football in high school, and I figure he must've beefed up for sports. But no matter how much weight and muscle he gained, he still had the same sharp, bright eyes. Eyes I suspected that could see through his big brother, Ethan.

Caleb walked to a small rolling cart set up as a bar. Someone had nestled a pitcher of martinis into a tray of ice. "Can I get you a drink?" He asked. "We have vodka martinis, cold beer, or just about anything in between."

"Jackson drinks scotch," Sandra said.

I joined her on the sofa.

Caleb searched the second shelf of the cart, held up a bottle of Glenlivet for approval.

I nodded.

"Soda, water, or on the rocks?"

"Neat."

He poured two fingers into a cut crystal glass. The kind of glass that weighs three pounds and costs more than I billed in a week.

"I wanted Ethan to stay here." Sandra pulled my attention from Caleb. Her voice, scratchy and raw, held the pain of a mother with a broken heart.

My heart rolled in sympathy. I hadn't prepared for Sandra's comment. I should have. I knew she'd be upset and likely blame me for allowing Ethan to claim the cabin as his residence. But using the excuse Ethan had left me no choice fell flat. So I sipped my drink and waited for the moment, heavy and pregnant with silent suffering, to pass.

"Ethan must've had his reasons for going to the cabin." Vernon reached for his martini. "How's he holding up?"

The image of Ethan dressed like a fifties gangster and

playing overlord to a bunch of gamblers popped into my head. Heat swamped my neck, and it took every ounce of strength I had to witness Sandra's distress and hear the worry in Vernon's tone and not call Ethan out for his deception.

I reined in my disgust. Ethan no longer deserved my friendship, but for now, he was still my client. "I dropped off his supplies. He seemed fine. Needs a good night's rest. We'll have our first strategy session in the morning."

Vernon sipped again. "What is your strategy?"

"To win." I tasted my scotch and bought a few extra seconds. "As we discussed earlier, the evidence against Ethan appears primarily circumstantial. And Grace's death hit him hard."

Sandra showed no indication she knew about the baby, so I assumed neither Vernon nor Caleb had shared the news of the pregnancy test. I turned to Caleb. "Jasmine told me about the threatening letter. She says she turned it over to you."

He nodded. "The GBI dispatched a courier. They should be here within the hour."

"So, the GBI opened a case?"

"Yes, after the first letter," Vernon said. "It's protocol when a state official or their family is threatened."

I considered mentioning my friend Howie, but then I'd have to explain DeMarco and decided to have that conversation with Caleb privately after dinner.

"I'm inclined to believe the threatening letters could have a connection to the fire." And the gambling. But for now, I'd tread lightly on that score.

I continued, "If introduced as evidence, the letters will throw doubt and hold weight with a jury."

I didn't plan for Ethan to stand trial, but again, that wasn't something I cared to discuss tonight. And to find the killer, I needed to investigate all possible evidence, which included the threatening letters.

I asked Caleb, "Any chance you can put a face on the letters any time soon?"

"We've processed the other three. I'm not holding out much hope the one that came today will be different."

"Sender likely wears gloves," I said.

"Here's the new one."Vernon passed over a white sheet of paper encased in a gallon Ziploc bag.

an eye for an eye

a tooth for a tooth

a son for a son

Old school cut-out letters filled the page. By the shine, they looked to be from a magazine or maybe a brochure—not newspaper stock.

I studied the paper, noted the letters cut to size and perfectly aligned. The kind of work a Type A personality would create. I turned the paper sideways, verified straight edges with no clear guidelines. No glue smears. No tattered edges. Neat to the point of obsessive. At first glance, the print on the envelope appeared to be laser, not ink-jet. I filed it all away for later.

I refocused on Vernon. "The threats could be a vendetta aimed at you personally. I'd like to review your recent cases, go back three years, see if anything matches."

"I've already checked out Dad's cases," Caleb said. "Nothing stood out."

"Won't hurt to take a second look. Will you grant me access?" I asked.

"Cases are digitalized and online. Call my assistant tomorrow, and she'll assign an ID and password. You'll have full access, but call me with any questions."

Reaching across the sofa, I took Sandra's hand. "I'd like to look over the legislative bills you've had a hand in passing. It's a long shot, but we need to cover all the bases."

"I'll notify my assistant. He'll supply you with whatever you need." Her dull eyes were no longer shiny with tears but she looked lost and forlorn or heartbroken. The look was the same.

Jasmine appeared at the door. "Dinner's ready."

I finished off my scotch and offered Sandra my arm.

She settled her hand over my bicep. "I want to see Ethan in the morning. I need to see for myself he's okay."

"Why don't you plan to come to the cabin for lunch?"

She frowned. I could tell she wanted to argue, but in the end, she only nodded. "I'll ask Jasmine to make a few of his favorites and bring them along."

The Benton dining room table could easily seat twelve, but we crowded around one end, with Vernon at the head. I sat to Sandra's right, Caleb across from his mom. The meal commenced without incident, and Jasmine, as usual, outdid herself. As if by silent agreement, we shelved further discussion of Ethan and his case. I got the impression everyone had more to say, just not in a group setting.

I wanted a few minutes alone with Jasmine and offered to help her bring in the dessert.

"You made banana pudding?" I gave her a quick one-arm hug. As a kid, banana pudding had been my favorite.

She smiled, handed me a serving spoon and four bowls.

I placed them on the counter. "I wondered if you could help me with something."

"Sure."

"I need to find someone who can spend more time at Dad's. Keep an eye on him without being obvious. My moving in is a good excuse to hire someone to cook and do more than his normal weekly cleaning."

"Colleen cleans for Zachary now. She's raising two grandkids. I imagine she'd appreciate the extra hours."

"Do you have her number?"

"Take in the dessert. I'll give Colleen a call and see if she's interested."

When I got back to the table, I found only Caleb.

"Mom's tired, and Dad insisted on seeing her upstairs.

They asked me to say goodnight."

"Gives me a chance to speak with you in private." I dished out the pudding, handed a bowl to Caleb. Unsure of how long I had before Vernon joined us, I dove in. "How much do you know about Ethan's side business?"

Caleb stared at me a moment. Until now, he'd displayed all the emotion of a cardboard cut-out replica of himself. A textbook, unflappable, cop face. Suddenly, his forehead creased, his eyes squinted, and agitation rolled off him like burning volcano ash down a mountain.

"We're talking about my brother," his tone anything but brotherly. "I have no idea what he's into, but I'm fairly certain, whatever it is, it's not legal."

Caleb issued traffic fines as a deputy sheriff, answered calls to rescue lost kittens, and occasionally jacked up a few teens for littering or skipping school. Loblolly wasn't exactly a hotbed of crime. But if Dad followed Ethan's card players to the cabin after he retired, chances were good the department suspected something was up. I couldn't rule out the idea Caleb might not be at liberty to share information outright.

"How long since you've visited your dad's hunting cabin?"

Caleb's spoon halted midair. "Six, maybe eight months. Why?"

"Does the name DeMarco mean anything to you?"

"No." His forehead creased. "Should it?'

No hesitation. Nothing in his body language to make me think he hedged the truth. Bringing Caleb into my confidence crossed the line of attorney–client privilege, but he had an in with the Blakeley PD, and I needed information. To get information, you had to give a little in return.

"My goal is to squash Ethan's trial."

Caleb's shoulders visibly relaxed. "Okay." He leaned his back against his chair. "No trial would be optimum. But if his case goes to trial, with the evidence only circumstantial, you'd win, right?"

I held his gaze, debated how much to say.

He leaned in. "I'm the first to admit Ethan's a top-rate asshat. And I wouldn't bet my next paycheck on him not burning down his business for the insurance or some other crazy scheme. But there's no way he killed Grace."

"I agree. And for reasons I can't go into, I don't think Ethan burned down his business."

"What aren't you telling me?"

I had no time to play games and made a snap decision. I needed Caleb's connections. "Ethan runs a high-stakes poker game out of your family's cabin. According to him, all the players are high rollers."

"How would Ethan know high rollers?" Doubt filtered Caleb's tone. "Not like he goes to Vegas."

"According to Ethan, a man named DeMarco is the frontman. This is where you come in. I need to know if the Blakeley PD knows about the illegal gambling. If this case goes to trial—"

"It'll be the end of Mom's career."

"And most likely your dad's as well." And my dad's reputation, but I held that close for now. "I have a GBI contact checking out DeMarco, so you have to keep this information to yourself for now. That means from Vernon and Sandra."

He nodded. His phone buzzed with a text, and he slid his phone from his pocket, read the screen. He frowned, looked at me, back at his phone. He rubbed the back of his neck. "Jackson—" He reread his screen a third time. "I don't know how to tell you this."

"What is it?"

"They've identified the fingerprints on the murder weapon."

"On the bat?"

"Yes."

IDing the fingerprints on the murder weapon could prove Ethan's guilt or go a long way in proving his innocence. My case was about to be blown wide open. I sucked in enough air to pop a lung, then blew it out long and slow. A ridiculous technique I'd read minimized stress. It never did anything but piss me off for failing to work. "Okay. Who's the lucky winner?"

Expecting Ethan, but hoping for a name I didn't know, it took a minute for Caleb's words to sink in. "What'd you say?"

"They have a positive match on the fingerprints—Zachary Taylor—your dad."

"My dad's fingerprints are on the bat?" The words cut me like a knife fresh off the sharpening belt.

Caleb stared at his phone as if he couldn't believe what he was saying. "This can't be right." He held out his phone to let me read his screen, but my vision blurred, and the letters swam together.

Dad's fingerprints on the murder weapon. Was that behind the Cougar's smirk in court? She thought she could bring down a senator's son and a thirty-year lawman, make a name for herself, and graduate to federal court.

This had to be a mistake—a mix-up at the lab. No way, not even on the coldest day in hell, would my dad have bludgeoned a woman to death.

Footsteps sounded to my left, and I turned to see Vernon walking into the dining room. He stopped, looked from me to Caleb.

"What's wrong?" he asked. His voice round and resonant, like he spoke into an empty jug.

I couldn't find enough air capacity to answer.

CHAPTER ELEVEN

I THANKED VERNON FOR the dinner invitation, claimed Dad needed me, and excused myself. Which was true—Dad *did* need me. He just didn't know it yet. I bolted so fast, I didn't even say goodbye to Jasmine.

Outside, the rain had eased into a steady drizzle, and I sped through town. Questions tumbling in my brain like rocks in a cement mixer. How had Dad's fingerprints ended up on a murder weapon? Was he framed?

Every client I represented on murder charges screamed the frame excuse. In my five years as a defense attorney, the age-old reason had never proven true.

But this time, something sure as hell happened.

Zachary Taylor was a Matt Dillon–Andy Griffith kind of lawman who had served Pine County for thirty years. So well liked, in twenty years of county elections, no one had bothered to run against him. I couldn't imagine someone holding a vendetta against Dad so intense they framed him for murder.

My mind searched for other possibilities. Nothing came to mind except the fake poker debt in Ethan's ledger and the mysterious Lou DeMarco. In reality, a mob-connected criminal had resources to pay a lab worker to frame Dad. But why? According to Ethan, Dad was clueless about DeMarco's poker racket.

But was he? Maybe Dad had uncovered DeMarco's racketeering and confronted him. Was that the reason

Dad insisted I drop Ethan's case?

Even if I could buy the far-fetched theory that DeMarco framed Dad, it made no sense for DeMarco to burn Ethan's business. And what about Grace? Made even less sense he'd kill Grace, a high school teacher.

I rewound my thoughts, focused on the basics—motive, means, and opportunity. Ethan admitted Grace's sister Naomi assisted him with the poker games, maybe Grace was involved as well.

There had to be a logical reason Ethan's girlfriend went to his dealership in the middle of the night. After I questioned Dad about the bat, Naomi was next in line. Now I'd have to comb through Dad's old cases as well as Vernon's.

I instructed my phone's digital assistant to send Caleb a text.

Please keep the fingerprint news quiet until I have a chance to talk to Dad.

How old were Dad's prints? Days, weeks, or months old? Please, God, let them be months and not days. I sent another text to Caleb.

Can you get a copy of the lab report?

I hit River Road and found it all but desolate. The two-lane highway followed the gentle bends of the Chattahoochee River, and other than a few slow snaking curves, the road was a straight shot. I picked up speed and headed for home.

Vernon and Sandra had received four letters threatening one of their sons. Which son was still a mystery, but my bet was on Ethan. And now, someone had framed Dad for murder.

Could the same person be responsible for both?

Death by bludgeon was a crime of passion—betrayal, hate, love gone wrong. No matter how hard I tried to make it stick, the theory DeMarco destroyed Ethan's business and brutally murdered his girlfriend didn't gel.

One thing I knew for sure—Dad wasn't the killer.

Rain rapped on the truck's roof like the restless drum of fingers on a tabletop. Long stretches of shiny blacktop closed in and brought more unsettling thoughts to mind.

Dad hadn't been himself for months. He'd seemed confused when I arrived and surprised to see me, even though less than four hours before I'd told him of my arrival, and confirmed my visit once again when he called me before the bail hearing.

The last time I visited, during the retelling of a favorite fishing story, Dad blanked at the ending. He'd tried covering his embarrassment with anger, but in the end, his eyes filled with tears, and he admitted his memory had begun to fail. The scene hit me hard. Other than my mom's funeral, I'd never seen Dad cry.

But the final straw broke last Thursday. During our weekly phone chat, Dad quietly confessed to getting lost on his way home from Blakeley. A route he could drive blindfolded. The guilt of waiting too long to return home had me hit with tsunami force.

I reeled with that same guilt now. I should've never accepted Dad's claim all was well. I had ignored the voice in my head shouting, *don't believe him, it's a lie*. I should have faced the inevitable, dropped everything, and rushed home to cherish every day I had left with the man who'd lived his life as a model for his only child.

A flash of chrome registered. I checked my rearview mirror, then moved to the right lane and slowed. A blue Chevy Tahoe parked on the side of the road was the same color and make as Dad's.

I made a U-turn, pulled behind the vehicle, and checked the license plate. The word SHERIFF centered on the bottom of the tag's frame confirmed my suspicion. I remembered my earlier unanswered call to his cell. It looks like I was right—he forgot his phone when he left the house.

I grabbed a flashlight out of the storage compartment, ignored the pelting rain, and approached the driver's side. I flashed my light through the window. Empty. Nothing in the backseat but an old sweater and Dad's brown tackle box. I opened the driver's door, his keys dangled in the ignition.

I scanned my surroundings. Pine forest lined both sides of the road. "Dad," I yelled. "Dad, where are you?"

I climbed inside his truck and turned the key. Nothing. I checked the gas gauge—empty.

Didn't make sense for Dad to start walking home in the rain. He didn't need a cell phone to call roadside assistance. I pushed the red button above his rearview mirror.

"On Star, how may I help you?"

"This is Jackson Taylor. This vehicle belongs to my father, Zachary Taylor. The truck appears abandoned. Has he called roadside assistance?"

"Let me check." A few seconds of dead air, then, "I show no record of a request for service. Would you like me to contact the police?"

"No, thanks. I'll make the call." I disconnected.

I hadn't passed Dad on my drive from town, so he didn't walk for help in that direction. No houses on this stretch of road until the River House Inn. He wouldn't walk seven miles home in the rain.

I called Caleb.

"I found Dad's truck on River Road. Mile Marker 98. He's not around. Can you send a deputy to the house and see if someone picked him up or if he walked home?"

"Will do."

"And can you check the River House Inn? He could be there. I have my mobile."

"I'll let you know what we find."

If Dad was walking home, the deputy would pick him up. Along this stretch of road, the river was less than a mile due west. An unexplainable urge to search the forest overcame me. Over the years, I'd learned the value of embracing instinct.

Dad's truck had a built-in storage box attached to the cab. It held a floodlight and a rain slicker with an oversized hood. I made use of both.

Sloshing through the ravine separating the road from the commercial forest, I couldn't shake the feeling time was critical. My heart pounded harder. Not faster—just harder and louder, making me aware of its beat in more than just my chest.

I walked into the forest. "Dad?" Inside the tree line, the towering trees silenced my voice. "Dad, it's Jackson. If you hear me, yell my name." There were hundreds of acres of pines. I'd need a megaphone and a full search team to cover this space at night.

News reports of older adults wandering away from home filled my head. Too often those incidents ended in hospitalization or death. I had to find him.

"Dad?" I yelled. "Zachary Taylor." I stumbled over a limb but righted. "Dad, it's me, Jackson."

After twenty minutes of searching with no luck, my worry turned close to panic.

Then I heard, "Jackson?"

Caleb's voice.

I swept the light behind me. A tall shadow, wearing a bright yellow parka, jogged in my direction. He carried a flashlight in one hand and a bullhorn in the other. I'd never been so thankful to see anyone in my life.

"Jenkins called," he said. "Zachary's not at home, and no one at the inn has seen or heard from him. Jenkins followed River Road back to your truck. No sign of him walking."

Hope plummeted, sitting like a two-pound sinker in my gut. I used the floodlight to scan a one-eighty. "If he walked into the forest, he'd likely be on this side of the road."

"Why would he come into the forest at night?" Caleb looked back towards the road and Dad's truck.

"I've no idea, but he's not at home and not on the road. And I have a bad feeling in my gut."

Caleb turned a three-sixty. "Zachary has problems with his memory, but he's not that far gone."

Six years was the average lifespan after someone was diagnosed with Alzheimer's, but not a guarantee. Some patients lasted less than two years. After his diagnosis, Dad didn't tell anyone for over a year. Not even me. "I think Dad's disease might be further along than we suspected."

"Best if we check both sides of the road." Caleb unsnapped the radio from his belt. He asked for two more deputies to assist Jenkins with a grid search on the east side.

With that settled, Caleb and I moved an arm's length apart. I swept the twenty feet in front of us with the flood light, and Caleb used the bullhorn to call for Dad. After each call, we stopped, waited for a response. After a few seconds of silence, we walked another five yards.

"Zachary Taylor?" Caleb spoke clear and even into the bullhorn. "If you hear me, call out."

We walked a steady pace through the forest, sweeping the floodlight, calling Dad's name, listening for his response. We must've repeated the drill a hundred times. Other than the occasional hoot of an owl and the soft rain falling through the trees, we didn't see or hear any sign of Dad.

My pulse should have been out of control, but it wasn't. I was afraid and anxious and as close to panicked as I could remember, but my head remained clear and focused.

I'd find him. He'd be okay. His mind might be confused, but Dad had great instincts. He'd never try to cross the river.

My blood pressure kicked up a couple of notches. It

had to be hitting two hundred by now. Who was I kidding? I was no longer sure of anything other than I had to find Dad.

Caleb stopped walking. "There's no guarantee Zach's not turned around and walking north or south, parallel to the river, or in the opposite direction. We need a full team and a search plan."

"Radio for backup."

"I can call in neighboring counties at sunup. Rain should ease up by then."

"We can't wait. I have a strong feeling about this. Dad would never leave his car on the side of the road with his keys in the ignition and the doors unlocked. He has to be confused. He may not recognize where he is."

Caleb removed his hat, shook off the water, and slapped it back on his head. "Zachary may be confused, but he knows every inch of this county like the back of his hand."

"Not anymore." I fought to restrain my growing dread. "Last week, he got lost coming home from Blakeley.

"From Blakeley?" Disbelief shot through his voice. "There's only one left turn between Blakeley and Loblolly."

I bit back a cutting response. Alzheimer's was complicated and not easily understood, especially by those left untouched by the disease.

"Dad's memory has holes. I think of them as empty pockets. He'll slide into one of the pockets and stay for a few minutes, sometimes hours. Eventually, he finds his way out and is normal again." So far, Dad had always found a way to crawl out, but one day he'd be stuck in one of those empty pockets for the rest of his life.

"He pretends things are fine," I said. "Even when they're not. Unless you pay close attention to what he says and how he says it, you think he's okay, maybe a little off, but nothing to worry about. He's a master faker, pretends everything is okay. But deep inside, he knows something is wrong."

I swept the light ninety degrees. "Dad? Dad, if you hear me, please answer." Honestly, I wasn't sure what Dad thought, how he felt about his illness. That's why I needed to come home. I needed to understand what was happening firsthand.

Caleb and I continued taking turns. Caleb yelling into the bullhorn, me screaming at the top of my voice until I was too hoarse for my words to carry more than five yards.

This search wasn't working. We had to do more. I didn't want to wait seven hours until sunrise to extend our reach. "Do you know anyone with a search dog?"

"Brenda Spears, one of our deputies, raises hound dogs. She runs them through trials for sport. We don't have much call for manhunts in Pine County."

"Can you call her? Ask if we can borrow her best sniffer."

Caleb placed the call, and Brenda agreed to meet us. By the time we made it back to the truck, she'd arrived with two bloodhounds. "I need Zachary's scent. A piece of clothing, an old shoe."

I grabbed the sweater from the backseat of Dad's truck. "Will this be enough?"

"Should be," Brenda accepted the sweater and stuck it beneath her raincoat. "I'll need something else for the second dog."

I fished a ball cap from under the seat. "Can you use this?"

"We'll give it a go.'

A thought dawned. I checked under the driver's seat, the glove box, then the extra storage compartment.

"What are you looking for?" Caleb asked.

"Dad's backup pistol. He never leaves home without it."

Caleb scanned the forest, then met my gaze. "He'll have it with him. It's an ingrained habit with the old guys to carry a weapon on or off duty."

I knew it to be true and read Caleb's expression loud and clear. I should've confiscated Dad's guns as soon as he told me of his diagnosis. But taking a weapon away from a thirty-year lawman was easier said than done.

According to the textbooks, Alzheimer's patients began wandering in stage six. The thought of a gun in the hands of a patient in stage six sent a cold line of trepidation down my spine. My brain argued—Dad still drove, he communicated well, he cared for himself. All the literature said those abilities disappeared by the sixth stage. But the medical journals also warned that while each patient exhibited similar symptoms, each developed differently.

Brenda knelt beside her dogs and encouraged them to smell Dad's sweater. "Don't worry, we'll find Zachary," she said.

"You've worked with my dad?"

She raised to standing. "I've had the pleasure of serving under your father for the past eleven years."

"He has Alzheimer's." I had to make sure she understood what we were facing. "And sometimes, he's not himself."

Even in the cover of darkness, I saw Brenda's face soften. "Yes, I know."

"He could be scared or paranoid. Not understand why people are following him. He could be hiding. Alzheimer's patients can turn combative without warning, and I'm fairly certain he's armed." I spit out my fears like gunfire.

She placed a hand on my forearm. "I'm a trained negotiator, and one of my team members is a paramedic. If we find him, he'll be in good hands."

The news someone on her team had medical training soothed my raw nerves. Even though Brenda might be a trained negotiator, I doubted her training covered a subject with Alzheimer's. But finding Dad trumped everything else, and I'd deal with rescue fallout after he was safe. "Just be careful. If you find him, he may not remember you. Call me, and I'll come."

"Okay." She pointed to the larger of the two dogs. "You and Caleb take Red. He's my best sniffer. I'll take Bluebell and work with the team covering the east side." The dogs stood by her side, their ears perked, a slight quiver in their bodies was their only sign of excitement. "If Red sniffs out Zachary's trail, he'll give a bark alert."

Brenda held Red by the collar and allowed the dog another long sniff of Dad's sweater. Then she motioned towards the forest and gave the command. "Search."

She handed the sweater to Caleb. "Now you give him the command."

Caleb held the sweater close to Red's nose, let him sniff, then, "Search." He added Brenda's hand signal. "Search!"

Red lifted his nose in the air

Brenda released her hold on the collar, and Red promptly stuck his nose to the ground, worked in a zig-zag, then a circle.

"Let him take the lead," Brenda said. "The weather poses a little obstacle, but Red and Bluebell work well in the rain."

She handed a plastic bag to Caleb. "Keep the sweater inside the plastic to protect it against the rain and transference of your scent. If Red needs a refresher, he'll stop and nudge your leg. Let him sniff the sweater again, then repeat the search command."

Red worked a tight circle, constantly scenting the ground. He swept a wider ring, then wider still, moving further into the forest. Forty yards inside the trees, he came to a skidding halt, bayed a long howling *rooooo*, and took off at a full run.

"He's on to something," Caleb yelled over his shoulder.

It took everything I had to match their pace and keep the floodlight aimed in Red's direction. With every step, I prayed for a miracle.

CHAPTER TWELVE

THE RAIN TURNED heavier, but Red moved on without complaint, showing a single-minded tirelessness rarely seen in humans. Tonight, I shared the bloodhound's steadfast determination.

I tightened the hood of my rain parka and focused on keeping Caleb and Red in the floodlight's beam. We quickly traversed the small shrubs and tall weeds surrounding us, but the occasional fallen tree required more maneuvering.

By now, Dad had to be cold and wet and tired, but most of all, scared. With his rain gear in the truck, if he wore a jacket, it had to be a light all-weather. Not ideal for a heavy September rainstorm.

Nose to the ground, Red angled sideways and headed down a slope. Until now, we'd traveled a ridge running parallel to the river, but this slight drop in terrain meant we were altering our course, shifting closer to the bank.

The water was fast this time of year, and the rain had turned the moss slippery. I hoped Dad had remained on high ground, didn't wander too close to the river, or worse, try to cross it.

Over the past few hours, the wind had changed and blew out of the east. The rain continued in a steady downpour, numbing my gloveless fingers. After stomping through an untold number of mud puddles, my drenched leather jackboots offered little protection against the descending temperature.

Red halted, sniffed the air. He ran back to Caleb and nudged his leg.

Brenda had said that meant Red needed to refresh his scent. Caleb removed Dad's sweater from the plastic bag and granted the dog his request.

I used the few seconds of downtime to check the time. We'd been in the forest for nearly three hours and almost two with Red. He'd alerted with strong bays three times, but we'd yet to see a single physical sign of Dad.

Red pulled away and began his scenting routine. He sniffed a tight circle, widened his territory and sniffed a few more rings, then lifted his nose and headed off. He scampered fifty feet, stopped, and howled a long eerie bay.

Caleb came alongside and pointed at the mud. "Looks like a boot print."

We were definitely closer to the river. The ground had softened, and if this print belonged to Dad, we'd finally be able to follow his tracks. I swung the floodlight a one-eighty.

The ground near us was covered in pine straw and gave up no more prints. But at the base of a nearby tree, pinecones were swept aside as if someone had made a clearing to sit. Red beelined to the spot. His entire body trembling with excitement.

During my last few visits, even though they were for only a couple of hours each, I'd noticed Dad losing his balance a few times in the yard. He always managed to catch himself before hitting the ground, but I knew he'd fallen at least once because a few months back, Sandra Benton emailed with the news Dad slipped, busted his head, and needed stitches.

I searched the ground surrounding the swept area, checked the bushes, and looked for any indication Dad had taken a spill. I couldn't imagine him traveling over this rough terrain, a carpet of pinecones three layers deep, without a flashlight.

Red concentrated on the tree trunk for another few seconds, then set off at a fast clip. An earthy smell rode the wind and made me think Red led us west, closer to the river. But with the rain and the zig-zag path we were following, I couldn't be sure. Then, we hit the turn-around.

Tree farmers maintained the strip of land between the forest and the river as a turning lane for their heavy equipment.

If lost, it made sense Dad would find the river and walk the mowed bank. Following the river south would eventually bring him to the River House Inn. Another three miles past the inn, he'd be home. If he walked north, he'd end up in Loblolly.

Thanks to the heavy rain, the ground near the river would be soft and muddy. Muddy footprints would speed up our tracking.

Red alerted again and broke into a full run. He shot Caleb a glance over his shoulder as if to say, *get a move on, human.*

Up ahead, I recognized three groups of trees. I knew this area.

Red bayed again.

I hurried to catch up with Caleb. "Dad fishes this area. He may have holed-up here. If he's confused, we could startle him. An animal is less likely to spook him."

"What are you suggesting?"

"Dad has a gun. I'm suggesting we not get shot. Let's hang back and let Red find Dad." I flipped the floodlight off. "Let's approach with your flashlight, it'll appear less intimidating."

"Lost people usually take the path of least resistance," Caleb said. "I'm betting your dad is walking the firebreak, not the riverbank."

"You could be right. But if he's lost, stress will bring on more confusion. He may be disoriented. And we have considered how a man who once knew every tree, path, and turn of this land will handle the realization he's lost." Lately, Dad grew agitated when he didn't understand something he thought he should know.

"He's beginning to have trouble with balance," I added. "And he needs a hearing aid but he's too stubborn to see a specialist."

We managed to keep the shadow of Red in our smaller scope of light. He paused, eagerly sniffing a drainage pipe running alongside a firebreak.

I remembered learning something called the chimney effect in school. The air would rise in open ground, dispersing Dad's scent above the tree line in multiple directions. Would that confuse Red?

I tried envisioning which way Dad might head from here. One of his favorite fishing spots was in this general area.

Red left the pipe and moved into an area of heavy brush. My eyes adjusted to the lesser light, and I searched for signs Dad passed through—footsteps or beaten down weeds. I found a bit of torn clothing in a stand of briars and a few bent and broken branches. But I had no way to know if the scrap of clothing was Dad's. I couldn't recall the shirt he'd worn at lunch and he could've changed before leaving for the diner. Maybe Sue Ellen would remember his clothes. It was late—

Red alerted. I rushed forward. Red sniffed a muddy trail with a row of solid footsteps. My heart soared with relief.

Within five minutes of walking the new mud-sucking path, my quadriceps quivered with fatigue. After three hours in the woods, Dad had to be exhausted.

The path leveled and dumped us in front of the river. Red scurried down the bank. He sniffed a stand of weeds before moving to a group of river rocks washed onto the bank. After a few seconds, he circled back to the weeds, then he sniffed the rocks again. He looked up at Caleb and whimpered before walking to the river's edge to satisfy his thirst.

"I think he lost your dad's scent."

I flipped on the floodlight and checked the bank. Ten yards down, I recognized a single pine tree with two trunks. It was a spot I remembered fishing as a boy. Dad called it Double Tree.

"Dad?" I called. "Dad, it's Jackson. If you can hear me, yell out."

Nothing.

Caleb walked to the water's edge and knelt beside Red. He offered another sniff of Dad's sweater.

After refreshing his scent, Red worked the area near the bank, scenting the rocks again, then a weedy area a few feet away. But he failed to alert. I had no idea if all the rain had finally affected Red's ability to track. And if Dad walked in the river, it could explain why Red lost his scent.

I pointed the floodlight towards Double Tree. "Dad fishes the area near that forked tree."

We trudged forward. Caleb encouraged Red to work the base of the pine tree, and I walked the area's perimeter searching for muddy footprints, broken branches, any sign of Dad.

"Maybe he recognized his fishing spot and backtracked or angled back towards his truck," Caleb said.

I tried to see the area as Dad would see it. The trees, the rocks, the dark cloudy sky. The open stretch of grass, peppered in muddy turning ruts made by the commercial equipment.

Dad getting lost in these woods would be as frightening and frustrating as getting lost in his own home. Based on what I'd discovered during my short hourlong visits and weekly phone calls, if Dad became confused, he either got angry or shutdown. The books warned that lost Alzheimer's patients often wandered in aimless circles becoming even more confused.

Red nudged Caleb's leg asking for another refresher. Caleb offered the now soggy sweater. "Search, boy. Search for Zachary."

We followed behind Red, who seemed to be trotting with renewed purpose back toward the river. He clambered over a pile of rocks, veered north, then stopped. He bayed a short alert and took off. We struggled to keep him in our sights. A few yards later, he stopped, giving a stronger alert.

Caleb and I ran to his side.

"What've you got, boy?" I squinted, tried to make out a definite shadow in the distance.

Red took off, moving so fast, we lost him in our beam. I had no choice but to use the floodlight. I flipped the on switch and swept the area.

An outline of a backhoe and a tractor with an attached mower came into view. The tractor had an enclosed cab—the perfect place to wait out a rainstorm. I cut my light.

Caleb started for the tractor.

I grabbed his arm. "No." The thought of Dad's firearm now uppermost in my mind. "Dad won't shoot a dog. But if he's confused and afraid, his instinct will be to protect himself. I can't be sure he'll extend the same courtesy to a human."

Caleb pointed right. "Let's use the trees as cover and get as close to the tractor as possible."

We jogged into the tree line, fast-walked until we pulled up even with the mower. I could just make out the shadowy outline of Red sniffing around the backhoe. He wasted no time working his way to the cab of the tractor, moved past the steps, then returned and sniffed the bottom stair. Smelling the air, he moved on again. A few seconds later, he returned to the running board and gave a strong alert.

"I think Dad's inside the cab."

Caleb glanced up at the sky. "That's where I'd wait out this rain."

"Stay here." I walked to within ten feet of the tractor. "Dad?" I yelled. "It's Jackson. Time to go home."

Red bayed again.

I turned to Caleb. "Call off Red."

"Red," Caleb patted his thigh. "Come."

Red sprinted to Caleb's side, and he gave the dog an entire body rub. "You're a smart boy."

The image of Dad, exhausted and scared, flashed in my head. I couldn't be sure he was inside the cab, but from Red's reactions, he had been at some point.

"Dad?" I walked closer, giving my voice a better chance of penetrating the vehicle without yelling. "It's Jackson. We need to go home."

No response.

I stepped onto the running board, crouched, and peeked through the side window. Both the driver and passenger seats were empty, but on the passenger side, there was a dark shadow on the floor. It could be just a heavy tarp or a box, or it could be a huddled body.

Dad wouldn't hunch down on the floor—unless he was hurt.

I cracked the door. "Dad."

"Stay away."

I recognized his gravelly voice, and my heart catapulted into my throat.

I inhaled a deep breath in an effort to keep my voice friendly and even. "Hey, Dad, it's Jackson. I'm here to take you home."

No response.

I slid the door another two inches, just wide enough to

stick my head inside the cab. "Dad?"

A shot rang, and a *swoosh* of air whizzed above my head.

"Stay. Away."

I jerked back and ducked. "Dad, it's me, Jackson."

Another bullet whizzed past no more than a hair's breadth from my scalp. I half-jumped, half-fell off the steps, and hot-footed back to the tree line.

"You okay?" Caleb asked.

"Warning shots over my head." At least I hoped that was Dad's intent.

"You think he knew who you were?"

"I couldn't tell."

I tried sucking air into my lungs in the hopes of restarting my heart. I ended up bending at the waist, gulping air as if I'd just completed an Olympic marathon. Not in a million years would I have believed I'd ever dodge bullets shot by my father.

"Did Zachary seem confused?"

"No idea. Dodging his bullets took precedence over assessing his mental capacity. But since he shot at me, I sure as hell hope he's confused."

Red whimpered and leaned against Caleb's leg. He'd completed his task and wanted to go home.

"Now what?" Caleb asked.

I scanned our perimeter, assessed the tractor, came up with nothing. "I have no idea. But in case Dad's watching, let's move deeper into the forest. I'd just as soon not give him another clear shot."

Caleb's phone buzzed with a call. He answered. "Yeah, Brenda, we found him. He's holed up in a tractor parked near a firebreak."

Brenda said something I didn't catch.

"Zachary fired the shots. Give us a few minutes to make a plan, and I'll call you back." He disconnected. "Brenda and her team will wait at your dad's truck."

I mulled over our situation. "I don't see a safe way to

force him out of the cab without risking a bullet."

Caleb appeared to have a sudden case of lockjaw.

I mentally swept through the stages of Alzheimer's. The first stage was no impairment, then mild decline, slight decline, moderate impairment, moderate severe decline, severe, and the last stage was very severe decline. Until five minutes ago, I'd believed Dad was somewhere between stages two and three, but now I wasn't so sure.

The next stage was severe decline. From this encounter, that stage seemed a more accurate level of Dad's condition. If that were the case, he'd remember the faces he saw daily more than a family member who visited sporadically.

Now that Dad had retired, his daily outings were limited to the occasional trips into town, his cleaning lady, and his nightly trek into the diner.

"Sue Ellen," I said.

"What about her?"

"Dad sees Sue Ellen almost every day at the diner. And he likes her. He might recognize her, and even more important, respond favorably."

Caleb shot me the same slack-jawed, wide-eyed look I'd expect if I suggested we take a quick trip to Mars. "I can't authorize putting an innocent life in danger."

He was right, of course. My gut swirled with a festering dread. Involving Sue Ellen was a wild-brained and very likely catastrophic idea. But I had to do something. "Just let me call Sue Ellen, see if she's willing to come out. She can stay in the tree line with us and use your bullhorn to talk to Dad."

Since Hank, the undersheriff, was on vacation, the final decision was Caleb's. A war of indecision played out in his eyes.

"No," he gave a quick head shake. "We bring in Brenda's team and surround the tractor."

"And do what?" I fought to keep my voice on an even

keel. "The more people involved, the more targets Dad has. If it's you, Sue Ellen, and me, and we stay inside the tree line, there will be fewer chances for things to go haywire."

Caleb's hell-no grimace tightened.

"Look, just let me call Sue Ellen and see if she's agreeable."

He glared at me, and I glared back, the longer our stare-down dragged on, the deeper my conviction. Caleb didn't have the experience to make a decision of this magnitude. And I understood his hesitancy. The fact Dad used me as target practice hit a new level of astonishment.

"Look, I swear to you, I won't make a move or say anything without your approval."

Finally, after what seemed an hour, but based on the beat of my heart, closer to ten seconds, Caleb nodded his approval.

I placed a call to Sue Ellen, explained our situation, and in less time than it takes to snap a finger, she agreed to help.

"Follow River Road south, approximately two miles past the city limit sign, you'll see Dad's truck on the side of the road. Deputy Brenda Spears will be waiting to escort you."

"I know Brenda," Sue Ellen said. "I'll be there in fifteen minutes."

"I really appreciate this, Sue Ellen."

"Honey, I love Zachary. There's nothing I wouldn't do for that stubborn coot. He's just a little out of sorts. You'll see, I'll bring him around in no time."

I got the impression this wasn't the first time Sue Ellen had brought Dad back into the real world. I only hoped she had the power to do it again.

CHAPTER THIRTEEN

SUE ELLEN CAME prepared for the rain. Navy galoshes, jeans, and a bright pink windbreaker. She'd covered her hair with a transparent plastic scarf that tied under her chin.

I gave her the rundown of what I needed her to do. Somewhere in the middle of my spiel, my words wobbled, and my heart constricted with gripping fear.

"Why do I have to talk to Zachary through a megaphone?" She shoved the bullhorn into Caleb's chest. "If he's upset, he'll calm down when he sees me."

I held my palm in the air to keep Caleb from arguing. Caleb was right. I had no right to ask this wonderful, generous human being, a woman whose friendship I'd cherished for over twenty years, to risk her life. "Sue Ellen, I'm sorry I dragged you out here. My request is much too dangerous."

She studied my face as carefully as a jeweler assessing the Hope diamond. "Why are you making this into a big to-do?"

"Please, forgive me. I was wrong to ask for your help. Caleb and I will take it from here. I'll ask Brenda to give you a ride back to your car."

She pinned Caleb with her mossy green eyes. "We're talking about Sheriff Zachary Taylor, right?"

Caleb ducked his head. "Yes, ma'am."

"Then you're blowing this out of proportion." She

started for the tractor.

"Wait." I grabbed her arm. "I know our concern may seem over the top, but earlier, when I tried talking to Dad, it didn't go well."

"What do you mean, it didn't go well?"

"He took a shot at me." I hoped my face exuded a calm I didn't feel. "I'm sure he only meant the shots as a warning, but—"

"He shot at you? Like with a gun?" Sue Ellen's voice came close to matching her wide, disbelieving eyes.

"Yes. But I'm sure it was meant as a warning."

She pushed her plastic scarf back an inch, offered up two squinting disbelieving eyes. "He shot at you." Her tone challenging as if I were a child stretching the truth, and there had to be more to the story.

I clamped my mouth closed, allowed my statement to stand.

After a few seconds, she pushed a slow stream of air through her teeth. "Well, I'll be."

"You might have noticed that sometimes Dad's not quite himself."

Caleb offered the bullhorn again.

This time she accepted it. "Everyone has off days. Zachary just has a few more than the rest of us."

"Dad sees you almost every day. I'm hoping he'll respond to your voice."

She patted my cheek. "You're a good son."

I was pretty sure Sue Ellen knew my visits with Dad had been the in-and-out-two-hour-max variety. Her forgiveness of my failures as a son prodded me from inside.

She held the bullhorn at eye level. "How do you work this thing?"

Caleb pointed to a white button on the handle. "Push here when you're ready to talk."

"Give me room." She shooed us back, but Caleb and I

didn't budge. She spared us a raised eyebrow.

We slid a couple of steps behind her.

"Zachary? It's Sue Ellen." Her voice blasted through the air. "You need to quit playing around with that tractor and come on out here. I need to talk to you."

Agonizing seconds ticked in slow motion and prickled the hairs on my neck. An immense underwater silence filled the air. It was as if the crickets stilled, and rain falling from the sky quieted. The world seemed in wait for the sound of Dad's voice.

The fear in my stomach clenched like a fist. I'd been so sure Sue Ellen could end this nightmare, but now I had doubts anyone could talk Dad into coming out.

In less than three hours, it'd be sunup. Shortly after, a maintenance crew would arrive for work. Noise and strange voices could turn this already dangerous situation catastrophic.

I gave a reassuring squeeze to Sue Ellen's shoulder. "Why don't you try again?"

She raised the megaphone. "Zachary Taylor, you promised, if I baked you a pie, you'd give me a tour of your rose garden. I made your favorite Dutch apple and drove all the way out here in the rain. Now, you need to live up to your promise."

We were out of options. This had to work.

"Look." Caleb pointed to the tractor.

I squinted. Couldn't be sure, but it looked like—yes, the door definitely moved.

"Sue Ellen?" Dad called through the crack.

She slapped the megaphone against my stomach.

I sucked in a breath.

She sprinted for the tractor.

"Wait." Caleb ran forward.

I managed to catch up, grabbed his shoulder, and held him in place. "Don't. You'll startle Dad."

Sue Ellen mounted the running board and swung the

door wide. She pulled Dad down to the first step. "There you are." She wrapped him in a hug. "I thought you were going to stand me up."

Caleb and I risked walking closer.

Dad laughed. "Well, I…" He seemed a little startled but not upset. "I must've forgotten our plans."

His gaze drifted toward Caleb and me, and his back stiffened.

Sue Ellen stepped down and pulled on his arm. "Well, come on then. Jackson gave me a ride out here. He'll take us back to your place."

"Jackson?"

I hurried forward. "I'm here, Dad."

His gaze swept past me to the open ground, he hesitated on Caleb for a few seconds, and his forehead furrowed. "Why's Vernon here?"

His question threw me for a minute, then I followed his gaze and realized he'd mistaken Caleb for Vernon.

Caleb did favor his father—same build, same hair color.

Sue Ellen tugged Dad's arm again. "That's not Vernon. It's his youngest boy, Caleb. They sure look a lot alike, don't they? Come on. It's raining cats and dogs out here."

Dad had piercing, all-knowing eyes. Even now, in the dark of night, when his mind had grown cloudy and erratic, I could tell he knew something was wrong.

Sue Ellen continued pulling him forward.

His gaze skittered about as if he'd awakened and was unsure of his surroundings. He looked from Caleb to me, then back to Sue Ellen. I saw the moment the quarter dropped, and he realized he'd disappeared into the empty cavern he seemed to visit more and more. His face turned pink, then red, then close to plum.

I felt his embarrassment in every part of me, crackling inside my bones. He'd stuck his gun inside the waistband of his jeans. "Dad, would it be okay if I looked at your pistol?"

His hand drifted to the butt. Worry clouded his eyes, and the crease between them seemed more pronounced. He offered an embarrassed smile. "Sure. You can look at it." He handed over his gun, butt first. His smile tightened, then fell away.

I shoved the pistol in the pocket of my parka. I had no idea if Dad remembered shooting at me, and I refused to consider what it must be like for a thirty-year lawman to have his gun confiscated.

Caleb stepped forward, extended his hand. "It's good to see you, Zachary."

Dad's shoulders relaxed, and he shook Caleb's hand. "Sorry to be a bother."

"Not one bit of bother. In this kind of weather anyone can get turned around," Caleb said. I detected nothing false in his tone. "We've all run out of gas at one time or another. Glad we came along."

Sue Ellen wrapped her arm through Dad's. "Come on, handsome. You promised to give me a tour of your rose garden. Besides, I'm so sweet I'll melt if I stay in the rain."

Dad just nodded.

"Brenda brought my truck to the firebreak." I flipped on the floodlight. "Follow me. It's less than five minutes away."

Sue Ellen and Dad walked a few steps behind Caleb and me. She told Dad about an upcoming ice cream social at the Methodist Church, her great-nephew's game-winning touchdown, and gave him the weather report for the next ten days. She rolled from one subject to the next without a break. Dad couldn't get a word in if he'd tried. I suspected that was Sue Ellen's intent. Allow Dad time to reorient himself to his surroundings with no time for questions and further embarrassment.

By the time we reached my truck, it was close to four o'clock. I got Dad and Sue Ellen settled into the backseat, and Caleb called me to the side.

"I can't thank you enough for your help," I said.

"I'm not going to file an incident report. But we can't ignore the new evidence in Ethan's case."

"At least give Dad a few hours to rest. He has to be exhausted." Dad's short-term memory lapses worsened when he tired or became overly anxious. At a minimum, he needed a nap before we tackled how his fingerprints ended up on the bat.

"There has to be a plausible explanation, but ferreting the answer out of Dad might take a bit of time. Can you call your contact and get a heads-up on what the district attorney plans to do with the information?"

"I'd imagine they're planning to drop the charges against Ethan."

His words twitched down my spine like a spider. "This case is nowhere near solved. And, if the detective heading the case—"

"Sterling. The detective assigned to Ethan's case is Matt Sterling." Concern wrapped his tone. "Sterling is a no-holds-barred officer of the law."

My focus had been on the Cougar, not the detective. Now that had changed. "If Sterling's smart, he'll drag his feet until he has a better grip on his case. There are too many holes, and too many people involved. He's already jumped the gun by using circumstantial evidence to arrest Ethan."

"But the bat—it's not circumstantial."

His point hit a bullseye. "There has to be an explanation for Dad's prints. I don't know what it is, but I promise you, I won't quit until I find the killer. I just need time to investigate."

Caleb's gaze flicked away and settled somewhere over my shoulder.

"Please don't tell your parents about the bat. They'll put pressure on the district attorney to drop the charges. Right now, the killer believes the police are focused on

Ethan. I want them to continue thinking that's true."

The gravity of my request was evident in the set of Caleb's jaw.

It was no longer raining, but my clothes were wet and my body chilled. I rubbed my hands for warmth. "I just need a little time."

"I'll call my contact and try slowing things down. But I don't know how much time I can buy you."

"Thanks, Caleb. I owe you." I jumped in my truck and left before he changed his mind.

Sue Ellen kept up a one-sided conversation, and I used the rearview mirror to study Dad. He stared out the window, lost in thought. I couldn't help wondering if Dad remembered shooting his gun. If so, did he realize he'd shot at me?

The rain started again, and within seconds a crushing downpour dropped from the sky, battering the top of the truck and turning the blacktop into a shallow lake. I hit my hazard lights and kept driving.

Dad didn't utter a word the entire trip home. As soon as I unlocked the front door, he mumbled an apology and headed for his bedroom.

Sue Ellen stood in the foyer. Her car was back on the highway with Dad's. "Give me a second, and I'll drive you home."

She shook her head. "Brenda said she'd ask one of the deputies to bring my car here. But I have the noon shift, so if it's okay with you, I'll crash for a few hours."

"Of course. The guest room is down the hall, second door on the left."

"Thanks."

Too wired to sleep, I made a pot of coffee and fried an egg sandwich. I had over a dozen texts from Kendra ranging from slightly irritated all the way to the drop-dead, pissed-off variety. Cell service in the forest was non-existent, but I wouldn't have answered her calls in the middle of the search.

I felt bad about the mix-up and owed Kendra an explanation. I shot her an email, apologized, briefly described the emergency, and hoped she understood.

With no time to waste, I got busy laying out my investigation.

At the moment, Vernon and Sandra were willing to share information, but I couldn't be sure how forthcoming they'd be once they learned of the evidence against Dad. And I couldn't expect Caleb to sit on the news for more than a day.

Dad considered the Bentons good friends, but had never cared for Ethan and trusted him even less. When Ethan and I were kids, Dad made it clear he disapproved of our friendship. If I asked to spend time with Ethan, Dad always found a few extra chores around the house. By the time I reached high school, buoyed by a foolish decision on my part, Dad's mild displeasure of Ethan had grown into strong dislike.

In tenth grade, Ethan and I had faked our science projects. When both projects ended up in the county fair, Dad showed up and immediately recognized mine as an elaborate figment of my imagination. Unimpressed with my blue ribbon, he grounded me for two months and demanded I admit my duplicity and accept a failing grade.

"Stealing is stealing," he'd said. "You stole your 'A,' and you've shamed our good name. If a man steals to feed his family, he goes to jail. What you did was far worse—you wanted to see if you could get away with theft. You'll take your failing grade like a man and be thankful I don't insist on expulsion."

Ethan, on the other hand, received no punishment. Vernon wrote off his son's bad behavior as boyhood antics.

But no matter how much Dad disliked Ethan Benton, he'd never purposely harm him. Whoever killed Grace had motive—a strong emotional motive. And the killer had opportunity—either they waited for Grace at the dealership or followed her inside. And the killer had means—did they bring the bat with them or find it on the property?

I started a list of questions for Dad:

—where was he the night of the fire?

—did he know Grace? If so, how?

—when was the last time he saw or spoke to Ethan?

—did he know Ethan's partner, Lou DeMarco?

—did he remember going to the cabin and witnessing Ethan's illegal gambling?

—had Dad mentioned the illegal gambling to his undersheriff, Hank?

—did he remember handling a bat?

I made another list of questions unrelated to Dad.

—where was Naomi, Grace's sister, the night of the fire?

—who owned the bat?

—who sent the threatening letters to the Bentons?

—were the letters written by the killer?

I set up my laptop and printer on the dining room table. I used social media to download photos and facts of all the pertinent players, then tacked everything on the wall. Along with the photos of Ethan, Grace, Naomi, Louis DeMarco, and Dad, I stapled a map of Pine County and built a timeline.

I waited until six forty-five before texting Caleb, asking for a photo of the bat. Even if they'd turned over the case to the Blakeley PD, the Pine County Sheriff's office would have a copy of the initial investigation.

Less than five minutes later, Caleb sent the photo. I blew up the print and posted it to the board. Louisville Sluggers retailed for around forty bucks, and every Little League coach and a slew of kids had at least one in their garage. Even I had one.

I sprinted through the kitchen and out the back door.

Dad never locked his shed, and I found my high school duffle bag filled with baseball equipment, right where I'd stowed it when I left for college.

I dragged the bag from the top shelf and emptied the contents. A pitcher's glove, a catcher's mitt, three baseballs, and four bats—a DeMarini, a Rawlings Quattro pro, an Easton, and a solid ash Louisville Slugger.

Every fiber in my body sighed in relief.

I stuffed everything back into the duffle, shoved it back on the shelf and went back to the dining room. I spent the next hour finishing my notes, emailing Vernon's assistant, and gaining access to his court cases for the past three years.

"Why is my photo on your murder board?" So focused on my work, I hadn't noticed Dad standing in front of my board.

I pushed out of my chair and walked to his side.

His expression, a mixture of shock and sadness, wasn't all that different from the one I'd seen on his face the day he realized I'd cheated on my science project.

I tapped the edge of DeMarco's photo. "Dad, do you know this man? His name's Louis DeMarco."

"You promised to withdraw from Ethan Benton's case." The pain in Dad's voice was a living thing, raw and coarse, and wrapped in anger.

"I'm sorry, Dad. I can't quit."

"Why?"

"Something's happened."

"What?"

This conversation wasn't going according to plan. "Let's sit down."

"I don't care to sit. What's happened?"

His dug-in expression left me no choice but to spit out the news. "Your fingerprints were lifted from the bat used to kill Grace Underwood."

At first, the news didn't seem to register. Then blood

drained from his face. "That's impossible." His voice might be fierce, but worry flickered in his eyes. "How could my prints be on the bat?"

"You must've come in contact with the killer. Do you remember touching a bat?"

"No." He massaged his forehead. "You need to steer clear of Lou DeMarco."

"How do you know him?"

"That's none of your concern. Just do what I say." He turned to leave, but his knees buckled, and he gripped the back of the closest chair. "My memory fails me sometimes." He sounded so sad and scared.

"I know—" I reached to embrace him, and quick as a rattlesnake, he gripped my wrist. For a moment we stood, struggling together—me fighting grief and guilt. Dad fighting demons slowly stealing his soul. Both of us battling the deep-seated pain that our life together was coming to an end.

Even if I fought with all my power to solve this mystery and prove Dad's innocence, we had no hope of winning the actual battle. We were powerless against the faceless, greedy enemy slowly erasing his world.

CHAPTER FOURTEEN

I DIDN'T KNOW IF my murder board would help me find Grace's killer, but for the time being, it shut down any hope of having a meaningful conversation with Dad. Probably not the brightest idea to use the dining room wall simply because it was empty and large enough for my purposes.

Before Dad stormed off to his shop, I'd floated the idea he'd been framed and asked again how he knew Lou DeMarco. He'd refused to answer, stomped out of the dining room, and slammed the kitchen door on his way to the shed.

I blamed my inability to read the room, or in this case, Dad, on my lack of sleep. I'd give him a few hours to collect himself before tackling the question again. But whether he liked it or not, we had to have the conversation, and it had to be soon.

I removed the photos, timeline, and maps from the wall. Then wasted a half-hour recreating a digital version of the same board on my laptop. Not the visual I preferred, but it'd have to do.

Sue Ellen walked in just as my cell beeped with an incoming call. I held up a wait-a-minute finger and answered.

"I talked to Colleen this morning," Jasmine said. "She's interested in working extra hours. Wednesday is her regular day to clean Zachary's house, so you can talk money and hours when she arrives."

"That's great. Any idea what time that might be?"

"I think she said ten o'clock."

I glanced at the time on my computer screen. Colleen would be here within a couple of hours. "I really appreciate your help, Jasmine."

"Anytime. Don't be a stranger."

We said our goodbyes, and I focused back on Sue Ellen. "I made a fresh pot of coffee. It looks like we're out of eggs, but Dad had a can of pop-open cinnamon rolls."

"So that's what smells so good." She followed me into the kitchen. "Just coffee for me, thanks."

I poured coffee into a mug, handed it to her, then refreshed my cup.

"Before I go, I'd like to say goodbye to Zachary."

"He's in the shed." I glanced out the kitchen window. The shed door stood open, no sign of Dad. "I'm afraid we got off to a bad start this morning."

She nodded towards the dining room. "Did it have anything to do with the collage you had pinned on the wall earlier?"

"Partly the wall, partly my choice of questions." I tried ignoring the guilt bumping my heart. It felt like I carried around enough to sink a boat. "It's complicated."

"Complicated, huh?" She opened the pantry, removed a go-cup, and transferred her coffee. "I've found life is chock full of complications. I'll stick my head in and say goodbye to Zach." She crossed the room, rose on tiptoes, and kissed my cheek. "I'm glad you're home."

As soon as she cleared the kitchen door, she called out to Dad.

I slid sideways to get a better view from the window.

Dad walked out of the shed, wiping his hands on an oily rag. He gave her an ear-to-ear smile, and I swear he looked surprised to see her. I couldn't make out what they said, but after a minute or so, she kissed his cheek and left.

My instincts about Dad having feelings for Sue Ellen looked accurate, and from where I stood, the admiration appeared mutual. Sue Ellen seemed comfortable in his house, and even knew where he stored his go-cups.

Earlier, Brenda had delivered Sue Ellen's car. It was likely word would get out and small town tongues would wag over Sue Ellen spending the night at Dad's. But knowing my father had a friend and ally, someone who cared more about him than grapevine gossip, settled in my heart as relief.

I could give Dad a few hours to absorb the fingerprint news, but Caleb would be itching to tell his parents that Ethan's prints were not on the bat. And I had no doubt Sandra would attempt to use her political power and pressure the prosecution to drop the charges against her son.

Either way, I expected a call from Detective Sterling sooner rather than later. I had no time to waste. As soon as the news leaked, the killer would realize his days of skating under the radar were over.

Dad looked up when I entered the shed, but his face gave nothing away. He pointed to the five-drawer toolbox to my right. "Hand me the Phillips head out of the second drawer."

I opened the drawer and stared at twenty screwdrivers lined up like soldiers in parade formation. I chose a medium Phillips head and handed it over. No one used the word talkative to describe Dad or me, and we often enjoyed companionable silence, unlike the kind filling the shed at the moment.

Dad knew as I did, once word leaked of Sheriff Zachary Taylor's involvement in a murder, no amount of truth would stuff that genie back in the bottle. He, of all people, understood that I had to get in front of the rumor mill. "You know I have to ask."

He unscrewed the handle on the blower. "I don't remember."

"You don't remember what?"

"Holding a bat." He shook his head. "I've tried. I can't remember any situation where I touched a baseball bat."

"So you think someone is framing you?"

"I want to say yes, but you and I know it may have happened."

Pushing him solved nothing. I moved on. "How about DeMarco?"

Dad unscrewed a cap on the blower and poured a pre-mixed oil and gas mixture into the tank. "What about him?"

"How do you know him, Dad?" I didn't squash my irritation.

"He called me a few weeks back."

"What'd he want?"

He screwed the cap back in place, threw away the bottle of oil, then wiped his hands on an old t-shirt he used as a cleaning rag. "He claimed I owed him gambling losses." His face reddened. "I never gambled in my life."

I waved away his concern. "DeMarco lied. You don't have to worry about his claims."

Dad met my gaze, studied my face, and then as if satisfied what I said was true, his shoulders slumped with relief. Up until now, he hadn't been sure whether DeMarco's claim was valid.

I couldn't imagine Dad's life now. What it would be like to have minutes, hours, even days of memory loss. And very soon, weeks, months, and years would vanish. His vulnerability had to be off the chart.

If DeMarco called Dad, Ethan must've told him about the Alzheimer's. And being the worst kind of human, DeMarco capitalized on Dad's weakness. Heat shot up my neck. I had a deep, compelling urge to invite Lou DeMarco into a dark alley.

"When I can't remember something, I put it aside," Dad hung the blower on a ceiling hook. "I do something unrelated to take my mind off trying to remember what I can't. Sometimes, it works, and the memory comes to my mind—but not always."

My father, so tall and proud and brave, standing before me admitting a weakness, splintered my heart in two. I may have kept my expression easy and pleasant, but my resolve turned granite. DeMarco overplayed his hand, and I would destroy him.

Most people see the world in black and white. It's so much easier to believe someone is all good or all bad. But I knew humans lived life in the grays. And as Dad often counseled, people might be basically good, but you'll do well to remember there is always a little vile mixed in. At this moment, I knew this to be true—because my capacity for hate shocked even me.

I showered, shaved, changed into gray dress slacks and a light blue oxford shirt. People seemed more willing to answer questions when an interrogator dressed the part of a successful lawyer.

As promised, Sandra's assistant forwarded a list of the senator's legislative bills. While I waited for Colleen, I skimmed through the records but found nothing worthy of instigating the types of threats mailed to the Bentons' home.

I spent another thirty minutes combing through Vernon's cases and had just finished skimming through the last one when the doorbell rang.

Colleen must've had a key because we met in the living room. She set down a bag of groceries on the foyer table and extended her hand. "You must be Sheriff Taylor's son."

No matter that Dad had given up his shield, to the locals, he'd always be Sheriff Taylor.

We shook. "Yes, I'm Jackson." She was medium height,

five-five or so, and had kind brown eyes and a ready smile. If I were to guess, I'd place her age as late forties.

"Jasmine called me last night and said you were interested in me working more hours?"

"Any chance you're available full-time?"

"Full-time?" She looked over the living room, then back at me. "It only takes four hours to clean this house, six if I do the laundry and press the Sheriff's shirts. I grocery shop for him on occasion, but that's a long way from full-time."

"I'd like to add preparing meals. And since I'm staying with Dad indefinitely, we'll have double the laundry."

She didn't comment, and I suspected I'd gone too far. "I can take care of my laundry. And cooking isn't mandatory. Most nights, Dad eats at the diner." I looked toward the kitchen, making sure we were still alone. "What I need is someone to keep an eye on Dad."

She waved off my concern. "I don't mind cooking or laundry, and I need the extra work. The problem is, I have grandkids living with me. What kind of schedule do you need?"

"I was hoping for eight to five, Monday through Friday. And maybe a half-day on Saturday?"

"You're moving home to Loblolly then?"

"Yes, at least for now."

She moved to the sofa, picked up a green throw, folded, and placed it over the back. "I can make the schedule work if you're okay with the kids coming here after school."

She straightened a stack of magazines on the table beside Dad's recliner. "They're well-behaved, and I'll see they stay out of your way. Lionel, my grandson, already does some yard work for Sheriff Taylor, and my granddaughter Alisha loves cleaning your mama's silver. That girl loves anything that shines." She picked up the TV remote, put it back in the charger.

"I don't see a problem with the kids coming here after school. Especially if Dad already knows them."

She offered a face-splitting smile. "Thank you, Mr. Taylor. You have answered my prayers."

"Please, call me Jackson. I'm sorry to be in such a rush, but I need to head out for a few hours."

She followed me down the hall and into the dining room. "Is there anything special you need me to do?"

I stuffed my laptop inside my briefcase. "Would you mind checking on Dad? He's working in his shed and hasn't had breakfast."

"I can make him breakfast." She carried the groceries into the kitchen.

"I left my contact numbers on the counter. I'll be home by five."

She opened the refrigerator and placed a half gallon of milk inside. Pulled out a carton of eggs. "Don't worry about a thing. We'll be fine."

Satisfied Dad was in good hands, I took my leave.

After reviewing Vernon's case log, my list of suspects had grown to six. Of the six people I needed to question, Naomi Underwood, Grace's younger sister, headed the list. Then Ethan and his pal Lou DeMarco, and lastly, the parents of three teen boys, who were found guilty and sentenced in Vernon's court. The first teen was convicted of grand theft auto, the subsequent a cocaine conviction, and the last was a kid who set the neighbor's barn on fire.

An eye for an eye.

A tooth for a tooth.

A son for a son.

Of the three cases, the only name I recognized was Dylan Thompson, the teen convicted of dealing cocaine. I'd played high school football with his older brother, Jed, and remembered his dad, a man Dad called Billy, who had never missed one of our football games.

Even though the suspect I found most interesting was

the firebug, all three teens had been arrested and charged during Dad's tenure as sheriff. Which meant I needed to vet all three.

Since I'd told Ethan to expect me this morning, I shot off a quick text.

Have to make a couple of stops. Be at the cabin by noon.

He replied with a thumbs-up emoji.

Based on the police report, Naomi lived with her parents in Magnolia Point, a small neighborhood community between Blakeley and Loblolly, fifteen minutes from Dad's house.

I turned off River Road and onto Highway 27, with one thought flashing in my head—if the owner of the bat was the killer, my dad's life was in jeopardy. I had to solve this case, and the Louisville Slugger was the key.

CHAPTER FIFTEEN

NAOMI UNDERWOOD'S PARENTS lived in a red brick ranch with two sky-scraping magnolia trees in the front yard and immaculately trimmed azalea beds flanking their front door.

I wheeled in behind a red MX-5 Miata. Ethan's skateboarding neighbor mentioned a midday guest driving a sick red MX-5 convertible. I filed the information under interesting and rang the doorbell.

Several social media photos of Grace Underwood included her younger sister, and I recognized the woman who answered the door as Naomi. "Can I help you?"

"I'm Jackson Taylor, Ethan Benton's attorney. First, I'd like to extend my condolences for the loss of your sister."

Her eyelids fluttered. "Thank you." Her voice registered a notch above a whisper.

Naomi's social media photos featured a vibrant woman with a girl-next-door beauty. Today she looked more like one of the white walkers on a *Game of Thrones* rerun.

"I'm sorry to show up without calling," I lied. Never give your subject enough time to think up probable answers ahead of time. "I wondered if I could ask for a few minutes of your time." And avoid saying the word question until you get in the door. I handed her my business card.

She stared at my card as if reading Latin. Then, something passed over her face—it looked a lot like pain. I got the impression she was trying to find the words to refuse politely.

"Ethan didn't kill your sister, and I intend to prove it." Stating a tenuous fact usually got my foot in the door, especially if the interviewee wanted to believe said fact.

Her lips quivered. "Ethan loved Grace." She studied my face as if measuring my sincerity. She'd find no dishonesty. I believed my statement.

After a few seconds, she stepped back. "You can come in, but I don't see how I can help you."

I followed her through the foyer, down a short hall, and into a bright yellow eat-in kitchen.

"Have a seat." She slid into one of four cane-backed chairs surrounding a small oak table overlooking a manicured backyard. Small talk didn't appear to be Naomi's forte.

I took the seat across from her, and within seconds realized my mistake. I'd chosen a seat facing a large picture window, and the glare seared into my eyeballs. I shifted in my seat and managed to dodge most of the beam.

Naomi absently wrapped a strand of hair around her finger and didn't seem to notice my discomfort, or notice me at all. Large clumps of her blonde hair had slipped from a rubber band, as if she'd slept, tossing and turning, and hadn't bothered to look in a mirror. "You want a cup of coffee or something?"

"Only if you're having one."

She pushed to her feet in slow motion, shuffled to a cabinet, and removed two mugs. The kitchen appeared spotless and smelled of lemons and disinfectant.

I took the opportunity to shift into a seat without direct sunlight. "Are your parents home?"

"No. They teach school. Today's their first day back since Grace died."

According to Facebook, Naomi graduated from the University of Georgia with a degree in English Lit. She seemed overqualified to fill a job as a receptionist for a used car dealer.

She placed a yellow mug of coffee in front of me. "You want cream or sugar?"

"Black is fine."

She slid into her seat. Her eyes were puffy and red, and she looked as if she'd been crying for days. "How's Ethan?"

"He's holding up." A tinge of guilt danced down my spine. Any halfway decent attorney would be at the courthouse filing a Brady motion to force the prosecution's hand, not playing a CSI detective. But Dad's fingerprints on the murder weapon had thrown my moral compass off by miles.

"I left a message on Ethan's cell. He hasn't returned my call." Naomi's eyes welled with tears. "The detective said Ethan's been arrested. Dad said they released him until the trial. I wanted to let Ethan know that I don't believe he killed Grace."

The sunlight cascading through the window gave Naomi's pale, taut, alabaster skin an almost ethereal appearance. She reminded me of a painting I'd once seen in an Atlanta art gallery: a blonde, blue-eyed woman standing at a window in an all-white room, watching a single red-tailed hawk soar in a blue, cloudless sky. The woman in the painting and Naomi shared the same expression, a wistful sadness rimmed in despair.

Her anguish over her sister's death was palpable, but I ignored the quick jab of guilt burning my chest and barreled ahead. "Ethan tells me you know about the poker games."

Her only tell was a slight flicker of her eyelids. She sipped her coffee, kept her gaze glued to the wall behind me.

"Did Grace know?"

"You should ask Ethan."

"I'm asking you."

A single tear fell over her cheek, then another. She wiped them away with her index finger. "Grace thought—" She stopped, rolled her lips in the way people do when they attempt to hold off tears. "I didn't tell Grace. Ethan asked me not to tell her. He said she wouldn't understand."

"But he trusted you with the information?"

She shrugged. "I worked for Ethan, and his business was in trouble. The games kept his car lot afloat."

Based on Ethan's bank statements, the games kept him substantially more than afloat. "Grace must've suspected something, right? That's why she went to the car lot in the middle of the night."

Naomi dropped her head into her palms. Her forehead came close to hitting the table.

"Is that why Grace went to Ethan's office?" I could only see the top of her head, but I thought she nodded, so I continued. "Did she ask you about the games?"

She raised, leaned against the back of her chair, and stared at me with red-rimmed eyes. "She was pregnant. She told us the night she died. My parents are devastated. They lost their daughter and their first grandchild. Mom's a walking zombie."

A lot like her daughter. "I know this is difficult—"

"Dad's not much better." Her voice shook with unshed tears threatening to erupt. "My parents hate Ethan."

"Because they believe he murdered Grace?"

"Dad never liked me working for him. He never trusted him," she said through rolling tears. "He and Grace fought about it the night she died."

That piqued my interest, but just barely. Grace's father murdering his daughter was a very, very long shot.

"I know the police charged Ethan with Grace's murder, but I don't believe it's true." Naomi grabbed a paper napkin from a holder on the table and blew her nose.

"Your dad and Grace fought the night she died?"

She took a steadying breath. "Yes. Jed Thompson filled his head with a bunch of lies about Ethan."

"Jed Thompson?" My interest now definitely piqued. "Why? What's Jed Thompson got to do with Grace or Ethan?"

"Jed and Grace dated a while back."

"How far back?"

She waved away my question. "They dated for like two minutes. Grace wasn't into him and broke it off."

"What did Jed tell your dad?"

"He told him about Ethan's illegal gambling. Dad was so angry. Angrier than I'd ever seen him. He demanded I quit my job and told Grace to break it off with Ethan. When she refused, he threatened to go to the police. I tried convincing him the gambling was only a rumor, and Jed was just jealous."

"So you lied to your dad."

"What was I supposed to do?" Her voice held the same pain as her eyes. "I couldn't admit I knew. My dad's a deacon of First Baptist Church in Blakeley. My mom teaches Sunday School. Grace's death has crushed them."

She turned sideways, bent at the waist keening with grief.

I didn't know her well enough to offer physical comfort, so I sat three feet away and waited for her to expel her misery.

After a while, she pulled herself together, grabbed another napkin, and swiped her tears. "I'm sorry. I just can't believe my sister is gone." Her face now a rainbow of dejected emotion.

"It's my fault," she said. "Grace would be alive if I'd only been honest. If I'd refused to work for Ethan, or quit when I learned about the gambling instead of helping him run his games." Another gush of tears.

"Did Grace find out you helped Ethan run games?"

She shook her head. "I lied to Grace, too. I lied to Dad."

She closed her eyes. "God, I've lied to everyone."

This conversation was going nowhere fast.

I remembered a quote hanging over my old boss's desk—you can't ride two horses with one behind. When deposing a client, focus on one topic at a time. "What did you lie to Grace about?"

Naomi wrapped her fingers around her mug but didn't drink. "Danny."

I ran the name through my memory bank, didn't make a connection. "Who's Danny?"

"A guy I sometimes date."

"What's Danny have to do with Grace?"

"Nothing."

I suppressed my growing impatience with a count of five.

Naomi fidgeted with her napkin, twisting and turning the paper into a tight roll. It seemed as if she fought an internal battle with her thoughts. I suspected she wanted to relieve her burden, and if I prodded and poked she'd spill her secret.

I changed tactics. "I'm having a difficult time understanding why a college graduate with an English Lit degree worked as a receptionist for a used car dealer."

Her waterworks started again. I'd hit a nerve. Good. "I would've thought you'd teach like your parents and Grace."

"I hated teaching." She blotted her tears with her crumpled napkin.

"So you tried it?"

"For a year. Teaching isn't for me. I wanted to earn an MBA. I'd never even worked in an office. Grace convinced Ethan to hire me."

"There's a kid who lives in Ethan's neighborhood. You may know him. He's usually riding a skateboard."

She lifted a shoulder. "Yeah, I've seen him."

"He says you visit Ethan's house." I waited. When she

didn't show signs of embarrassment or irritation, I continued. "If you worked at Ethan's office, why did you leave the dealership to meet him at his house?"

Her gaze hardened. "We weren't screwing around if that's what you're implying."

I raised my hands, palms up. "I didn't say that." But from her reaction, someone had.

She pressed her lips into a straight line.

I segued into a new topic. "Do you have any idea why Grace went to the dealership in the middle of the night? Was she looking for something?"

Naomi untwisted her now wet napkin and began tearing tiny pieces from the edges. "We had a big fight."

"You and Grace?"

"Everybody—Mom, Dad, Grace, me—a family screaming match."

"Why?"

"Grace ran into Danny and learned I lied about going out with him. She confronted me and wanted to know where I'd been all those nights."

"You mean the nights you worked the poker games with Ethan?"

She nodded.

I wondered if Naomi found the deception of keeping the secret from her sister thrilling? Or, maybe she and Ethan *were* having an affair.

"Were you honest with Grace?"

"Not then. I told Grace it was none of her business. But she kept pressing me. And like an idiot, I told her I was working. That's when things got bad."

"I'm not following."

"When I helped Ethan run the games, I wore sexy dresses. Ethan called it eye candy. It was just part of the ambiance he thought we needed to create."

Eye candy sounded like something Ethan would say.

"I mean, he never allowed the players to get out of

hand or anything."

Yeah, Ethan was a real stand-up gentleman.

"Grace and I always shared our clothes, and the dresses weren't our normal style. They were shorter and tighter than I usually wear. She'd believed me when I told her Danny picked them out."

Naomi kneaded her forehead. "Then Grace saw Danny, and he asked about me, said he hadn't seen me in months. That's when she accused me of having an affair with Ethan."

"But you weren't."

"No. I'd never sleep with my sister's boyfriend."

"Was this fight on the night your sister died?"

"Yes."

"Before or after Grace met Ethan for dinner?"

"After. She broke up with him that night and called me to pick her up at the Loblolly Diner. She was wound tight. On the way home, she was crazy mad. I'd never seen her that angry. She accused me of sleeping with Ethan. When I denied it, she tossed back my lies about Danny. She kept bringing up a text from Ethan on my phone."

"What did the text say?"

"He asked me to meet him at his house at noon."

"Did you meet him?"

"Yes, he had a meeting and needed me to set up that night's game. So I swung by his place and picked up liquor and snacks. Grace wanted to know why I needed to go to Ethan's house when I saw him at work, and I couldn't come up with a reasonable answer."

"What happened then?"

"She accused me of sleeping with Ethan in front of our parents. It was awful, but I had no choice. I had to admit working the games. My parents went ballistic. Grace accused me of lying, but Dad said he believed me because he'd heard rumors Ethan ran a gambling racket."

She ran her fingers back and forth over her forehead. She probably had a headache from crying.

"Grace announced she was pregnant and stormed out of the house. That was the last time I saw her."

Quiet tears streamed over her cheeks. "It was the last time any of us saw her."

"Do you have any idea why Grace would go to Ethan's office in the middle of the night?"

She closed her eyes. "Yes."

I waited for her to say more, but the only sound in the room was the clock ticking on the stove.

"Naomi, why did Grace go to Ethan's business?"

After a shaky breath, she said, "She was looking for my journal."

"You keep a journal?"

"A stupid habit since grade school." She pressed her hand against her mouth as if holding in a new round of tears. "Grace knew if I had an affair with Ethan, I'd write about it in my journal."

"You kept your journal at work?"

She nodded. "A few weeks ago, I found Grace rummaging through my nightstand. She claimed to be looking for a pen. But she'd been moody and sullen, and I got the feeling she didn't like me working for Ethan anymore."

"Did you write about the poker games in your journal?"

A barely audible thrum emitted from her throat. She nodded again. "The morning after I found her in my room, I stuffed my journal in my purse. A few days went by, then at dinner one night, Grace casually asked if I still wrote in my journal every night. I knew she'd been snooping again."

"Ethan says Grace didn't have keys to the office. Did she use yours?"

"No. I still have my keys."

"Any idea how she got in?"

"No, but during our fight, she asked me where I was hiding my journal. I knew she'd looked in my nightstand again. I was angry, told her it was none of her business. She must've gone to the office to check my desk." Tears streamed over her cheeks. Her eyes resembled shattered marbles.

I got no indication Naomi's tears were fake or that she was lying. On the contrary, her level of despair, erratic explanations, and clouded thoughts matched actions of the grief-stricken, not the smooth story style of a practiced liar.

"Does anyone in your family own a baseball bat?"

Her forehead wrinkled. "The police asked the same question. Grace and I played tennis in high school, not softball. We don't own any bats."

"Anyone at the car dealership keep a bat in their office?"

The wrinkles in her forehead deepened. "Why would they?"

"Some people use them for protection."

"I've never seen one at work."

I mulled over my next question for a few seconds. "Do you know my dad?"

Her eyes widened. "Sheriff Taylor? Yes, I know him."

"Did you give him a ride home?"

Her cheeks pinked. "Yes. One night he showed up at the cabin during one of the games. Ethan asked me to take him home." She gave me a sad smile. "He seems nice. Doesn't talk much."

Everything Ethan said had checked out, and I'd run out of threads to pull. I thanked her for seeing me and said my goodbyes.

I sent a quick text to Caleb. He'd promised to send me a copy of the new lab report due in this morning. Analytical chemistry could prove a fingerprint's age, and since Detective Sterling hadn't called, and Dad had no memory of handling a bat, I was betting the incident with

Dad and the bat wasn't recent. Which meant Dad's prints were immaterial to Sterling's case. But absolving Dad of Grace Underwood's murder was not my biggest concern.

I had to find the owner of the Louisville Slugger before they learned about Dad's prints being on the bat. Before they realized Dad could identify them as the killer.

Jed Thompson and I had played baseball in high school. Jed might have a bat. Hell, half of Pine County likely owned bats. But according to Naomi, Jed had dated Grace—*for like two minutes.*

The guy I remembered from high school, big and burly, was more teddy bear than grizzly. Nevertheless, I made a mental note to add Jed Thompson to my growing list of suspects.

My next stop—the hunting cabin. It was past time to level with Ethan about Dad's prints.

CHAPTER SIXTEEN

MY DAY MIGHT'VE been half over, but I'd only managed four hours of sleep in the last forty-eight. I needed a serious jumpstart before meeting with Ethan.

I stopped at the Red Rooster Mini Market on Highway 27 for a jolt of caffeine. The manager seemed to believe offering coffee sizes in Italian allowed him to provide truck-stop brew at Starbucks prices. I swallowed my pride and shelled over four dollars and seventy-nine cents.

Back in my truck, I stole a few minutes to sip my overpriced *grande* and jotted a few notes from my conversation with Naomi.

My phone rang with a callback from Caleb.

"Any news on the age of Dad's fingerprints?"

"According to the lab report, range is within the last ten days."

"Ten days?" I'd counted on months, not days. I'd assumed Dad didn't remember the bat incident because it happened so long ago.

"My source says Sterling asked the lab to narrow the window."

My brain kicked into high gear. "Do you know which lab?"

"No idea. Why?"

"Sterling might ask for a tighter range, but unless he uses a GBI or FBI lab, his request will likely disappear down a black hole. Has he had any luck nailing the owner of the bat?"

"Not yet." A woman's muffled voice said something I didn't catch. "Ask her to hold on," Caleb heaved a sigh. "I gotta go. Mom's on the other line. I've already dodged three calls from her this morning. According to Brenda, she's now at the spitting nails stage." He disconnected before I could ask him to keep Dad's fingerprints under wraps for a few more hours.

I checked the time on my phone—one-ten. My day wasn't just zipping by; it was close to evaporating. I ignored Ethan's warning, saved thirty minutes' drive-time, and turned on the Goosehead Bridge cutoff.

Goosehead was one of the oldest covered bridges in the Southeast, and the gateway to Old River Road, which ran parallel to River Road, the main artery into Loblolly. The bridge had new wood mixed with the old, and looked as if it had undergone a recent repair.

After crossing, I glanced in my rearview mirror and spotted something wedged into the right corner rafter. Curious, I braked, exited my vehicle, and confirmed my suspicion—a security camera with built-in solar panels.

The county used cameras to monitor traffic, but it was unlikely this backroad warranted a county census. Not a giant leap to assume the security setup was behind Ethan's warning to stay off the bridge.

Lou saw your dad on the surveillance videos, Ethan had said. At the time, I assumed he meant from a security camera hidden inside the cabin.

I snapped a few photos of the camera setup, then continued down the two-lane dirt road surrounded by hundreds of acres of pine trees. Almost identical to the type of woods Dad got lost in last night.

Dad—I should check in. I activated the digital assistant on my phone. "Call Dad."

"Home or mobile?"

"Home."

Two rings later, Colleen answered.

"How are things?" I asked.

"I'm glad you called. Sheriff Taylor's lawnmower is missing. He asked me to call the police, but he can't remember the make or model of his mower. He said you might know?"

Each time I faced a real-life reminder of Dad's failing memory, it was as if someone shoved a hand through my chest wall, gripped my heart, and squeezed. "No one stole his mower. He asked me to drop it off at Bubba's shop yesterday."

Paranoia reared hard in Dad's disease. If Colleen tried convincing him the mower hadn't been stolen, he could turn irate and distrust anything she said. "It's probably best to tell him I wanted to surprise him and have his mower overhauled. Let him know Bubba said it would be ready tomorrow afternoon."

My phone pinged with an incoming call. I recognized Kendra's number and hit ignore.

"Other than the missing mower, is everything okay?" I asked.

"Right as rain."

"Okay. I'm going to be a couple more hours." In my ear, I heard a beep-pause-beep. New voicemail. "Call if you need anything."

I slowed to a stop and tried Justin Cramer's cell, my buddy at the GBI. I wondered if he'd dug up anything interesting on DeMarco. My call went to voicemail, and I left a message.

A message popped on my phone screen—new voicemail. I tossed my phone in the cup holder and ignored Kendra's message for now. I had murder on the brain, not strategizing ways to split marital assets.

I crept down a rutted road in serious need of a backhoe to smooth out the potholes. It'd been years since I'd visited this part of the county and nothing on Old River Road stood out as familiar. But then, two trees with a double row of yellow fluorescent tape came into view. I assumed something that obvious marked the turn for Ethan's poker players.

I turned onto a trail large enough to accommodate a single vehicle. A hundred yards down, I spotted another tree marked with the same type of flagging tape. Then, roughly a hundred yards farther, two more trees were flagged. No way a player would get lost. This strip of land had enough fluorescent to night-land a plane.

I crested a small hill and spotted Sandra's white Mercedes 450 S class by the cabin's back door. She stood on the deck, one hand on her hip, the other shielding her eyes.

I parked beside her car and hopped out. She strode towards me, shoulders back, her face set on grim. Even at a distance, she looked well past ticked.

"Hi." I kissed her cheek.

"Have you talked to the district attorney about dropping the charges?"

"Not yet. I wanted to review a couple of things with Ethan first."

"You realize Ethan's fingerprints aren't on the murder weapon." Her ratatat cadence shot like gun fire.

"That's true, but the police found the bat two blocks from his office—"

"And how did the bat *happen* to end up with Zachary's prints?"

Her challenging tone gave me pause. I knew Sandra's patience rested at rock bottom, but so did mine. To bring the conversation down a notch, I slowed my cadence. "I have no idea, but I plan to find out."

I might have sounded comforting and in control, but indignation swirled in my gut. I didn't blame Caleb for bringing his parents up to date, but I resented Sandra's insinuation Dad had anything to do with Grace's murder.

"Mom, chill." Ethan leaned against the door jamb, barefoot, shirtless wearing a pair of jeans that threatened to slide below his hips at any minute. I'd seen jonesing addicts look healthier. "Let Jackson inside the cabin before you mount your attack."

Sandra's mouth pulled so tight her lips looked stitched together. My phone buzzed with a call. I checked the screen. Kendra again. I pressed mute and stuffed my phone in my back pocket.

"I'm sorry." She pushed her hair off her forehead. "I didn't mean to attack you. I'm just—"

"Worried." I patted her back. "Your reaction is understandable. Let's go inside, and I'll bring you up to date."

The smell of barbecue hit me as soon as I stepped through the door. Sandra had stopped by Smokey's Barbecue on the way to the cabin. Three giant Styrofoam cups filled with sweet iced tea sat on the kitchen counter, along with an assortment of Styrofoam food containers. Evidently, Smokey hadn't bought into the need to reduce his carbon footprint.

I was starving but knew questions had to be asked and answered before we shared a meal. So I grabbed a tea and walked into the living room. "I stopped by the Underwoods and had a chat with Naomi."

Sandra perched on the only chair. "Why would you see Naomi before the district attorney?"

"Among other things, I wanted to know if anyone in her family played baseball or owned a bat."

"You could've accomplished that with a simple phone call." Sandra's face was a billboard of exasperation. I suspected if I Googled "pissed-off," a photo of Sandra's expression would pop up.

"Asking in person allowed me to gauge Naomi's reactions."

Ethan sat across from me on the sofa and propped his

feet on the coffee table. "How's she holding up?"

"She's grieving for her sister. Mr. and Mrs. Underwood went back to work today, but if Naomi's any indication, the family is in deep mourning."

"We all mourn Grace," Sandra said with a touch of admonishment. "I'd begun to think of her as my daughter-in-law."

I hadn't considered Sandra's feelings for Grace and made a mental note to watch my words. "The way I see it, we need to determine who owned the bat and whether it was a weapon of opportunity." I faced Ethan. "Was the bat yours?"

"Mine?" He frowned. "No."

"How about one of your employees? Anyone have a kid playing Little League?"

"I only have two employees. Naomi and Corky. Corky doesn't have any kids."

In any case, I would add Corky to my list of people to question. "Have you and my dad had words recently—other than the one night we spoke about?"

"No."

"You had words with Zachary?" Sandra asked. "When?"

I kept my focus on Ethan. "Have you said anything negative about my dad to anyone?"

"No."

"You sure?"

"Yes, I'm sure. Why?"

"I'm betting the owner of the bat murdered Grace, burned down your business, and set you up to take the fall. Along with putting you in prison for life, he's also ruining the reputation of Zachary Taylor."

Sandra sat in silence. Black circles rimmed her eyes, and exhaustion seemed to seep from her pores. She reminded me of my mom during chemo.

Ethan stretched his neck from side to side. Then, he stood and shook his arms like a fighter preparing for a bout. "So, how do we find the owner of the bat?"

"We strategize."

"How?"

"Arguably the greatest general in history, Sun Tzu, claimed there are nine different battlegrounds. The most dangerous is desperate ground—that's when the only way to win a battle is to fight without delay, in a place with no shelter and no possibility of easy retreat."

"Thanks for the Asian history lesson, but what does that have to do with me undergoing the needle?"

Sandra flinched at Ethan's reference to lethal injection.

"Grace's killer believes he got away with murder," I said. "And as long as you're under arrest and proceeding to trial, they have no reason to think differently. However, the second I demand the D.A. drop the charges against you, we will throw the killer onto desperate ground."

I let that idea sink in for a few seconds, then added, "The longer we keep them from knowing I'm on the hunt, the better my chance to solve the murder. And remember, this is a person who brutally killed an innocent woman and burned down the building on his way out. There appears to be no moral line they refuse to cross."

"Jackson, you're not a detective." The voice of motherly concern replaced Sandra's earlier irritation. "You can't go head-to-head with a killer."

"Either someone doctored the lab report or Dad knows the killer. Unfortunately, Dad doesn't remember holding a bat."

"Why would anyone set up Zachary?" Sandra asked.

Ethan's eyes met mine. The secret we shared straining the air between us. "I don't have the answer, but I won't rest until I do."

"So you're not planning to ask the district attorney to drop the charges against Ethan?" Sandra didn't seem happy, but at least she wasn't issuing threats.

"The best thing I can do for Ethan is to solve the murder. My chances are better if the killer doesn't have a reason to believe he's being pursued."

"Ethan's murder charge doesn't affect just him. Vernon's reputation and mine are on the line."

I leaned forward, took her hand in mine. "Give me forty-eight hours. If I haven't figured this out in the next two days, I promise to file a Brady motion and force the prosecutor's hand."

I waited for Sandra's nod of concession before turning to Ethan.

He nodded.

Relief surged through my body. I stood. "I need to get going."

Sandra jumped to her feet. "I brought lunch."

"I can't—"

"Nonsense, you have to eat." She hurried into the kitchen and shoveled barbecue brisket, baked beans, and coleslaw onto a paper plate.

I ate standing up and scarfed my food in record time.

Ethan followed me outside. "I checked with my security company. Someone remotely disabled my office system an hour before the 911 call."

"How about your house system?"

"House system was uninterrupted. Naomi's the only other person who has the code to the office, but she doesn't know my password to access the security system online."

"On the night Grace died, did she accuse you of having an affair with Naomi?"

He frowned. "Why do you ask?"

"I'm trying to understand why Grace went to your office the night she died. Naomi suspects Grace was searching for a journal."

"What kind of journal?"

"Naomi's diary."

His eyelids blinked, then blinked again. "But—"

"I checked Grace's college yearbook. She was in three computer science and engineering clubs, and taught computer science at the high school. Naomi thinks Grace hacked her phone and read a text from you. If the security cameras were disabled remotely. I'm betting Grace hacked into your account, disabled your building security, then used your keys to enter the building. The killer must've followed her in."

I gave Ethan a minute to mull over my suppositions. "Grace had your keys. How did she get them if you activated your home security system?"

He chewed on his bottom lip, then blew a short breath. "She used the side door."

"That's what I think. If Grace hacked into your account on the security company website, she could've opened the lock. She knew your habit of leaving your keys in the ignition."

Ethan scrubbed his hand over his face. "Damn."

"Grace met someone at your office, or they followed her inside the building. Since the lab report says Dad's fingerprints were no more than ten days old, and he doesn't remember holding a bat in his hands, I like DeMarco for the killer."

"That's crazy."

"He's the only person with enough pull and connections to doctor a lab report."

"He wouldn't..." Ethan raked his fingers through his hair. "Makes no sense. Why would Lou kill Grace and burn my office?"

"Did you know DeMarco called Dad?"

Ethan slumped against the deck railing. He shook his head. "What'd he say?"

"Claimed Dad owed him money. And, knowing Dad, he didn't back down. Did you tell DeMarco about Dad's Alzheimer's?"

Ethan closed his eyes as if dreading his answer. "He saw your old man on the camera. When he learned he was the ex-sheriff, he didn't believe me when I said your dad wouldn't be a problem. I had no choice but to tell him why."

"By camera, you mean the one on the bridge?"

Ethan seemed a little surprised I knew. "Cameras are Lou's way of keeping track of the players."

"So there's more than one?"

"Three that I know of." He shrugged. "But I'm sure there's more."

I laughed, but there was no humor behind it. "You saying DeMarco doesn't trust you?"

"Trust isn't a concept Lou embraces."

"Is DeMarco in Atlanta?"

Ethan looked alternately puzzled and panicked, two traits he rarely exhibited. "You aren't planning to question him?"

A shadow at the window caught my attention. Sandra would wonder what we were discussing.

"I *am* planning to question him. In fact, I want you to set up the meet. Tonight. In Atlanta." I checked my watch. "Anytime after seven."

"Jackson." Full-out panic skated through Ethan's voice. "Not a good idea."

"Whoever involved my father in this murder will live to regret it. If that's Lou DeMarco, so be it." I stepped off the porch, turned back. "And don't mention the reason for my visit."

"What excuse can I use?" Not often I witnessed Ethan Benton off balance. Maybe it was losing Grace, or maybe it was facing life behind bars for her murder—whatever the reason, his entire body had gone rigid.

Realization hit me like a well-swung axe. Crossing DeMarco was scarier to Ethan than going to prison.

"Don't give him a reason, just set up a meet."

CHAPTER SEVENTEEN

THE TOWN OF Loblolly had two restaurants—well, one restaurant and a barbecue shack across from the now defunct sawmill. Chet, the owner of the Loblolly Diner, located on Main Street, used the old *Happy Days* TV show as his design inspiration.

I opened the door to Fats Domino's "Blueberry Hill" blaring from the corner jukebox. Sue Ellen, in a bubble-gum pink uniform, worked behind a long counter with red leather stools. It wasn't too surprising to find the counter and all but one of the booths empty at three-thirty in the afternoon.

I slid onto a stool at the far end.

"Hey, handsome. What's your pleasure?" Sue Ellen removed a stainless container from under the rotating arm of a stand mixer.

"Milkshake sounds good."

She poured a strawberry shake into a fancy fluted glass, plopped a cherry on top, and added it to a tray of four others. "Okay, just give me a sec to deliver this order."

Behind me, eight booths overlooked Loblolly's city park. She carried the shakes to a group of women playing Mahjong in the last booth, then hustled back. "Vanilla, chocolate, or strawberry?"

"Chocolate."

She scooped vanilla ice cream, chocolate syrup, and some kind of powder into a stainless cup and worked her magic. She slid the shake across the counter. "How's Zachary?"

"Snoozing in front of the TV."

She chuckled. "Watching *Gunsmoke*?"

"That's the one." I took a moment to savor the drink that no ice cream shop in Atlanta came close to duplicating. "I have a big favor to ask."

She stopped wiping the counter. "Bigger than your last one?"

The heat of embarrassment slid up my neck. Involving Sue Ellen in last night's shooting fiasco had the makings of catastrophic. Before I could piece together another apology, she smiled. "Jackson, I'm teasing. What's up?"

"I need to make a fast trip to Atlanta. After last night, I don't feel comfortable leaving Dad alone. I'd ask Colleen to stay over, but she has kids. My meeting is related to Ethan's case, and it's time sensitive."

When she didn't say anything, I added, "I confiscated all Dad's weapons."

She rolled her eyes. "I'm not worried about Zachary shooting me."

"I'll drive back to Loblolly after the meeting. I can be home before you wake in the morning."

"No." She shook her head.

It might've been presumptuous, but I hadn't considered Sue Ellen would turn me down.

"No telling how long since you slept." She scrubbed an imaginary spot on the counter. "And now you're planning to spend six hours driving back and forth to Atlanta?"

I had no Plan B. "I have a late evening meeting." Canceling would set me back days, maybe weeks. "It's important that I talk to this guy face to face." I wanted to look into DeMarco's eyes when I grilled him.

"Then you need to overnight in the city and get a decent night's sleep. Tomorrow's my day off, and I can stay with Zachary until Colleen arrives."

Cool relief swamped me. "I can't thank you—"

She waved me off. "No need for thanks. I enjoy spending time with your dad. I'll call Colleen and let her know I'll be over after my shift." She pointed to my drink. "You want me to put that in a go-cup?"

"That'd be great."

I had my overnight bag with me, and if I left now, I'd have time to check into a hotel and grab dinner before I met with DeMarco.

I thanked Sue Ellen again, hopped in my truck, and stuck my cell in the holder. Six new messages from Kendra scrolled over my screen. I'd forgotten my phone was still on mute. I skipped over Kendra's first five messages and played the most recent.

"Jackson, you can't avoid me forever." Kendra's voice hit a couple of notches above steamed. "We have to talk. Either call me back by four o'clock, or I'm driving to Loblolly."

I checked the clock on my dashboard. I'd reach Atlanta by seven. I instructed my phone's digital assistant to place the call.

Kendra picked up on the first ring. "About time."

"I'm sorry. Today's been a real headache."

"We have an offer."

"Offer?"

"For your half of the business. Isn't that what you want? I assumed you'd be happy I found someone to buy you out."

"I am pleased. Who made the offer?"

"No one you know."

Most likely a relocating attorney. "What's he offering?" My assumption the interested party was male might seem chauvinistic and less than *woke* but Kendra disliked sisterhood competition.

"Two hundred thousand."

Less than my investment. "Does that include my interest in real estate?"

"No."

Taylor & Vine's downtown location was the reason Kendra needed a partner. The mortgage, taxes and insurance absorbed forty percent of our firm's monthly billing.

"I'd rather have a full buyout. I sent a package to three attorney's who have an interest. I'll reach out in the next few days and get a feel for where they stand."

Selling my half-interest in Taylor and Vine would tide me over until I could build a new practice in Loblolly, but I couldn't stomach a fifty-percent loss. "Ever hear of negotiating?"

"Did you receive a formal offer?"

"Yes."

"Is the guy relocating?" He was probably low-balling.

"The offer isn't from a practitioner. It's an out-of-state firm looking to expand."

A cautious tingle skated up my neck. Not many firms looking to move into Atlanta would choose to buy into a two-lawyer practice specializing in divorce. "You received a firm offer to join a larger firm?"

She hummed a sigh, then, "Look, I'll drive down tonight and explain everything in person."

"I'm not in Loblolly."

"Where are you?" A little surprise and a lot of irritation swam through her tone.

"I'm on my way back to Atlanta."

"Oh." Her voice returned to all business. "When will you be in the office?"

"I'm not coming into the office."

"Okay, then when will you be home?"

"I'm staying in the city."

"Seriously? Why?"

Kendra was in the middle of a massive condo refurbishing project and I'd agreed to let her stay at my house during her renovations. We'd been dating for a few months and she spent most weekends at my house anyway. But, two months had turned into four, and a few weeks ago we'd agreed mixing personal with business didn't work for us.

"Jackson, you can stay at the house. I'm not going to jump you."

A tremor trailed down my spine at the husky timbre of her voice. I'd hurt her feelings and that wasn't my intention. My decision to sell my interest in our firm had nothing to do with ending our personal relationship. But our split was only a few days old—new and untested.

"I have a late meeting. It's easier to stay in the city."

Kendra's reputation as a go-for-the-juggler lawyer served her well in court, it just wasn't my style. And the more time we'd spent together, the more her natural assertiveness crept into our relationship. And, as she so eloquently stated, the more small-town boring I became. Before long the differences we'd once found enchanting and interesting, had turned annoying and tedious.

"Where are you staying? I'll drop off the contract." Kendra's words broke into my thoughts. She sounded distracted and ready to end our call.

"Four Seasons."

"You're booked at the Four Seasons?" This time, her surprise was more than warranted. We'd often debated five-star hotels and my stubborn refusal to agree to spring for luxury over a reasonably priced hotel—how nice can a five-hundred-dollar room be?

"Client's choice, not mine." Ethan—or more likely, DeMarco—chose the Four Season as our meeting place.

"What time do you plan to arrive?"

I checked my GPS. "Seven-thirty, with traffic eight."

"I'll meet you at the Garden Table at eight-thirty. We can have a drink, and I'll explain why you *should* accept the offer."

I owed her at least a sit-down meeting. "I'll arrange a table."

I booked my room, reserved a table for eight, then called Howie Sinclair, a realtor friend who lived in my Atlanta neighborhood.

"I'm thinking of listing my house."

"I think that's a great idea." His voice sounded close to giddy. "I have a couple of motivated clients looking for rustic charm. What's your asking price?"

A skidding reluctance pushed its way forward. "Let's start with an appraisal and see where it leads."

"We could do that."

I had a sudden need to ease into selling. I'd worked with an architect for a year to get my house design perfect. Pored over plans, studied every detail, and required nothing less than perfection from my builder.

"Market's hot, and appraisers are slammed right now," Howie said. "How about I work up a comparable analysis, put out a few feelers, and test the market?"

A sense of loss filled my chest as if the life I'd built over the last five years was silently slipping away.

"Hello?" Howie's voice bellowed in my ear. "Did I lose you?"

"No, I'm here."

In reality, the only parts of my Atlanta life I'd loved was my house and working as a prosecutor. I'd given up working for the D.A. in lieu of a partnership that offered more money and fewer hours. I lasted less than six months. All I had left was the house—a house was no reason to remain in a city holding no future, or at least none I wanted. "Okay, work up a comparable."

"I'll start right away and email a report tomorrow," Howie said. "I appreciate the opportunity. Your place is going to sell in no time."

If the market was as hot as Howie claimed, I should let Kendra know my plans tonight. She'd likely view the news as an eviction notice.

CHAPTER EIGHTEEN

I HIT THE OUTSKIRTS of Atlanta and battled my way into midtown, fighting a fierce thunderstorm. By the time I turned my truck over to the Four Seasons valet, I only had thirty minutes to shower and meet Kendra at the rooftop restaurant.

I dashed through the double doors and met a line of people ten-deep waiting to check in. Three desk clerks smiled, nodded, and attempted to exude relaxed demeanors while frantically typing on their computers. Within seconds, I caught the rumbling complaints of slow service.

"The power shortage from the thunderstorm threw our system into reboot mode," a female clerk explained to a man holding a cranky toddler on his hip. "It should only be a few more minutes."

At this rate, I wouldn't have time to shower. I debated changing our dinner to a breakfast meeting, but I had too many suspects to interview tomorrow to give up my morning. I needed to be back in Loblolly before ten.

A group of six suited men and women rushed into the lobby. Their umbrellas dripped puddles of water at their feet.

My cell buzzed. The name Howie Cramer popped on my screen, my GBI contact.

"Got a bead on Lou DeMarco." Howie wasn't a shoot-the-bull kind of guy. I liked that about him.

"Is he made?" Not that it would affect my decision to meet with DeMarco. But if the guy had mob protection, I might frame my questions with a little more care.

The check-in line snaked forward. I assumed the computers were back online.

"Not yet," Howie said. "DeMarco's still a low-level hood who made his way to Atlanta via Vegas. A poker hustler who accumulates high-rollers like pushers collect junkies."

Low level—good to know.

I heard horns blowing. Howie must be driving. He grumbled something, then, "Although, DeMarco has collected a few big names on his roster. He offers his clients total obscurity. According to my source in bunco, he has a mix of high-rolling businessman, a few B-list film stars, and a couple of A-list TV actors."

"Is he running drugs or prostitution?"

"As far as I can tell, not in Atlanta—not yet anyway."

"Okay. Thanks for checking. I owe you one."

"Is there a chance we can meet tomorrow?"

"About DeMarco?"

"Yeah." His quick confirmation caught my attention, and I was tempted to accept. "Sorry, I gotta head back first thing."

"Just a quick meet— it's important."

I owed him, and anything on DeMarco had the potential of affecting my case. "I'll try and move appointments around but it'll have to be early. I need to hit the road by eight."

"You won't be sorry. Word on the street is the Bianchi family in Chicago made DeMarco an offer."

Bianchi headed one of the most powerful organized crime families in the country. I glanced around, lowered my voice. "I'm in public. I'll pick up this via text."

I disconnected my call, opened a text thread, and typed, *The Bianchi family is moving into Atlanta*?

Three seconds later. *Not if we take down DeMarco.*

I have a ten-thirty meeting.

With?

DeMarco.

You have a morning meeting with DeMarco?

No. We're meeting tonight.

Because?

Ethan Benton is my client.

You like DeMarco for the murder?

The man in front of me stepped to the counter, and I moved to the front of the line.

I typed, *He's on my suspect list.*

Four seconds later, *You really think DeMarco blazed his partner's business and bludgeoned his girlfriend to death?*

I like to look a crook in the eye when I ask him questions.

And I had another bone to pick—DeMarco would pay for messing with Dad.

One of the desk clerks waved me forward.

I slipped my American Express card from my phone case and handed it over, then read Cramer's text.

DO NOT SCARE DEMARCO OFF TONIGHT!!! Call me after your meet-up.

Interesting demand, my curiosity won out. *Early breakfast?*

Where? When?

The clerk tapped her finger on the digital screen. "Sir, if you'll sign your name…"

I did as she asked, picked up my room key, and rolled my overnight bag to the elevator.

I'll meet you at six-fifteen at the Silver Skillet.

I threw my overnight bag on the Four Seasons' overpriced bed and debated a shower or a simple change of clothes. No doubt, Kendra would arrive fashionably twenty minutes late, allowing me time for a shower.

I ended my shower with sixty seconds of cold spray to remove the last of my no-sleep exhaustion, dressed in record time, and stepped off the elevator with three minutes to spare.

Kendra sat at a corner table nursing a martini. My first clue she considered this meeting all business. Notorious for arriving late to any social function, Kendra made a point to be the first to arrive at all business meetings.

She turned her cheek for a kiss.

I obliged, then slid into a chair.

"You look like hell," she said.

"Thanks. You look gorgeous as usual." It was true, she did look beautiful. She wore a flimsy black number that I knew showed off her legs.

"Thanks." Her smile, dazzling and beautiful, didn't reach more than my eyes. A few months back, that same smile held the power to knock me to my knees.

She sipped her martini and considered me over the rim. "I don't know why you're staying in a hotel instead of driving twenty minutes home and sleeping in your bed."

Probably not the best time to tell her I was selling the house. A waiter carrying an empty tray walked past, back-stepped, and placed a napkin on the table. "What can I get you?"

A double, single-malt scotch sounded perfect. But I'd need a clear head for my meeting with DeMarco. "A Cabernet, please."

"Any particular label?"

"House is fine." How bad could the house wine be at a five-star resort?

The waiter left, and Kendra leaned in, her forehead creased like a folding fan. "You never drink wine before dinner."

"I usually forgo all alcohol at business meetings."

I nodded at the blue file to her right. "You bring the agreement?"

She slid the file across the table.

The server delivered my wine, and I spent a few minutes looking over the contract from Wilcox, Savage and Knox. According to the contract, the firm was headquartered in Chicago.

The contract appeared standard fare, a straight-up buy-in. The offer was eight hundred thousand for a forty-nine percent share of the firm, annual bonuses not to exceed twenty percent of net earnings, leaving eighty percent for Kendra and I to split. Except Kendra wanted me out. And there was no real estate included in the sales price, which meant Kendra and I would continue to own our office building, a prime downtown location. Pretty sweet deal.

The offer included accounting services and tax services. All Kendra would need to run the law firm was a receptionist and a good paralegal. This offer explained a lot. Kendra's offer of two hundred grand was to buy me out. She wanted to keep me out of the negotiations. "Is the firm aware I won't be on the masthead?"

"I'll break the news when you agree to sell."

"You could get pushback."

"Not when I explain you've taken on a high-profile murder case that has no hope of winning."

Her offhand rebuke bounced off without a ding. "Since you know nothing about my case, you have no idea if I can win."

"I know if Ethan Benton is found guilty, the verdict will be debated on every news channel and newspaper in the state, maybe the entire Southeast. If you're still my partner, our firm will suffer. That kind of press takes years to live down. Taylor and Vine specializes in high-profile divorces. You had no right to accept a murder case that will leave a black mark on our firm without my consent."

"I don't plan on losing."

Kendra's eye roll came close to hitting her hairline.

In all honesty, I hadn't given a moment's thought to what losing the case would mean to Taylor and Vine's reputation. But this was no time to wallow in self-reflection. And no time to let Kendra get under my skin enough to make a knee-jerk decision. "I'll look over the contract and let you know my verdict."

Her face flushed, an argument wouldn't be far behind. "I'm willing to negotiate."

I laughed. "I'm sure."

Her mouth firmed.

I raised my palm in the air. "Relax. I'm not opposed to negotiating a sell-out. I even called Howie Sinclair about putting my house on the market." Lack of sleep had made me restless and blunt, and more than ready for this meeting to end.

"You're putting your house on the market without consulting me? You agreed to let me stay for two more months, maybe three." She shot me a look that said, I'd like to cut your throat while you sleep and bathe in your blood. Kendra's temper zoomed zero to sixty in three seconds flat.

"I haven't signed the listing agreement. I'll uphold my promise. I'll tell Howie I can't close before the end of the year."

Her fake smile grew so wide it came close to cracking her cheeks. "Well, isn't this just peachy. Not only are you bailing on our business, you're throwing me out on the street!"

"I just said you can stay in the house until your condo is ready."

"And let Howie parade clients through my bedroom on a whim? I don't think so."

"No winning this argument." I finished my wine in one gulp, grabbed the file, and stood. "I'll be in touch."

Our eyes met and held for a good five seconds. Then her face morphed into an all-business facade. Her expression flattened, her breathing slowed. "I'd appreciate your answer within twenty-four hours."

"I can't promise twenty-four hours, but I won't leave you hanging. I'll be in touch." I pivoted and headed for the door.

I ordered room service. Enjoyed a T-bone and a Caesar salad and purposely arrived ten minutes late for my meeting with DeMarco. We'd agreed to meet in the bar.

Two men who could easily double as linebackers for the Atlanta Falcons sat with their backs against the far wall. I figured them for DeMarco's goons. Only one man in the bar fit Ethan's description of DeMarco. I slid into the booth across from a short, stocky built man with dark hair and a mustache.

Describing someone's height as tall, medium, or short was usually relative to the person making the claim. At six-four, most men measured shorter than me. Ethan had referred to DeMarco as short. Ethan stood close to five-ten, and even though DeMarco was seated, I'd estimate Ethan had a good four inches on him.

DeMarco nursed his drink and made no secret of studying me. Based on the color of the liquid, I'd guess bourbon. He raised his index finger and a female server appeared at my side. He tilted his head toward the woman, silently indicating I should order.

Grab control and grab it early. "Nothing, thanks."

The waitress glanced at DeMarco as if asking permission to exit.

He offered a curt nod, and she scurried away.

DeMarco's puffed chest and raised chin tipped into a Napoleon complex. He sipped his bourbon. "You a teetotaler?"

"This isn't a social call."

"No?" He took another sip, then ran his thumb and

index finger over his mustache, once, twice, three times, as if his stash were a lapdog in need of petting. "What is this, then?"

"Let's call it a conversation to clear the air."

He sat back, continued stroking, as if he and his pet dog were considering my words.

"Ethan Benton has retired," I said.

His mustache twitched and told me I'd struck a nerve. "From the car business?"

"No. The poker business."

His eyes squinted into button-hole slits. "If Ethan decided to give up the game, why are you bringing me the news?"

"He's on house arrest."

"And Ethan agrees with your retirement plan?" His glare had enough heat to savage a tank.

"If he hadn't, he'd be looking for another lawyer. I don't represent clients on racketeering charges."

"Just murder and arson." DeMarco smiled.

"Consider this a friendly notice to find a new partner."

He slugged down the last of his bourbon. Raised a finger and pointed to his glass. He caressed his mustache. "And if I refuse?"

"I'm not following."

"If I refuse to release Ethan from our agreement?"

I shrugged. "I suppose you could always take him to court. Maybe you'll luck out and score a judge that'll honor your verbal contract for an illegal gambling racket."

The waitress dropped off his second drink and scuttled away.

I leaned in. "One more thing before I go. Do not make the mistake of contacting my father again."

He joined his hands together and made a steeple of his index fingers. He placed them under his chin as if he were Confucius contemplating a philosophical truth about the universe.

"Consider this your only notice."

DeMarco smiled, but it was neither friendly nor accommodating. "But I so enjoy my conversation with your befuddled father."

Boiling heat filled my veins. *Do not scare DeMarco off tonight!!!* Cramer's message played like white noise in my head. "You make the mistake of contacting my father again and you'll be in search of a surgeon."

"Is that a threat?" His over-the-top laugh grated my skin like eighty-grit sandpaper.

It was as if a firecracker exploded in my chest. I had to fight to keep my voice even. "A threat may or may not happen." I threw a twenty on the table and stood. "You'd be wise not to confuse a threat with an absolute promise."

He shot out of his seat, slid a money clip from his pocket, and threw a hundred-dollar bill on the table, walked five steps, and turned back. "You and I will meet again, Jackson Taylor."

I beamed the kind of smile that was anything but amiable. "You can damn well book it."

I don't think he heard my response. He was too busy motioning for his goons to follow him to the exit.

CHAPTER NINETEEN

THE SILVER SKILLET was as close to the Loblolly Diner as I'd found in Atlanta. The architecture reminded me of a Steak 'N Shake, white brick, black trim. A neon sign in the window claimed the diner opened in the mid-fifties. If I were to guess, based on the drop-down fluorescent lighting and the decorating style— leather booths covered in harvest gold and avocado green—the last remodeling occurred in the seventies.

I'd always been drawn to the southern cooking and the all-day breakfast beginning at six o'clock. I arrived within minutes of the doors opening and snagged a corner booth. Cramer walked in ten minutes later to a packed crowd.

He slid into the booth across from me and scanned the menu. "What's good here?"

"This your first time?"

"Yeah."

"Can't go wrong with the Farm House Special." Eggs any style, sausage gravy over two fluffy biscuits, and of course, the southern staple, a side of grits.

He studied the two-page menu with the concentration of a kid with a hidden treasure map. "Not big on grits, I'm more of a pancake man myself."

We placed our orders and settled in with coffees.

"How did it go with DeMarco?" Cramer asked.

"It went."

"You didn't scare him away?"

"No, but he didn't look as smug when he left the bar as when I arrived." I recalled DeMarco and his goons scurrying away. Despite my best effort a smile crept over my face.

"I could use your help nailing him."

"My help? I've only had one conversation with the guy." I scanned the room, spotted our server taking an order two tables down. I had a feeling I'd need more coffee for this conversation.

"Tell me about DeMarco's relationship with Ethan Benton."

I caught the server's attention, pointed to my cup. "That'd fall under client privilege."

He waved me off. "Okay, I'll give you my take."

The server delivered a thermal pot of coffee. "You guys look like heavy drinkers." She laughed at her joke. A joke I'm sure she repeated twenty times a day.

Cramer and I offered the obligatory chuckle, then I topped off our cups. "Your party. You want me to dance, you need to supply the music."

He leaned back in his seat. "This is how I see it. Ethan Benton runs games for DeMarco. Lou offers anonymity, so the game has to be in a secure location. I figure it's the cabin Ethan claimed as his residence when you bailed him out."

No surprise Cramer knew this detail. Easy enough to access court records, but I kept my face blank and didn't bite.

He smiled, offered a lazy shoulder roll. "Seemed kind of odd your boy owned a house in a gated community and used a backwoods cabin as his lockdown site. I can always put eyes on the property and test my theory—"

"Is that a threat?" I was starting to regret taking this meeting.

"No. No." He gave a quick head shake. "I'm just theorizing."

"Cut to the chase. What do you want from me?"

"I want to offer your client a deal."

"What kind of deal?"

"He gives me a heads-up on the next poker game and—"

"So you can bust him on racketeering? I'm having difficulty spotting the silver lining in your deal." I air-quoted "deal."

"My boss would do a lot to stop the Bianchi family from moving into Atlanta. Shutting down DeMarco is the quickest way to accomplish his mission."

Our food arrived. I used the time to consider my options. It didn't take a soothsayer to see where Cramer and his boss were headed. They wanted Ethan to be their snitch and agree to give up DeMarco.

Dad's prints on the murder weapon wouldn't sway a good prosecutor. I no longer worried Dad would be dragged into Ethan's trial or charged with murder. The bat might not have Ethan's fingerprints but he had no alibi. His keys were found at the scene, and the prosecutor would assume and convince a jury he wore gloves when he killed Grace. Both solid reasons a request to dismiss wasn't the slam dunk Sandra believed.

If forced to go to trial, I'd muddy the water with Ethan's home and office security records, but in the end, we didn't have a cake walk defense. And if Cramer moved forward on this operation and busted Ethan on racketeering, Ethan was looking at a minimum twenty year sentence on the illegal gambling charge alone. "What are you offering?"

"You think your guy's guilty?"

A soft-ball question. What defense lawyer admitted his client murdered his girlfriend? "My client is innocent."

"Then I'm willing to throw my resources into the mix and help you win your case."

Using the GBI's resources to find the killer could be useful. And there was a good chance Ethan wouldn't walk on the murder and arson charges. The prosecutor might claim Ethan played a part in setting up Dad. I'd briefly considered then discounted the idea. But if I were the Cougar, it might be my strategy. If a twenty-year racketeering sentence were tacked on, Ethan would grow old in prison. "What if Ethan's found guilty?"

"If Benton agrees to work with us and he's found guilty on his current charges, I'll testify on his behalf. A GBI agent asking the court for leniency will go a long way with the judge."

Using GBI resources had the potential of speeding my investigation tenfold, and solidify Ethan never stood trial. I figured Cramer didn't know about my dad and the fingerprints. Or maybe he did, and held the ace up his sleeve to seal his proposal.

Just so happened I had my own ace. "I may have a way for you to nail DeMarco without Ethan's help."

Cramer shoveled a mouthful of pancakes, chewed. "I'm listening."

"There's a camera filming ingress and egress from the cabin."

"You mean like a security camera?"

"Exactly."

"No way DeMarco's players agreed to being filmed."

"Equipment is well hidden." I slipped my phone out of my pocket, found the photos I'd snapped, and handed him my phone. "The camera's located in the middle of a pine forest, hidden under the eaves of a covered bridge, about three miles from the cabin. The players arrive at night. I doubt anyone would notice."

His eyes lit up. He set his fork aside, grabbed my phone and enlarged the photo. "This setup has to be DeMarco's handiwork."

"It is. According to Ethan, Lou has trust issues and keeps

a close eye on the parade of cars attending his games."

I could practically see Cramer's mind whirling with possibilities. "We trace the camera back to DeMarco, and we hammer one more nail in his coffin."

"You get a warrant for the IP address on the camera—"

"And we grab DeMarco's digital security files." Cramer's head bobbed up and down like a cork caught in a class three water rapid. "We'll have the evidence his players are tied to ongoing illegal gambling racket and not just a one up."

"And if they were my clients, I'd advise cooperation."

Cramer beamed a game-winning smile. "Beautiful! All I need is for Ethan to oversee one more game." He handed me my phone and dug into his stack of pancakes with renewed gusto.

Patterns of illegal activity of this type fell under RICO, a federal law making it illegal to acquire, control, or profit from a business through crime. The players would face federal charges, and Ethan's money laundering fell under RICO, not the State of Georgia.

I blew a slow stream of air. "There's a problem."

"What?" Cramer paused his fork halfway to his mouth. He suddenly looked constipated. "Your client won't be arrested. I'll clear it with the prosecutor. Let him know Benton's our guy?"

I backtracked, rethought my position. I hadn't considered this scenario. My concern had focused on closing down the games to keep Ethan from accruing a racketeering charge. But if Ethan received immunity first, then… "You'd give Ethan written immunity?"

"Of course."

Immunity would be the best possible outcome. Even if Ethan never ran another game, there was no guarantee the feds wouldn't bust DeMarco in the future. With Ethan already on the feds radar, he'd likely be dragged into their case. Which meant, if there was any way possible, I needed to work with Cramer. "Ethan retired from running DeMarco's games. I delivered the news last night."

Cramer's face drained a couple of shades lighter. "That's the reason you met with DeMarco?"

The GBI heading a RICO case had career-making consequences, which explained Cramer's crestfallen face. He slumped in his seat, drummed his fingers on the table to a tune only he could hear. Then his eyes lit with a eureka sparkle. "What's to keep Benton from telling DeMarco he's changed his mind."

DeMarco's taunt, *'I so enjoy my conversation with your befuddled father,'* played in my head, shooting heat up my spine. "I have to admit, I'd take strong personal pleasure in bringing Lou DeMarco down."

Cramer pounded his fist on the table. "Then let's do it."

Ethan had shown resounding fear when I announced my intention to meet with DeMarco. Maybe he'd be relieved if I offered him the chance to refrain from rocking his illegal boat. "Might work. I'll talk to Ethan and let you know."

I finished the last of my biscuit and sausage gravy, then drained my coffee. "I have to hit the road."

"DeMarco will have Benton's phone tapped."

"Already handled that problem." I tossed a twenty on the table. "I have another favor."

Cramer gave me the stink eye. "You're getting heavy."

I leveled a get-real gaze. "You take down DeMarco and you'll owe me for a good while yet. But, this favor is personal. My law firm, Taylor and Vine, has an interested investor, a law firm out of Chicago. Can you run them through your system?"

"Chicago? Sounds a little serendipitous."

"I agree." An offer from a firm in Chicago flashed as a strong coincidence for me last night, too. "The Chicago firm is Wilcox, Savage and Knox, P.A."

Cramer's barking laugh wafted through the room. "I don't need to run the firm through our system. It's a boutique firm with one client. Guess who?"

"The Bianchi family."

He pointed at me. "Give the man a cigar."

"DeMarco must've assumed I'd learn about the games," I said.

"And he was smart enough to come clean with Bianchi."

"Bianchi figures, if we were partners, he could pressure me to keep the illegal gambling racket in Pine County a secret." The idea of Bianchi believing I could be bought burned my pride.

This buyout would never happen once Kendra gave them the news I was no longer in the picture. Wilcox, Savage and Knox's buy-in offer amounted to nothing more than a power play aimed at me. Bianchi wanted to own me, literally. And I suspected DeMarco wasn't the only one who knew Dad visited Ethan's game.

I placed three calls to Ethan. Twice on the burner phone I'd given him, and once on his cell. All three went unanswered. He must sleep like the dead.

I called Dad's to check in. Sue Ellen answered the phone.

"I'll be in Loblolly in a couple of hours, but I need to swing by and see Ethan first."

"I need to talk to you."

Her solemn tone turned my mouth dry. I swallowed a gum-ball sized lump. "Is there a problem?"

"No." She released a heavy breath. "Not exactly."

My heart bumped. "What is it? Is Dad okay?"

"He's fine." She didn't sound fine. She sounded worried. "Take care of your business and we'll talk when you get here."

"Is Colleen nearby? I may need her to work late."

"Her granddaughter had some kind of stomach bug, and since I was already here, she stayed home today."

I'd abused Sue Ellen's friendship enough. "If you need to go—"

"I'm available until three," she said. "Jana called in with the same symptoms as Colleen's girl, and I need to cover the dinner shift."

"I promise to be home by eleven."

"Okay, gotta run. I'm making Zachary pancakes."

I spent a few minutes mentally reshuffling my day. I needed to concentrate my efforts on IDing the owner of the bat. I had to find the killer before they learned the police knew Dad handled the bat. Before the killer realized Dad could identify him. I'd planned to interview four people on my suspect list—the three boys convicted in Vernon's court, and Corky, Ethan's salesman. No way I could get four interviews completed by midafternoon. I called Caleb.

"Any of your deputies work security after hours?"

"A couple, why?"

"I want to hire round-the-clock surveillance on Dad's place."

"Really?" By the tone of his voice, Caleb thought my idea waded into overkill.

"Doug Larson still install security systems?" I asked.

"Yeah." He stretched the word into three.

"Send me the names of your deputies who want extra income. They know Dad, and if possible, I'd rather not use rent-a-cops."

"If you're worried about Zachary wandering away, Jasmine might know someone who could sit with him when you're not at home."

"Not worried about him wandering away."

"Then why—"

"Word of Dad's fingerprints on the bat will eventually leak, probably sooner rather than later. And after the other night, I confiscated his guns. It's too risky to leave him alone without backup."

After three seconds of silence, I said, "If the killer gets word the police found Dad's prints on the murder weapon, they'll realize Dad can identify them."

Caleb grunted, then, "Yeah, I thought about that, but surely no one would take on Zachary."

I couldn't shake off Sue Ellen's voice when she said we needed to talk. Her tone sounded antsy, and solid-as-a-rock Sue Ellen didn't throw easy. Something must've happened. "Maybe no one would take Dad on six months ago, but now…too many people know about his diagnosis. I'm running out of time, and I could use your help on Ethan's case."

"Anything you need."

"I'm on my way to the cabin to talk to Ethan. Can you meet me at Dad's house at three o'clock?"

"See you then."

In my years of prosecuting criminals, I'd found actual killers very different from the TV variety. Very few murderers planned their crime. Especially crimes of passion like Grace's murder.

The theory I found most probable—Grace's death was the result of misdirected anger. My gut said the murder and the fire were executed by the person sending threats to Vernon and Sandra. Statistically, emotional killers were rarely methodical. They made mistakes. Mistakes I planned to expose.

Without the luxury of time, I'd have to begin my interviews via phone. I'd start with the easiest, the father of one of my high school friends, Jed Thompson. Of the three cases on my list, this one had the lightest sentence. Which equated to the least likely parent to hold a grudge against Vernon. And Jed and Grace had a history, even if was only a few dates. I needed to cross him and his dad off my list.

I start with the father and go from there. Four years ago, Vernon sentenced Jed's sixteen-year-old brother Dylan for possession with intent to sell. The police confiscated thirty-one grams. Three grams less, and Dylan would've faced the lesser charge of possession. I suspected that's why Vernon gave Dylan six months in rehab instead of a stint in juvie.

Using my phone's digital assistant, I placed a call to the Thompson residence, and spoke with Dylan's father, Billy. Vernon's four-year-old file listed Billy Thompson's occupation as shift manager for Pine Forrest Products, the defunct sawmill.

After a brief introduction, Mr. Thompson said he remembered me from my football days with Jed. I also remembered Mr. Thompson. Looking back, he'd always seemed pleasant and friendly, if a little on the quiet side.

"I'm representing Ethan Benton," I said. "I'm not sure if you're aware, but the fire that destroyed his car lot has been ruled arson."

"A shame about the Underwood girl."

A tingle ran up my spine. "So you knew Grace Underwood, Mr. Thompson?"

"Sure. We live in the same neighborhood as the Underwoods."

"I wondered if I could speak to Dylan."

"Dylan?" Mr. Thompson's voice adopted an edge of irritation. Fatherly protection maybe?

"I just have a couple of questions." If the father held the grudge, the kid would be easier to break.

The seconds ticking by was my first clue the conversation had veered a hard left. My earlier spine tingle took on heat. "Mr. Thompson?"

He inhaled a breath that came across shaky. But hard to tell over the phone, could be a spotty connection.

"You can't talk to Dylan." His voice was gruff with an emotion I couldn't quite discern.

When he didn't offer more, I said, "Would you mind if I dropped by the house in a couple of hours?"

Dylan was now an adult. His father's refusing to let me talk to Dylan punched my curiosity up a notch.

"Dylan's dead."

It took a few seconds for his words to register.

"I'm sorry, Mr. Thompson. I didn't know." Dylan was dead? I couldn't have bungled this conversation more if I'd set out to make an enemy. Before I gathered my thoughts, apologized for my insensitivity, and asked for Jed's contact information, Mr. Thompson disconnected our call.

I spent the next hour berating myself for going off half-cocked like an unprepared rookie. Dead. I did the math. Dylan should be close to twenty. I mentally added new questions under Dylan's name. How did he die? How long ago? Where?

CHAPTER TWENTY

I PASSED THE WELCOME to Loblolly sign and turned onto Old River Road twenty minutes earlier than expected. Crossing over Goosehead Bridge, I checked my rearview mirror and verified the security camera was still mounted under the right eave.

The rumble of an engine filled the air, followed by an emerald green Lamborghini shooting around a curve. The driver whizzed by. His brake lights flashed and his car slowed to a stop. Then, as if changing his mind, he revved his engine and sped over the bridge.

The traffic on Old River Road was primarily locals and heavy machinery used in harvesting lumber, not race cars with price tags starting at three hundred grand. Farmers checking their crops or hunters checking their cabins drove pick-ups. The chance a local farmer owned the Lamborghini, by my estimate, fell somewhere around a million to one.

The Bentons had the only cabin with an entrance well-groomed enough to welcome a car sporting a ground clearance of roughly four inches. I sent a quick text to Cramer.

Any chance DeMarco has a green Lamborghini?

When I arrived at the cabin, someone had parked Ethan's black Escalade by the back door. I wasn't surprised. Even though his monitor chained him to a hundred feet of the cabin, residing in the middle of nowhere without the means to leave in an emergency would make a person feel pretty darn vulnerable.

I knocked twice, then opened the door. No one bothered to lock doors in town, much less in the forest. I walked into the empty kitchen. "Ethan?" Living room was empty, so I checked the hall. Noticed the bathroom door closed and debated interrupting. After a few seconds, I rapped on the door. "Ethan, it's Jackson."

"Be out in a minute." Ethan mumbled something else, but the only words I made out were *damn* and *privacy*.

I grabbed a bottle of water out of the fridge and stood at a window overlooking the water. A shame no one used the cabin for anything but illegal poker; the fishing in this part of the river had always been pretty decent.

After I closed Ethan's case, maybe Dad and I could trek up this way, make camp, and enjoy a few days of fly fishing. The water would've cooled off by now. April and May would be a better option for camping, but I wasn't sure if Dad would be fishing come spring.

Guilt hit hard and fast. Chances were good the GBI would seize this property under the Equitable Sharing Program. News of a high-profile bust would travel fast and give the press another hit on Vernon and Sandra.

Damn Ethan, his parents didn't deserve this nightmare.

"Ethan is difficult, but he acts out for attention," my mom had said more than once. "*Be patient with him. He needs someone like you in his life."*

After Mom died, I carried around an unreasonable obligation to stick by Ethan, as if that's what Mom would expect of me. I treated the obligation like a secret and never shared the reason for my continued friendship with Ethan—not even with Dad. I had no idea why kids shouldered secret burdens, I just knew they did. As a prosecutor, I witnessed kids protecting parents, their siblings, their friends.

Once I solved this case, my days of helping Ethan were

over.

My phone buzzed with a text from Cramer.

DeMarco has a registered Lamborghini Gallardo, Yr 2021, tag#: LMD1082. Call me!!!

The toilet flushed and I still hadn't come up with a way to incorporate DeMarco's visit into my spiel to convince Ethan to turn state's evidence.

Ethan emerged from the bathroom a second later. Obviously, personal hygiene hadn't been on his morning to-do list. His jeans looked as if they'd endured twenty-four hours of continuous wear, and his hair was in desperate need of a comb.

Hit hard and fast. "What did Lou want?"

Ethan showed no outward signs of surprise.

I waited. A guilty conscience usually filled silence with chatter. But not Ethan. He firmly locked his jaw. Although, a war played out in his eyes—truth or lie, truth or lie. He took on the same stance he had in tenth grade when the principal caught us sneaking back into school after grabbing burgers and shakes for lunch. In tenth grade, we were too stupid to think Chet and Sue Ellen would rat us out.

Ethan slunk across the room and plopped on the sofa. "Lou and I had some unfinished business. By the way, Lou doesn't much care for you."

"Feeling's mutual."

"Games are set up for the week." He propped his feet on the coffee table. "It's too late for me to back out."

I raised a brow.

He heaved a sigh and raked his fingers through his hair. "Damn it all, Jackson. I can't say no. Lou's connected."

I swallowed the words on the tip of my tongue and reshuffled my argument. Ethan running one more game was exactly what I wanted. Now, I didn't have to disclose the bust and worry about Ethan snitching to DeMarco. Best of all, when Cramer arrested Ethan, his shock would be real. No one would suspect a setup.

No reason to worry about Ethan taking a deal once he heard racketeering convictions carried a minimum twenty-year sentence. When he realized his parents had no pull with federal charges, Ethan would jump at Cramer's deal.

I was under no legal obligation to advise Ethan of my conversation with Cramer. As a ward of the court, I had a fiduciary responsibility to report a potential crime or risk accusation of assisting. "Racketeering and money laundering isn't in my wheelhouse. You get busted, you find another attorney."

He swung his legs to the floor and stood. "Lou has everything under control."

If Lou thought his fake poker debt against Dad and Bianchi's buy-in of Taylor and Vine had everything under control, he was in for a life-changing surprise.

"Give me your game schedule. I want to make sure to steer clear."

"Tuesdays and Thursdays."

"You have a game tomorrow night?" For good measure, I added the expected disappointment to my tone.

"Can you do me a solid and make a liquor run?"

Man had nerve, I'd give him that. I had no intention of doing any more solids for Ethan. "I make a habit of not assisting clients with breaking laws."

"My players expect booze."

"Ask whoever delivered your car to buy your supplies."

"No way I can explain that much booze to Corky." His whine grated on my last nerve. "And Naomi's not taking my calls."

Smart girl. "Why aren't you answering the burner I gave you?"

His gaze skated around the room before he shrugged. "I thought it'd be better to turn it off while Lou was here."

He was lying. I'd been a prosecutor long enough to recognize the signs. The tightening skin around his eyes, shifting his bare feet, his normal sarcastic tone disappearing into friendly and accommodating.

I'd bet a month's pay DeMarco exchanged the SIM card. By now, the burner I gave Ethan had a tap.

"Keep both your cells on. I don't have time to drive out here every time I have something to tell you." I chugged my water and tossed the bottle in the trash on my way out of the cabin.

"Hey."

I looked back.

Ethan stood in the doorway with his palms in the air. "Well?"

"Well, what?"

"What did you come out here to tell me?"

Caught flat-footed, my mind searched for a plausible reason to drive thirty minutes out of my way. "Checking to make sure you were still alive. Keep your damn phone on."

I jumped in my truck and left. Once I hit River Road, I called Cramer. "Next game's scheduled for tomorrow night."

"That's great. We'll be ready," Cramer sounded like a kid learning a new puppy was in his future. "I'm on my way out to Goosehead Bridge to grab the IP address off the camera."

"DeMarco made an appearance at the cabin."

"Yeah, after your text, I figured something happened. What'd he say?"

"Nothing to me. He was leaving when I arrived."

"Probably best not to rock the boat."

"Ethan decided not to cross DeMarco. He'll be as surprised as the players tomorrow night."

I gave Cramer a minute to absorb the change. When he didn't comment, I added, "It'll play better, and I stay uninvolved. I want to let Ethan think he made the deal with you on his own."

It took Cramer so long to respond, I started to think he had a problem. "Yeah, okay. I can make that work."

"I need you to keep him locked up a few days."

"Not sure that'll fly since Benton's father is fishing buddies with the governor."

"You said you'd help out any way you could. I need this."

"You mind me asking why?"

"Even if I believed Ethan capable of brutally killing his girl, he'd never burn down a business that allowed him to wash his money. As long as the real killer thinks Ethan's behind bars—."

"The killer has no idea he's being hunted."

"Exactly."

"Okay, I'll drag my feet. Maybe swing three days."

I would have three uninterrupted days focused solely on the killer. "I'll take it. Let me know when the bust goes down, and I'll brief Ethan's parents. I'll try and give you a few hours before the senator bends the governor's ear."

"Roger that."

When I got to Dad's, he and Sue Ellen were sitting on the sofa watching *Gunsmoke*. I stuck my head into the living room. "Hey, I'm home."

Sue Ellen patted Dad's knee. "Well, I better get a move on. Chet's expecting me to work the dinner shift." Her gaze remained on Dad, waiting for a reply.

He stared straight at the TV screen. He didn't seem so much engrossed in the program as unaware. His glassy eyes looked vacant. Like they did when his mind wandered into one of the deep empty pockets in his brain.

Sue Ellen followed me out of the room, and the welcoming, homey scent of cinnamon and orange pulled me towards the kitchen. A dish towel covered a pan of what I hoped were homemade sweet rolls. I lifted the edge of the faded cotton cloth towel. Score!

"I'm just about to spread glaze over those."

I pointed to one of my mom's plastic containers lined with wax paper. "Probably won't need that. Caleb's on his way over and between the three of us, doubt we have leftovers."

"I sliced leftover pot roast and stored it in the fridge. Plenty enough for sandwiches." She busied herself putting away dishes drying in the rack.

"What did you want to talk to me about?"

She folded her drying towel, then turned and faced me. "It'll be easier to explain if I show you."

I followed her into the dining room. She opened the china cabinet and removed my grandmother's soup tureen. "I was going to use this bowl to serve the pot roast last night and found these."

Lifting the lid, she removed at least thirty rolls of tightly wound slips of paper, along with a single brown nymph used as bait on a fly rod. At first glance, I thought the paper was old adding machine tape, then realized the size was off. She slipped a blue band from the roll and straightened the pages. The edges were torn and looked ripped from a notebook. Similar to the kind Dad carried in his front shirt pocket.

Cops lived by notes. They jotted times, dates, names, anything they might need for a case or regurgitate later as evidence in a court of law. Every cop I knew had a note-taking system they lived by. Their notes were valuable and protected, filed away in case files and never destroyed. When cases were microfilmed, the cop notes were copied and followed the cold case. During my time in Atlanta, a surprising number of cold cases were ultimately solved using notes written by the investigating officer.

If Dad had stored his case notes at home, Caleb could take them back to the station. I picked up the top sheet and read,

My name is Zachary Jackson Taylor.

My wife's name is Anna Marie Cumberland Taylor.

I have one son—Jackson Cumberland Taylor.

My birthday is January 15, 1955.

Anna's birthday is March 10, 1959.

Jackson's birthday is June 6, 1988.

I worked for the Pine County Sheriff's office for 31 years.

I was sheriff for 20 years.

My wife died on 10-10-20 or 2021 or 2019???

She had cancer.

I slid into a chair, set the page aside, and read the next sheet.

My name is Zachary Jackson Taylor.

My wife's name is Anna Marie Cumberland Taylor.

I have one son—Jackson Cumberland Taylor.

My birthday is January 15, 1955.

My wife's birthday is March 10, 1959.

My son's birthday is June 6, 1988.

I worked for the Pine County Sheriff's office for 32 years.

I was sheriff for 26 years.

My wife died on October 10, 2019.

She had cancer

Each page exactly the same. The shocking heartbreak of reality hit me. These were Dad's mental exercise to commit slowly ebbing facts to memory. I picked up another roll, slipped the band off, and found similar lists of personal facts. This roll of twenty or so pages included the names of his parents and grandparents.

Sue Ellen sat in the chair beside me. "I counted sixty-eight rolls," she said. "I opened enough of them to know they're all about the same. He lists dates and names of his family. I can't imagine how long it took him to write this many."

Tears filled her eyes. She picked up the sheets from the first roll, bound them together, then slipped the blue band in place. She gathered the rolls, put them back inside the soup tureen, placed the fishing tie on top, and closed the lid. She gently placed the dish in the china cabinet.

"Come to his office. There's some other things you need to see."

I wasn't sure my heart could stand anything more, but I followed her down the hall, passing the living room with *Gunsmoke*'s theme playing on the TV. I glanced in.

Dad still sat on the sofa staring into space.

The home office adjoined the master bedroom. Sue Ellen opened the bottom drawer of his desk and pulled out a spiral notebook. "After I found the notes in the dining room, I snooped in here." She handed me the top book, at least ten additional books were stored underneath.

I flipped the cover, read the first page, then thumbed through the pages. They all looked similar to the first page. I turned back and read.

Today is Tuesday, September 19.

I had Raisin Bran for breakfast. Jackson is home. He says he's going to stay but I can't remember for how long. I need to ask him.

Colleen cleaned today. Her little girl came. She helped Colleen. Her son pulled weeds in the rose garden. I don't remember if I paid him. Ask Colleen.

I can't remember if I ate lunch.

Sue Ellen came for dinner. We watched TV and pruned the roses. She cooked pot roast. We watched a movie. She made popcorn.

I flipped the pages and found more of the same. "These are like a daily journal."

"I think he writes down the things he wants to remember, things he's afraid he will forget. I don't know why I thought you should know..." A tear escaped, and she wiped it with her finger. She gave me a small, sad smile. "He's such a good man. I'm so mad." She pounded her fist on the desk. "I'm not ready to let him go."

I folded her into my arms, as much to offer comfort as to receive. "Thanks for staying with him last night. And for saving me the night before. You're a true friend to us both."

She pulled away and studied my face. "Please tell me you're not thinking of sticking him in a home and going back to Atlanta."

"No. I'm here to stay." If nothing else, the last ten minutes solidified that decision. No way I'd leave Dad again.

A door slammed.

She grabbed a tissue from a box on the desk, wiped her eyes. "That's Zachary. He's probably looking for me." She pointed at the book in my hand. "Put that back."

I nodded and she hurried out of the office.

It was as if every muscle in my body turned to stone. I slumped in Dad's chair, slipped my phone out of my pocket, and found the phone number for Doug Larson Security.

Could Doug design a system to keep bad guys out and a good guy in? And how in the hell was I supposed to convince Dad his life was in danger over an event he couldn't remember?

Doug didn't seem surprised by my request to install a security system. Nor did he mention Dad's illness. But when he said he'd prioritize the work order and agreed to stop by the house on his way home, I was fairly certain word of Dad's diagnosis was common knowledge.

I removed the stack of journals from the drawer. They came close to filling the entire file drawer. I thought about taking a few to my room to read. Even though Dad made an entry last night, it was unlikely he'd notice a couple were missing.

I clutched the stack to my chest—a son's curiosity had no right to intrude on a father's privacy. I'd ask permission before reading any more. I placed the books, one at a time, back in the drawer. Each book felt like an arrow stabbing my aching heart. I shut the drawer and went to find Dad, hoping I could find the words to explain why I planned to turn his home into his personal jail.

CHAPTER TWENTY-ONE

"SHERIFFS DON'T NEED fancy security systems." Dad's eyes flashed with the stubborn anger Mom had claimed I inherited. "This is Loblolly, not Atlanta. People respect private property in my town."

Remnants of our lunch were strewn across the kitchen bar. Dad's half-eaten roast beef sandwich, an empty bag of chips, an open jar of mayonnaise. Surprisingly, the entire pan of cinnamon rolls remained untouched. My appetite competed with the string of knots lining my stomach. The knots won hands down.

So much for not riling him. He hadn't bought into the general need for home security, so I had no option but to go to Plan B—convince him he needed personal protection.

The problem with Plan B—spoken in the vernacular of a teenager—it suuucked!

I rose, searched the cabinet over the sink for a bottle of Tagamet, and dry swallowed two. I couldn't solve this case sitting at home. And I couldn't leave Dad until I knew he was safe.

I switched tactics. "I could use your help on my case."

The anger in Dad's eyes simmered into something akin to a distrusting wary. "You promised me you'd walk away from Ethan Benton's case."

Jesus. We'd already been through this, had he forgotten our conversation in the shed? "I know I promised to withdraw, and believe me, I wish I could. But I can't, and I need your help." At least his eyes no longer shot fiery darts at my chest. "Will you at least look at my notes, and see if I've missed anything?"

He collected our used paper plates and threw them in the trash. "Yeah, I guess I can take a look." He pretended to begrudge the favor, but at heart Dad was born to solve crimes. My father was a county lawman with the mind of a big-city detective.

"Let's set up in the dining room." I sprinted to my bedroom and grabbed my laptop, the file with the police reports, and my notebook. Talking through the case with Dad would not only give me a solid sounding board, the exercise allowed me to gauge his critical thinking skills and short-term memory loss firsthand.

I sat at the dining room and motioned Dad into the seat next to mine. I pulled up the murder board I'd stored on my laptop. "I've asked for Caleb's help. He should be here within the hour."

"Caleb believes his brother is innocent."

"So do I."

Dad grunted his response.

"Look, I haven't stuck my head in the sand. I know Ethan lives on the backside of honest. But hear me out before you assume he's a murdering arsonist."

I waited for Dad to nod his grudging assent.

"Some of what I'm going to share is confidential." I didn't need to remind Dad of his fiduciary responsibilities. After thirty years in law enforcement confidentiality was all but seared on his brain.

Short-term memory was Dad's nemesis. But at this moment, his demeanor appeared normal, his eyes were clear and assessing, and during lunch, he hadn't seemed confused about anything except me not giving up Ethan's case.

I removed copies of four letters from my file. "Over

the past several weeks, the Bentons have received these notes by mail."

His eyes skimmed the first page. "Does Hank know?"

"Yes. Caleb opened a file and involved the GBI."

Dad nodded. "Protocol for a threat on a senator. How long in between the notes?"

"Not sure. Caleb will know for certain, but Jasmine mentioned the first one arriving over a month ago, the last one day before yesterday."

"So they received one after the fire?"

Good deduction. He was focused. "Yeah."

"Are the notes postmarked?"

"Yes. Different cities, but all within a hundred miles of Loblolly."

"The last message could've been mailed before the fire." Definitely thinking clearly. "You think Grace's killer is the sender?" His tone indicated he had his doubts.

I leaned back against my chair, considered if I might've jumped to the conclusion too quickly. "I think it'd be a helluva coincidence otherwise."

Dad set the letter aside. "Okay. What else you got?"

"Grace and Ethan argued six hours before the fire. Grace's sister picked her up from the diner, and Ethan went to Al's Place. Ethan claims, and Al agrees, he drank steady until closing."

"Guessing he drove home." Dad's opinion of Ethan wove through his words.

I shrugged.

"Alone?"

"Yes, which leaves him no human alibi." I enlarged the timeline on my computer. "But I assessed Ethan's security system, and his garage door sensor and outside camera logged his arrival at two-twenty."

Dad shuffled through my file, pulled out the initial police report. "911 call came in at three-twelve AM. Gives him plenty of time to drive back to his car lot."

"Maybe, but not in his car. The outside camera logged no movement other than a stray dog and a raccoon walking by his house. The next vehicle in Ethan's driveway was a police car at six forty-eight the next morning notifying him of the fire."

"And a dead body," Dad said.

"Right. The garage door wasn't raised from the time Ethan arrived home until the police searched the garage the following day. But by that time, Ethan was already in county lockup."

"He could've switched off his security system the night of the fire, turned it back on when he got home."

"His system records shutdowns. No record of one."

"Maybe Ethan figured a way to scam his system. Some kind of work-around. Doesn't he have some kind of computer science degree."

"He does." I'd also considered the idea. "But he was drunk, and according to Al, having a hard time walking. Takes a clear head to hack into a complicated security system."

"You always had a blind spot for Ethan."

"I didn't, not really. I know what he is. I also know what he's not."

"Bludgeoning murders are the result of heightened emotion or carried out by a psychopath," Dad said.

Cop school 101. "Agreed. I just don't believe Ethan is a psychopath and I don't think he has the stomach to bludgeon a woman carrying his baby."

Dad mouth firmed. He still wasn't convinced.

I went back to the full murder board that displayed photos of Ethan, Grace Underwood, her sister Naomi, Corky, Ethan's salesman, Lou DeMarco, and the fathers of the teen boys convicted in Vernon's court.

Billy Thompson, whose son had died.

Kevin Durban, the father of the boy charged with arson.

Lamar Chesney, the father of a car thief.

And Dad.

Dad leaned forward. "I'm on your case board?" This time around his voice was more curious than resentful. A shot of adrenaline zipped through me.

Dad didn't remember our earlier conversation about the murder board and the bat. I didn't look forward to rehashing the conversation but I had no choice.

I dug the lab report out of my file. "You're on my board because your fingerprints were found on the murder weapon."

His face turned purple and shiny, like an overripe plum. His expression went from insulting to irate and morphing into shock in the span of three seconds.

He pressed his fingers into his forehead. "You told me that already. I remember now."

"It's the reason I didn't withdraw from Ethan's case."

He cradled his scalp, dug in his fingers. "Why the devil can't I remember holding that bat?"

I gripped his shoulder. "No one believes you killed Grace Underwood. There's a reasonable explanation. We just have to figure it out." I gave him a minute to let my words sink through his self-anger.

He stared at the report. "The victim was beat to death," he said as if talking to himself. "I didn't even know her." His voice shook, but not with anger. Then a deep sigh washed away the last of his fury. He met my gaze. "I forget so many things."

"You remember a lot, too. Let's focus on what we know and what you do remember. I checked my gear in the shed, the bat that killed Grace is not my old Louisville Slugger. Which means you had to have run into someone you knew and for some reason handled their bat."

"Hello?" Caleb's voice carried in from the hall.

Sue Ellen must have left the front door unlocked. Amazing Doug Larson could make a living installing security systems in a town where no one worried enough to lock a door.

Except Ethan, who turned his home into mini Fort Knox.

Caleb walked into the dining room, beamed a smile. "Zachary." He stuck out his hand. "Good to see you."

Dad rose, shook Caleb's hand. "Glad you're here.

"Dad and I are reviewing the case."

Caleb nodded, pulled out a chair. "Three heads are better than two, even if one of them is mine."

"We need a copy of the 911 call reporting the fire," I said to Caleb.

"We have it on file. I'll ask Brenda to email a copy."

"Okay, let's get started."

Caleb slipped his notebook from his front pocket.

I stole a glance at Dad. He stared at the lab report listing his name. I got the feeling his mind was somewhere else and focused back on Caleb. "My gut says the anonymous 911 call came from the killer."

"Because?" Caleb asked, his pen poised and ready to write.

"Anonymous call at three o'clock—"

"Three-twelve," Dad said. My heart did a slow roll. He never ceased to amaze me.

"Right, three-twelve. Loblolly's dead at that time of the night. The only downtown bar closes at two, so there's no reason to be in the area."

"Could've been kids," Caleb offered.

"Do deputies patrol downtown?"

Dad straightened in his seat. "Every hour." He looked at Caleb for confirmation.

"That's right," Caleb said. "Sturgis pulled duty that night. Said he didn't notice anything unusual, and he would've mentioned seeing teens out that late."

"And why was the call anonymous? In general, anonymous callers don't want to get involved or be questioned by police. The average Joe passing by and spotting the fire wouldn't know Grace Underwood's body was inside the building. So why not give your name? Unless you had something to hide."

"Seems a likely theory," Caleb said.

Dad was the harder nut to split. He sat stone-faced, offering no opinion. But he was listening.

"In the letters sent to your parents, the reference *'a son for a son'* gives the impression the sender is a father, and his son has been harmed. Your Dad had three fairly recent cases involving teen boys, so their fathers check at least one box on the sender's profile. I'd like you to interview them for means and opportunity."

Caleb flipped a page in his notebook. "Names?"

"Kevin Durban, son Ronald, and Lamar Chesney, son Derrick. And, we need to talk to Corky."

Caleb's pen screeched to a stop. "Corky? Ethan's salesman?"

"Is there more than one Corky in Loblolly?"

Caleb shrugged. "I just don't see it."

"I don't know Corky, but Ethan claims he doesn't have keys to the office and doesn't have a kid playing ball. But he is still the most logical person to make a copy of Naomi's or Ethan's key. And a bat could be his weapon of choice for a home invasion. I know it's a long shot, but we need to mark him off our list." I stood. "Anyone else want coffee?"

"I'll take a cup," Caleb said.

"How about you, Dad?"

He got to his feet. "That coffee is from this morning. I'll brew a fresh pot."

He sounded tired, and I fought to push down my guilt. I needed as much from him as he could summon. And working a case could be just what he needed to feel useful.

I turned back to Caleb. "When you conduct your

interviews, start with small talk. Ask about their kids, especially the boys who came before your dad in court. Find out where they live now, how they're doing. And find out if any of them played baseball or if the father happens to be on a city or church team. We find the owner of the bat, we find the killer."

Caleb's gaze strayed to the kitchen, then back to me. He raised a brow, clearly asking if Dad knew the owner.

I shook my head.

Caleb's phone dinged with a text. "Brenda's sent the 911 call." He pressed play.

I closed my eyes and focused on the voice reporting the fire. Not a voice I recognized offhand. "Doesn't sound like a teen."

The deep voice, almost a baritone, calmly stated there was a fire at Benton's Used Cars. When the operator asked his name, he hesitated for a second, then disconnected.

Dad walked in with three mugs of coffee. "Did you trace the burner?"

"Yes, sir," Caleb said. "Purchased two months ago at the Walmart in Blakeley."

Dad sat, sipped his coffee. "Who buys prepaid phones?"

"Parents buy them for their kids to limit charges," Caleb said.

"Criminals who don't want their calls traced," Dad said.

"And people who have money problems and can't get credit." I made a note in my file, then asked Caleb, "Can you run a credit report on the three fathers and Corky?"

Caleb scratched a note in his book. "You only gave me two fathers who fit the profile."

"The other one is Billy Thompson. I talked to him yesterday. His son Dylan died last year. I want to take that interview." I wanted to apologize in person for my inconsideration.

Dad picked up the lab report again. "I've known Billy

Thompson since elementary school. Quiet, stellar fly fisherman. Salt of the earth. He wouldn't hurt a bug."

"And Mr. Thompson doesn't hold a grudge against my dad," Caleb said. "Dad and I went to Dylan's funeral. At the gravesite, Mr. Thompson told Dad how much he appreciated all he tried to do for his boy."

"Naomi mentioned that Grace and Jed, Billy's oldest son, were an item for a while."

Caleb frowned. "Jed and Grace might've gone out a few times, but as far as I know, they were never serious. And Jed's a stand-up guy, volunteer fireman, coaches Little League."

"So he probably owns a bat or two."

Caleb raised both palms. "Hell, I have a couple lying around. Who doesn't?"

"Evidently, your brother."

The doorbell rang. "That should be Doug Larson about the security system." I turned to Dad. "I need you to let me do this. News of your prints on the murder weapon will leak out. You might not remember touching the bat, but the killer will think you can identify him."

I left to answer the door. Dad didn't give his permission, but by the firm set of his lips, I knew he wouldn't refuse.

Caleb followed me down the hall. "Until we find Grace's killer, I'll put twenty-four hour surveillance on Zachary."

I breathed a sigh of relief, and gripped his shoulder. "Thank you."

"But just so you know, if Zachary asks why one of our deputies is sitting on his house, I'm claiming you twisted my arm."

CHAPTER TWENTY-TWO

I STOOD IN THE kitchen staring into the fridge, marveling at the lack of provisions for two bachelors with limited cooking skills. Dad's answer to cooking—a trip to the Loblolly Diner. I could cook, but ninety percent revolved around a gas grill, tin-foiled baked potatoes, and bagged salads. The garlic bread was optional.

After meeting with Doug on the new security system, Dad retired to his bedroom for a nap. The day had taken its toll, and I wasn't sure he had the energy to dine in town tonight. Going anywhere with Dad resulted in a parade of locals stopping by the table to shake hands and, as Dad would say, shoot the bull. Elected small-town sheriffs wore two hats, lawman and politician. My father had always seemed to enjoy both equally.

I grabbed my keys and wallet and stepped outside. With Colleen off today, I didn't feel comfortable leaving Dad without someone in the house.

True to his word, Caleb assigned round-the-clock surveillance, and Steve Sinclair, a young deputy who looked no more than a year out of high school, caught tonight's shift. Steve seemed to confuse security details with stakeouts and had parked at the end of our long winding drive.

He saw me coming and stepped out of his patrol car. "Mr. Taylor."

We shook hands. "Please, call me Jackson. Wondered if I could impose on you for about an hour?"

"Sure, what can I do?"

"I'm headed into town to grab dinner. Would you mind staying inside the house until I get back? Dad's taking a nap." Unsure how much Caleb had explained, I didn't elaborate.

"Be glad to."

"And in the future, I'd rest easier if you parked a little closer to the house. You're welcome to sit on the porch or under the oak in the front yard. Dad knows you're here, and he's fine with it." Or almost fine. At least I didn't think he'd bite the kid's head off for hanging around.

He followed me back to the house, and I left him watching an old *Seinfeld* episode.

On the way into town, I called Caleb to see how his interviews were shaping up.

"I talked to Ronald Durban's mom," he said. "His dad's a deacon at the Baptist church, and they had some kind of meeting this afternoon. I plan to go back in the morning to speak with Mr. Durban, but I don't think he's our guy."

I held off asking why for the moment. "Did you get an update on the son from Mrs. Durban?"

"Ronald goes to school at Valdosta State."

If that were true, he'd certainly straightened out. "We need to follow up. Verify Ronald's still attending and in good standing." I knew from experience, without a warrant, his grades were off limits. "It'll be easier for a cop to verify than an attorney."

"I'll handle it. Ronald's mom made a point of letting me know she and Mr. Durban think highly of your father and my dad. She said Zachary arranged to get Ronald in the boys' work farm in Richland instead of sending him to juvie hall. According to Ms. Durban, Ronald came back a new kid."

"Did she seem overly zealous?"

"Overly zealous?"

Caleb had less than two years of experience as a cop, none as a detective. "Did you get the feeling she might be trying too hard to convince you how much she and her husband liked your dad?"

"Oh, I see where you're going. Was she faking? No. I don't think so. She mentioned her son sent a thank-you letter to Dad before leaving the work farm. I checked. Dad remembers reading it."

A letter to the judge could've been encouraged or even required by the program manager. I made a mental note to follow-up.

"Mrs. Durban believes Ronald was in with the wrong crowd," Caleb said.

"Yeah. That's every parent's go-to response when their kid falls off the rails."

"I hear you. I'm on my way to meet Corky. He bowls in a league and agreed to meet up for a beer."

I thought about suggesting a different venue, but Caleb wasn't questioning Corky in an official capacity, so the bar environment wasn't a bad idea. "Might be better if you limit your drinks to one."

"I planned to have a Coke. But Corky loosens up after a few beers. I'll know everything he knows inside an hour."

I laughed. Caleb had the makings of a good detective. "Stop by the house after, and we'll have a cold one."

As soon as I stepped into the diner, the odor of Wednesday's special slammed my nostrils. I detested liver and onions worse than bologna, although Dad was a big fan of both.

I stopped to say hello to Mayor Duncan and Stella Campbell, the city clerk. We chatted about Stella's daughter, Candice, my high school sweetheart, now living in Savannah. After a few minutes, I made my way to the bar and spent a few minutes bringing Sue Ellen up to date.

After ordering all-the-way burgers for Deputy Sinclair

and me and the special for Dad, I spotted Mathew Finn sitting alone in a window booth. I walked over.

Mathew had finished his meal and was working his way through a slice of a lemon meringue pie.

"Jackson." He half-stood. We shook, and he waved me into a seat. "My goodness, it's been five years since I last saw you."

I slid in across from him. "I'm glad I ran into you."

"Heard you were in town representing Ethan Benton. Gotta say I'm glad Vernon called you instead of me." His forehead wrinkled. "But I was surprised you took the case. Thought you were working in Atlanta as a prosecutor. Didn't realize you'd switched sides. Not that we're not all on the same side of law and order..."

Mathew rambled on for another few minutes about the law and how we had to work together. More often than not, he tended to have one-way conversations, requiring nothing more than a warm body to listen. I waited for him to come up for air and jumped in. "I planned to call you later this week."

"Really?"

The idea seemed to please him. "I've decided to move back to Loblolly."

Mathew's smile dropped like a cartoon anvil.

"I want to spend time with my dad."

His face softened. "Yeah. I heard Zachary has Alzheimer's. It's a heartbreaking way to go. My mother-in-law died two years ago. In the end, she didn't know me, or my wife, not even her grandkids. She started gibbering words that didn't make sense. By the time she passed she couldn't speak at all. Sadder than sad that was."

His description of his mother-in-law's last days landed with a heavy ache of realization that I'd soon witness the described nightmare firsthand. I inhaled a breath, pushed the thought away, and forced myself to refocus on my reason for sitting down. "As I said, I'm moving home and wondered if you'd be interested in adding a lawyer to your firm?"

Mathew Finn speechless was a condition I'd never witnessed in all the years I'd known him. To call him dumbfounded would be a significant understatement.

"I'm not looking for a salaried position," I clarified. "I'm willing to rent an office and build up my end of the practice."

He collapsed into the back of the bench as though someone had knocked the breath from his lungs. We sat in silence for a few seconds, then he heaved a deep sigh. "I just don't know what to say." His voice so low, I had to lean forward to hear him. "I'm flattered, of course. Real flattered. And you'd be an asset to any firm. But to tell the truth, with the mill closing, there's hardly enough work in Loblolly for one lawyer."

As Dad said when I opted for law school, attorneys were on every corner—dominating TV commercials, billboards, advertisements plastered across buses and park benches in every town in America. I'd never considered there might be one-lawyer towns left in America.

"And would you be happy writing wills?" Mathew looked at me as if he already knew the answer. "Closing what little real estate is selling in these parts isn't enough for part-time work, much less two lawyers. I don't think I could support a wife and kids if I had to share the business. And if you open shop, even if it is my firm, some of the local business is bound to come your way."

He was right. In fact, I'd counted on my roots in the county to pull in business.

"You've worked in a fast-paced city for years. Loblolly will bore you to tears." His voice had taken on a lecturing tone as if I were the junior partner in need of a few lessons in our industry.

He swept his palm through the air as if banishing the idea and forked the last bite of his pie, chewed. "You bagged the only murder trial we've seen in ten years. We haven't had a homicide since Peavy found a dead vagrant in his pine field over five years ago. Your dad always believed someone dropped the guy over the county line after the fact."

More than a few of Mathew's points hit home. I had a sudden need to take my leave, go home, and mull over this life-changing decision with Dad.

A deep yearning gripped my heart and squeezed. The days of talking problems into a solution with Dad were coming to an end. And like Sue Ellen, I was nowhere near ready to let him go.

On the way home, I stopped at the meat market and bought a couple of rib eyes and baking potatoes. The market didn't carry bagged salads, so I gathered the necessary rabbit food for a chopped salad. At the last minute, I added a six-pack of beer.

On the way to the register, I noticed the owner had recognized a niche market and stocked a reasonably good supply of quality cigars. I added two of his best to my order and stepped into the checkout line.

Tomorrow night, Dad and I would barbecue steaks and enjoy a good cigar. The idea brought back memories of earlier bonding times we'd enjoyed when I came home on college breaks.

Pivoting, I walked back to the cigar display and traded in the two singles for a box. From now on, I planned to make as many father–son opportunities as possible.

Dad was awake when I arrived home, rested and in a good mood. I could tell he was fond of the young deputy Steve. While we ate, he asked about Steve's parents, if he had a girl, and if he'd worked on his casting since the last time they went fishing. It took Dad less than five minutes to get around to quizzing Steve about his future and if he thought law enforcement was his calling. The question caught the young deputy off-guard. He stuttered a couple of maybes and not sures, but then admitted he really liked being a cop.

That's when Dad got serious, extolling the importance of Steve having a five-year plan that would naturally build into an entire life plan.

I sat back, kept quiet, and let Dad have his fun. I'd found most kids under twenty didn't understand the concept or even why anyone needed a plan for their life.

Steve deftly ducked most of Dad's questions, and I wasn't at all surprised when he claimed the need to return a phone call and left.

As an only child, I'd been under Dad's microscope hundreds of times. I often complained of living in a fishbowl, with nowhere to hide from what I believed at the time to be unreasonable expectations. As an adult, I now knew Dad's expectations were the catalyst for my professional success.

I rose from the table and stacked our take-out containers. "While I was in town, I bought a box of wannabe Cubans. You up for a smoke?"

"Sure." His smile turned a little sly. "I believe I have a bottle of brandy around here somewhere."

We lit our cigars, sat on the back deck in two wooden rockers overlooking the pine forest, and sipped our drinks. The only sounds riding the air were mating crickets and a hoot owl claiming his territory.

After a few minutes, I broke our comfortable silence. "I'm thinking of moving back to Loblolly permanently."

Dad puffed on his cigar and considered my news. "What changed your mind?"

I'd opened this discussion door without planning for the inevitable conversation my decision would cause. I tiptoed away from the elephant stomping a circle around us. "Bottom line, I don't like living in Atlanta and don't see myself remaining indefinitely. So, building a practice in the city seems counterproductive."

We continued rocking, puffing, and sipping for another few minutes, then Dad's rocker slowed. "Is Kendra planning to join you here?"

He landed his question at mid-inhale, and I came close to choking on cigar smoke. Kendra had accompanied me on a couple of visits, but Dad had never mentioned her before.

"No," I said. "Kendra likes living in Atlanta." Imagining Kendra relocating to Loblolly, a town she referred to as podunk, brought on a chuckle. "But to be fair, Kendra's not invited."

Dad's rocker picked up speed. "Any other reason you've decided to move back home?"

I propped my feet on the bottom rung of the railing and screwed my courage. "I want to spend time with you."

"While you still can?"

My heart turned over. Dad's question was more statement than a question and required no response.

We sat in comfortable silence. Soaking in the quiet and our time together under a starlit sky. Enjoying a fall evening with a good cigar and a glass of fine brandy.

I'd often thought every life had a soundtrack. Tunes that reminded a person of their past. Carefree summers of a youth spent on a beach or throwing a baseball. Fly fishing on a river. Springsteen's song about his hometown always reminded me of tagging along with my father on Sunday mornings to pick up the *New York Times*—the only day he read an out-of-town paper.

The tune by Harry Chapin, with lyrics depicting the life of a father who never made time for his son, elicited memories of the day I announced my acceptance into

Duke School of Law. Chapin's song never comes to my mind because it resonates—just the opposite. Dad was never too busy to throw a ball, or go fishing, or attend my games in high school.

On the day Dad learned I had no plans to follow him into law enforcement, he struggled to hide his disappointment. But he never discouraged my dreams. And when I hear Chapin's song, the image of my father's hearty, back-slapping congratulations, delivered with a broken smile, never fails to pop into my head.

Tonight, sitting here with Dad, the song played like a loop in my head. I couldn't help but wonder if he realized just how great a father he had been. How great a father he still was.

"I'm going to miss you, Dad." The words slipped from my lips before I could pull them back.

After a few seconds, he cleared his throat. "I know, son." His voice low and graveled with emotion.

We let the moment lie in silence.

Finally, Dad doused his cigar and turned to face me. "I need you to promise me something."

"Anything," I said without hesitation.

"When the time comes, I want you to let me go. I mean, physically let me go. Won't be long now, and I won't know who you are. That's when you'll know it's time to let go."

My throat filled with tears. "We have time yet."

"In my desk, you'll find a brochure of a real nice place in Blakeley. That's where I want to live out my life."

The tears in my throat backed into my eyes. I sipped my brandy and fought for control.

"I need you to promise me, son."

I swallowed another healthy gulp and allowed the burn to travel down my throat. I used the time to gather myself.

"Dad, when the time comes, I'll think back to tonight and remember what you asked of me. But that's the only thing my heart will allow me to promise."

CHAPTER TWENTY-THREE

I WOKE TO BIRDS chirping in my ear. It took a few seconds for my sleep-deprived brain to realize I'd left my phone on the adjacent pillow. I cracked an eyelid and slid my cell closer. Sandra Benton? At six-thirty in the morning?

I swung my feet to the floor and cleared my throat. "Good morning, Senator."

"I'm on my way to Atlanta for a staff meeting. I want to tell my people you've filed a Brady motion for discovery, and the charges against Ethan have been dropped." Sandra, a stickler for propriety, could canonize an etiquette bible in her sleep. Dispensing with good morning gave clear notice of her current mood.

But my conscience heard the maternal angst swimming in the quasi-demand. A mama bear's fighting instinct ran through the senator's veins. I wasn't at all sure her heart or her political career would survive Ethan's upcoming racketeering arrest.

"How long will you be in Atlanta?"

"Just for the day. My son's murder charge is scintillating news. Reporters camp in the coffee shop across from my condo. They roam the halls of the capitol. They wait outside my favorite restaurants."

To save my hearing, I held the phone three inches from my ear.

"Hoping to throw the bloodhounds off my scent, I

scheduled today's staff meeting in my aide's apartment. This madness has to end today!"

"I've arranged for a courier to deliver the motion to the clerk's office at eight o'clock this morning."

Sandra blew a slow, uneven breath. The kind holding back a bucket of tears. "Good. I'll set up a press conference for this afternoon and announce the charges have been dropped."

"No press until we receive verification from the court." I sucked in a deep breath and searched for the words that would keep her from unwittingly committing career suicide.

I embraced a softer tone. "I can't promise the prosecutor will drop Ethan's charges. The murder weapon and accelerant *were* discovered in his garage. That's damning evidence."

"But Zachary's fingerprints—"

"Dad's fingerprints are on the weapon, but the lab report listed the time span as ten days."

"I know, but surely the judge..." Her voice broke. "Ethan's innocent—"

"Filing the Brady motion is our first step." A stab of guilt hit my gut. Ethan's subsequent arrest was hours away. Placating Sandra with filing a motion was self-serving and disingenuous.

And worst-case scenario, if Sandra touted her son's innocence to reporters today and the racketeering charge leaked tomorrow, the press would swarm like bees to a honey hive.

"Senator, you have to promise no press until I give the okay."

I timed the seconds of her silence by the beat of my heart. After five, I said, "Sandra? You have to promise me."

"I'm calling the judge."

"She won't take your call." Or would she? I had no idea. I was no stranger to influential people circumventing the law. And I also knew their back-door antics worked more often than not. But in this case, it would undermine her credibility.

"Don't call Judge Larson. If she identifies your actions as strong-arming, you'll damage our case." My tone came across just shy of berating. I dialed it back. "As soon as I confirm the motion's filed, my next call is to the prosecutor. You'll be my second call. Until then, stay away from the press. Safe travels, Senator." I disconnected before she pinned me down further.

I pushed away my last strain of guilt. I had no choice but to manipulate the players and keep them from unwittingly crashing and burning. I had a plan, but success rested on me finding and exposing the killer. Keeping Dad safe took precedence, and if that required using the Brady motion as a stopgap to rein in Vernon and Sandra, so be it.

After the bust, Vernon would understand the importance of Ethan working with the GBI. Staring down twenty years in federal prison would be a sobering incentive. I'd put a bug in Vernon's ear—make compliance contingent on anonymity, which would make Ethan's identity and the location of the bust confidential, making confiscation of the family cabin off the table.

At this point, DeMarco and the Bianchi family hadn't joined forces, which meant DeMarco would be left to deal his hand. Behind bars, a low-level hood offered no serious threat.

If Ethan made a deal with the GBI and I exposed the real killer, Ethan would be a free man. But for my plan to work, I had to break the murder case, and at the moment, I was at a standstill.

Last night, Caleb had bailed on the beer invite and emailed a summary of his bowling alley conversation with Corky. Nothing stood out as questionable. Corky knew Grace in passing, his only sport was bowling, and he had a long-time girlfriend he planned to marry later this year. The only blemish on his squeaky clean record—a three-year-old speeding ticket. Nothing about Corky fit the profile of a murderer or an arsonist.

My gut also said the Bentons' threatening letters were the key to finding Grace's killer, which meant I needed another pass at Vernon's log. A case must've slipped by me. But plowing through court documents required coffee and a place to spread out. I pulled on a pair of sweats and headed for the kitchen.

The door to Dad's office stood open. He sat at his desk and looked to be reading his journal.

"Care for fresh coffee?"

He raised his head, squinted, then shook a no. I got the impression he was focused elsewhere, the curt headshake equating to *go away, I'm busy*.

My curiosity buzzed, and I walked over. "What are you reading?"

He opened another book. "My journals."

My pulse quickened. Last night, I'd considered searching for an incident that could explain Dad's prints on the bat. In the end, I refused to dishonor his trust and resigned to ask permission to look through his journals today. "Are you looking for anything in particular?"

"Made a list of people I've conversed with over the last three weeks." He blew a frustrated breath. "On a couple of days, I forget to post."

"You find anyone interesting?"

"Not really." He handed me a lined piece of notebook paper. His list filled half the page.

I scanned the names: Sue Ellen, Chet, Colleen, her grandkids noted as Colleen's boy and Colleen's girl. There were entries for Caleb, and Brenda, who I assumed to be Brenda Spears, the deputy who owned and trained bloodhounds. He'd lunched with his undersheriff, Hank, a couple of times.

My gaze stopped and held on to an entry logged six days ago. "Billy Thompson?"

Dad shuffled through the pages of his open book. "Yeah. I tried to remember where I saw him, but I can't pull it in. I made a note we talked about fishing. I kind of remember the conversation. Must've been at the diner."

Dad's gaze drifted left. His forehead creased as if trying to remember the scene in his mind. "Billy said he tied a few custom flies. He had a nymph the trout were hitting pretty hard. He offered to give me one. Seems like we talked out by his car." He rubbed the back of his neck. "I must've left that fly in my truck because I don't remember seeing one lying around the house. Can't for the life of me remember what it looked like."

I had a good idea where Dad stored Billy's fly. "Let me grab some coffee, and I'll be right back."

On the way to the kitchen, I swung by the dining room and removed my mom's covered bowl, lifted the lid, and removed a small brown nymph fly sitting on top of the rolled-up notes Sue Ellen had found.

I pocketed the bait, then poured two coffees. On the way back to Dad's office, I grabbed my notebook out of my bedroom.

"I think I found your fly." I handed him his coffee and laid the nymph on his desk.

He fingered the tail, didn't ask where I'd found it, and I didn't say.

I sat in one of the brown leather wingbacks in front of his desk and shuffled through my notebook until I found the list of questions I'd made and had yet to ask.

He set his journal aside, then picked up the bait. "Sometimes, I can't even remember what I ate for breakfast."

I made a point of not looking up. "Yeah. Sometimes I can't remember mundane stuff either."

I could tell he was embarrassed by his laugh, but he seemed relieved that I'd made light of his admission. No need to stew about something we couldn't change. "Do you date your journal entries?" I knew the answer but didn't want him to know Sue Ellen and I had snooped.

"Yes." He opened the top desk drawer. "I use my calendar and the weather channel to keep track. Weather channel gives the date and time at the top of the screen. I figure as long as I know what day it is, I can't be too far gone."

The sadness in his voice crept into my heart and squeezed. I waited for a second, let the hurt settle, then said, "Based on your journal entries, can you tell where you were on the night of the fire? That'd be September eighth."

He found the page, used his index finger to skim his entry. "Had Raisin Bran and a banana for breakfast. Mowed the lawn and went to the diner for supper. It was a Thursday."

I jotted his answers in my book, checked my next question. "And you said yesterday you didn't know Grace, right?"

"Don't remember meeting her."

"Do you remember the last time you saw Ethan?"

He looked at the ceiling. After a second, he sighed, shook his head. "Not really."

"Do you remember going to the Bentons' hunting cabin a few weeks ago?"

"No." He rubbed his forehead. "Did I?"

"Yes, I believe so. That visit was behind DeMarco's call to you."

I pushed aside the stab of anger that accompanied the vivid memory of DeMarco's reference to Dad and refocused on my list of questions. "Before you retired, did you suspect Ethan was involved in illegal behavior?"

"I wouldn't call it illegal. We fielded a few complaints of Ethan refusing to live up to verbal warranties on his vehicles. Is that what you're talking about?"

"No. Did you and Hank ever suspect Ethan might be involved in illegal gambling?"

"Gambling? No, not that I recall. I'm fairly certain Ethan wasn't on the department's radar if that's what you're asking."

If Dad didn't suspect Ethan ran a gambling scheme, why did he show up at the cabin? "You been out to Old River Road recently?"

He shrugged. "I go fishing out that way a couple of times a month."

I tried concocting a scenario in my mind that would lead Dad from a fishing trip to the Bentons' cabin. He could've witnessed unusual vehicle activity on Old River Road. He was a cop. He'd naturally investigate. But it didn't matter how or why Dad ended up at the cabin, so I moved on.

"Speaking of fishing, how'd you like to get a line wet?"

"Sounds good."

"I have a few things to take care of, but I can be free by four." I left him searching his closet for a fishing net.

I thought about checking in with Ethan but decided to let that sleeping dog snooze for the day. I'd made it clear, if he were arrested for racketeering, I wouldn't represent him. Didn't matter. I'd be the one call he made from jail. Within minutes of Cramer confirming the bust, I'd be knocking on Vernon and Sandra's door relaying the shocking news. Until then, I had a pile of work.

Using the dining room as a makeshift desk, I laid out my notes on Vernon's cases. I grabbed two of Colleen's fresh-from-the-oven buttered pecan muffins and settled down to work.

Caleb interviewed the parents of Joey Chesney, the seventeen-year-old teen who stole his neighbor's truck. Learned Chesney took his girlfriend on a joyride for her sixteenth birthday. The police report confirmed Joey brought the vehicle back the following day.

Lamar Chesney, the teen's father, credited Judge Benton with the wisdom of sentencing his son to community service instead of sending him to juvie jail. Caleb found no indication Joey's parents had anything but glowing admiration for Judge Vernon Benton.

My phone buzzed with an incoming call. Kendra's number popped on the screen. "Hey, what's up?"

"Have you made a decision?"

"About?"

I could hear her eyes rolling over the airwaves. "Selling your interest in our firm."

"I'm willing to sell my interest, but not for you to join up with Wilcox, Savage and Knox."

"Why?"

"Have you investigated the firm you're thinking of joining?" No way Kendra would purposely sabotage her career by aligning herself with a mob firm.

"What do you think?" Sarcasm dripped from her response. She often dished out scorn as a cover. I got her reasoning. I walked away from her and our firm, and she wanted to make it final.

"Wilcox, Savage and Knox have only one major client?"

Silence, then the sound of high heels clicking on a wood floor. A door slammed. If she wanted privacy, she must be at the office. More walking, then, "Why do you care?"

"Why do you think a law office handling only the Bianchi family's legal battles wants to own forty-nine percent of a firm specializing in divorce?"

When she didn't answer, I added, "You do know the Bianchis are a well-known mob family, right?"

"Yes, I know." She blew an exasperated breath. "I turned them down. But I still want you out."

We'd finally reached the crux of her plan. "I'm not opposed to selling, but it'll have to wait until Ethan's case is over."

"Murder trials take years."

"Not this one. It'll be over inside a month."

"Fine, but I'm holding you to a month. Check your email. I sent questions on your open cases. I need help picking up your carnage."

"There is no carnage in my files." I accessed Kendra's email and opened the attached document. She'd listed my open cases with at least ten pages of questions. "This will take the rest of the day."

"You're the one dumping twenty-three cases on my desk. I'm juggling my caseload and yours. The least you can do is complete the prep work."

She was right. I owed her clean files and copious notes. "I'll get back to you by tomorrow."

"Focus on the Casselberry file first. The hearing is the day after tomorrow." Dead air was the only clue she'd ended our call.

I reneged on my fishing invite with Dad and asked for a rain check. I spent the rest of the day and into the early evening getting my files transfer ready. At six-thirty, I compiled my notes and emailed them to Kendra, and went in search of Dad.

I found him in the kitchen with Colleen, who'd made enough chicken cacciatore and Greek salad for ten people. Dad invited Bruce, the deputy pulling the evening security detail, Colleen, and her grandchildren to share our meal. Since I had the dining room table covered in paperwork, we set up outside on the deck.

I had no idea how Dad explained the twenty-four-hour security detail to Colleen, but the reason he'd given must've satisfied her. So far, neither she nor the kids had mentioned the police car in our driveway.

After dinner, Dad and I insisted on cleaning up, and Colleen gratefully ushered her group out the front door, promising to see us by eight in the morning. Bruce settled back on the front porch swing.

In the kitchen, I washed and Dad dried.

"I'm expecting a call," I said. "Good chance I'll need to go out for a couple of hours."

"You seemed busy today."

"Just working on my Atlanta cases. Kendra's agreed to step in and assume the reins."

"Nothing on the murder?"

"No." Frustration seeped into my voice. "I'll take another look at Vernon's cases, and tomorrow I plan to run down Billy Thompson."

Dad dried the last plate, folded the dishtowel, and laid it over the edge of the sink. "Billy Thompson isn't the kind of man who beats women to death. He's a giant of a man but has the heart of a Good Samaritan."

"How'd his son die?"

"His youngest?" Dad's forehead furrowed. "Let me think—"

My cell phone rang, and I recognized Cramer's number. "Give me a second. "I walked into the dining room and out of earshot. "How'd it go?"

"Like clockwork. Your boy's demanding to talk to his attorney."

I checked the time, eight-fifty. "Can you hold him off?"

"We're still an hour out of Atlanta. Figure another hour for processing. I'll let him make his call around midnight."

"That should work."

"I'm counting on you to convince him to pony up."

"I'll lean on his dad and brother. That and the twenty-year sentence should be enough to bring Ethan around." I disconnected and went in search of Dad. I found him in the living room watching a John Wayne and Maureen O'Hara movie. One of my favorites. Any other time, I'd join him.

"I need to leave. I may be gone a few hours. I'm going to invite Bruce inside the house until I get back."

"I don't need a babysitter."

I picked up the remote, paused his movie, and sat in the chair across from him. "Dad, word your fingerprints are on the bat is going to leak. Probably has already. You might not remember who owns the bat, but the killer doesn't know that."

"I can take care of myself."

"I know you can but humor me. Besides, Bruce is bored sitting outside. He'll appreciate an invite to watch a movie."

Dad waved his hand, which I took as his okay.

Just as I suspected, Bruce jumped at the chance to wait inside.

I called Caleb, asked him to meet me at his parents'. On the way, I plowed through a battery of choices to deliver the news of Ethan's arrest. I finally decided my best option was a simple truth—their son was a selfish jerk who lived under the impression he was exempt from the laws that governed the rest of us.

Maybe I'd temper my words, but in the end, that'd be my message. I had no doubt the news I wouldn't represent Ethan on the new racketeering charges would break the last string on the fraying rope binding me to friends I considered family.

CHAPTER TWENTY-FOUR

MY TELEPHONE CALL to Caleb had been curt and to the point. "I'm on my way over. You need to wake your parents." By the time I arrived, the entire house was ablaze in lights.

Caleb answered the back door. "Since Ethan isn't answering his phone, I'm assuming this middle-of-the-night meeting is about him."

Over the years, I'd learned it was best not to answer absolute statements, especially if they were true.

"Did he bolt?" Caleb's tone held equal measures of anger and disbelief.

"No, he didn't skip bail."

"Then where is he?"

"On his way to Atlanta."

"Atlanta?"

"Let's find your parents, and I'll fill you in."

Caleb stood aside, and I walked through the mudroom and into the kitchen.

Sandra and Vernon were sitting at the dark pine breakfast table perched on the edge of their seats. I no sooner cleared the doorway, and Sandra pounced. "What's happened? Where's Ethan?" Even in her white silk robe, scrubbed face, and messy hair, she appeared regal. Her face conveyed her expectation—whatever the problem, it was mine to fix.

A snifter of brandy sat inches from Vernon's right hand

as if he suspected my news would require fortification. He wore a burgundy robe over light blue pajamas, and his eyes were puffy with sleep. The lines framing his eyes appeared deeper than I remembered just two days ago.

I considered sitting, then changed my mind. This conversation was akin to swaying a jury during summation. Standing would send a subliminal message of the gravity of the situation, giving me a better chance of winning my desired outcome. "Ethan's been arrested. Again."

Blood seeped from Vernon's face. He reached for the bottle of brandy.

"Arrested?" Sandra's voice bounced off the ceiling. "What about the motion? You said—"

Vernon laid his free hand on his wife's forearm. She glanced in his direction, then promptly closed her mouth. Must be their marital signal to stay quiet and listen.

Caleb stepped behind his mother and laid a calming hand on her shoulder.

Vernon topped off his brandy and sipped. "Go on."

"I received a call from a GBI contact. He informed me of a raid on a high-stakes poker game. They made a dozen arrests. Ethan was one of them."

I had no way to know how the Bentons would react to the news. Dad always advised that it was best to take tiny steps in a dark room, so I pushed down my desire to offer more.

During the following seconds, all three Bentons exhibited signs of stunned shock. Vernon's skin, already a couple of shades lighter than usual, drained to ashen. A reasonable response after receiving word his thirty years of public service had been flushed down a toilet by an ungrateful and spoiled adult child.

Sandra's pupils darkened and then increased to the size of nickels. If I had to guess, I'd say her innate instinct to protect her oldest child's reputation battled with self-preservation. At this point, I wasn't at all sure which would win.

Caleb's reaction was less noticeable. He maintained the flat, unemotional face of a cop. His only tell was a slight flare of his nostrils and a tightening of his jaws.

"I don't understand," Sandra said. "Ethan's confined to the hunting cabin. If he wasn't at the poker game, how could he be arrested?" She turned to Vernon. Understandable. For years she'd relied on her husband for all things legal.

Vernon, appearing in deep thought, did not explain.

In the quiet that followed, where the only sound came from the refrigerator's soft hum, Sandra couldn't sit still. She pushed the hair from her face, straightened the collar of her robe, steepled her fingers, then, as if realizing she was fidgeting, clasped her hands to her lap.

I turned my attention to Caleb. As if he felt the heat of my stare, he glanced in my direction, then gave a slight nod of understanding.

Vernon inhaled a breath. Soul-deep disappointment encompassed his release. Vernon and Caleb looked so much alike. Both were tall and lean with agility that came from spending years on a tennis court. They simultaneously aimed their wary blue eyes at me.

Time to offer up the next shock. "It seems Ethan runs a gaming program for a man named Lou DeMarco."

"DeMarco?" Vernon rolled the name over his tongue. "Never heard of him."

"He's out of Vegas. Word on the street says DeMarco is hooking up with the Bianchi family out of Chicago."

I didn't think Vernon's face could turn any whiter, but I was wrong.

Sandra fell against the back of her chair as if her spine had snapped in two. "Ethan's involved in illegal gambling?" I imagined she, too, envisioned the crash and burn of her hard-earned political career.

"My source advised you should expect racketeering

charges."

"Racketeering?" Vernon kneaded his forehead. "That's a mandatory twenty-year sentence."

Sandra moaned, reached for Vernon's hand. "But if Ethan wasn't at the game—"

"He was at the game, Mom." Caleb's voice cut through the air like a samurai's sword. "He runs his games out of your cabin."

"Ethan wouldn't do that." Sandra looked at me for confirmation.

"I'm sorry to say, he does."

"Can the GBI confiscate the property?" Caleb latched on to the obvious and gave me the opening I needed.

I raised both hands, palms up. "There's precedence, but—"

"How long have you known?" Vernon asked.

I'd prepared for the question, knew this would be a sticking point. "I stumbled onto a game the night Ethan made bail."

"And you said nothing?" Sandra said.

"I said a helluva lot to Ethan. Demanded he give up the games. I also went to Atlanta and met with DeMarco and personally gave him the news Ethan would no longer run his games."

I let that settle for a minute, then said, "But in the end, Ethan's fear of crossing DeMarco won out." I walked across the room, chose a pod of extra bold coffee, popped it into the coffee maker, and pressed start.

While my coffee brewed, I lined up my argument. "If Ethan's charged with racketeering on top of murder and arson, you'll be crucified in the press, Senator.

I cut my gaze to Vernon. "And you, Judge, might find your next election isn't a landslide to victory."

Caleb joined me at the counter. He handed me my full cup, slid a pod in place, and shoved a mug under the spout.

While Caleb's cup brewed, I leaned against the counter, determined not to make the first move. Best to let Vernon and Sandra absorb the consequences to their lives before I threw them a lifeline.

Vernon raised his glass to his lips, then realized it was empty. He poured a refill.

Sandra stared into space as if she were miles away.

I found a juice glass, poured a shot from Vernon's bottle, and nudged the glass against her hand, then took a seat at the table.

She cradled the brandy between her palms, stared at the contents as if she wondered where it came from, then slowly sipped. She sipped again, and color slowly spread across her cheeks.

Behind me, Caleb paced the kitchen. The heels of his boots clicked against the hardwood floor. I realized the only unreserved talker in the Benton family was Ethan.

"How long has Ethan run his game?" Vernon finally asked.

I thought back to the day I viewed his bank statements. Long enough to make a pile of money. "Can't say for sure, but it's been going on for a while."

Caleb halted mid-stride. "The gambling, the fire, the murder—they have to be connected." He swung his gaze in my direction. "Right?"

"At first, I thought so. But after my talk with DeMarco, I changed my mind."

Caleb shook his head. "It all seems too coincidental not to be intertwined."

"How does Ethan wash his money?" Vernon asked.

I nodded. "Exactly. Why would DeMarco destroy the business that washed the dirt off his earnings? I think the murder and fire are connected, but I don't like DeMarco for either one."

"I have to call Jeffrey. We need to get in front of Ethan's arrest." Sandra pushed to her feet.

"Your aide Jeffrey?" I asked.

"Yes. He needs time to prepare a press release."

"Wait." I grabbed Sandra's hand and held her in place. "You have a better option."

"Did your GBI friend put an offer on the table?" By Vernon's tone, he'd reached the same inevitable conclusion—Ethan had to cooperate.

"I floated the idea of cooperation. My guy seemed agreeable." I knew better than to push. For this to work, cooperating with the GBI needed to be a family decision.

I relaxed against the back of my chair. "This is how I see it. The big player is DeMarco. If Ethan agrees to cooperate, he's in a unique position to ask for anonymity for himself and the location of the bust."

Sandra came back to life. "Can you swing it?"

I shook my head. "Not me. I'm sorry, but I will refuse to represent Ethan on this charge."

Tears sprang into her eyes. "Jackson, you can't abandon us now. We need you."

"You don't need me. You need Ethan to do the right thing." For once in his lousy life. "It's up to you, as his family, to apply enough pressure to make him see reason. But with Ethan staring down twenty years in prison. I doubt it'll be a hard sale."

My phone buzzed with an unlisted number. "This will be Ethan. Tell him you'll be in Atlanta first thing in the morning. Instruct him not to talk to anyone until you get there. Don't say anything about making a deal. Wait until you see him face-to-face. I'll arrange for you to meet with the arresting agent this afternoon."

I laid my cell in the center of the kitchen table and placed the incoming call on speaker.

CHAPTER TWENTY-FIVE

THE BENTONS LEFT for Atlanta and I drove home, set my alarm, and crashed. Nine o'clock came early, but after a hot shower, two cinnamon bagels, and two cups of strong coffee, I'd reached semi-human status.

I poured a third cup, made my way to my makeshift desk in the dining room, and cruised through my email. Cramer had a two o'clock meeting with the Bentons and forwarded the deal he wanted to make with Ethan. I'd pushed for, and Cramer had agreed to anonymity, no jail time, and a three-year probation. I was comfortable Vernon would steer the negotiations to a favorable conclusion. Cramer reiterated his promise to hold Ethan in custody for the next three days. There was no mention of confiscating the cabin.

That part of my strategy had gone according to plan. But the following email from Judge Larson's aide, ordering me to the judge's chambers at eight o'clock tomorrow morning, threw me into a tailspin. The attending parties, listed as the district attorney, the prosecutor, and me.

I suspected Sandra had ignored my advice yesterday and called the judge, which instigated this summons. I had no doubt my father's fingerprints on the murder weapon would be on tomorrow's agenda.

Before I fully digested the ramifications of the summons, Sue Ellen called.

"Janice Nelson says she heard from Corrine Beasley,

who heard from her nephew, that Zachary is a suspect in Grace Underwood's murder."

My heart ricocheted against my breastbone.

"Is it true?" she asked.

"No."

"Then why is Corrine's nephew spreading it around?"

"Exactly what did Janice say?"

"Corrine's nephew works for the sheriff's office in Blakeley. He claims the police have evidence of Zachary's involvement in the murder. I said flat out it was bull-hockey, but you know, mouth-of-the-south Janice, she insisted Corrine's nephew had no reason to lie. What's going on, Jackson?"

A brewing headache building behind my eyes ballooned. "It's too complicated to explain over the phone. I'm meeting with the judge tomorrow morning. I'll get everything straightened out." I sounded far more confident than I felt.

How far would the killer go to ensure Dad kept his secret? "The evidence against Dad is circumstantial," I said, as much as a reminder to myself as to calm Sue Ellen.

If she'd heard the rumor, chances were half of Loblolly had heard it as well, and the other half would be in the loop by nightfall.

"Circumstantial? What's that mean exactly?" she asked.

"It means the evidence is questionable and on its own not strong enough to initiate an arrest." But possibly strong enough to get Dad killed.

"Does Zachary know about this?"

"Yes, he knows." But in Dad's current mind-set, he didn't seem to grasp the seriousness of being the only person who could identify a killer who'd beat a defenseless pregnant woman to death, then burned the building as he exited the scene.

Sue Ellen exhaled enough carbon dioxide to keep a rain forest alive for five years. "I'll swing by after my shift and bring him a slice of pie."

Pie—the cure-all medicine of the South. "You're a good friend, Sue Ellen."

I had to make sure Dad remained close to home until I solved the case. Short of taking away his keys, I wasn't sure how to accomplish the feat. And Colleen needed a heads-up before she heard the rumor from someone else. If she knew the risks, even with a cop sitting on our front porch, she might feel uncomfortable letting the kids come here after school.

I resigned to speak to Colleen today and turned my attention to an even bigger issue, Hank, Dad's undersheriff. Hank was scheduled to return from vacation on… Wednesday.

I glanced at the top of my computer screen. *Today* was Wednesday!

I had to catch a break in this case today. I couldn't count on Hank continuing to approve round-the-clock surveillance to protect Dad against a killer that the police believed was my client.

I put aside Sue Ellen's news for the time being and refocused on my work. I still believed the murder and fire were connected to the threatening letters the Bentons had received. If my suspicions were true, the likely place to find the killer's name was in Vernon's files.

The only outlier in my theory was Grace's murder. The coroner estimated ten blows to Grace's skull. I might be able to make a case the killer murdered Grace to frame Ethan. But a savage killing of that magnitude spoke of heightened emotion, not the cold, calculated deed of a parent who believed their child had been unfairly treated.

If the injured parent had the stomach for killing, and in truth, few people did, why not choose Ethan or Caleb as their victim? None of the cases I'd pulled so far measured up. I needed to review Vernon's case log through a new lens. Increase the time scope from three to five years, up the maximum age from twenty to thirty, and search for any connection with Grace Underwood.

My new statistics added forty-three cases to my list. But offhand, I found no new cases with a connection to Grace. I grabbed a bottle of water from the fridge and went to work.

Sometime around two, Colleen delivered a lunch tray with a ham and cheese sandwich, potato salad, and a glass of iced tea. I welcomed the break. My empty stomach had growled in protest for the past hour, and my eyes burned from the strain of reading trial transcripts on a laptop screen.

Dad meandered by, pulled out a chair, and joined me at the table. I recognized the fishing fly in his hand as the one Billy Thompson had given him. Interviewing Thompson was still on my to do list.

"We never set a new time to go fishing," Dad said.

Guilt jabbed my conscience. I'd locked Dad, an avid fisherman, inside his house. He had to be close to stir crazy. "I'm sorry. I got tied up." Taking a quick estimate of the number of files left to review, I said," I have a couple more hours of work, but we should be able to hit the river by four-thirty." I'd visit Billy Thompson after supper.

I pointed to the fly in his hand. "Is that the bug of the day?"

"Thought I'd try it out and see." He picked up a sheet of my handwritten notes. "Lanny Scroven." He repeated the name I'd written at the top of the page. "I remember this case. Kid tried outrunning two of my deputies. Gave them a real chase through town."

"Report says he was charged with reckless driving."

"Seemed more than fair since Scroven plowed into Larry Pittman's new King Ranch truck."

"Why'd Scroven run?"

"Had a couple of beers at a friend's house, and his truck

had an expired tag." Dad snorted a laugh. "He ended up passing the breath analyzer, and the ticket for his expired tag cost him thirty-five dollars. But I heard Larry's insurance popped him with a repair bill of five thousand dollars." Dad tossed the sheet back on the table.

I picked it up, moved it back to the "no" pile. "Sue Ellen called. She's planning to stop by after work."

"That's nice." Dad smiled. "She usually brings pie."

"Yeah, she said something about that. She also said rumors are flying connecting you to Grace Underwood's murder. She didn't mention the bat, but…"

Dad exhaled his frustration. "I've racked my brain over that bat. I can't for the life of me remember touching one in the last few years, much less the past few weeks." His forlorn expression sliced my heart. "I'm sorry, son. I just can't seem to recall holding a bat."

"I know. But until we figure this out, I need you to stick close to home."

He nodded. "Okay, and I'll keep trying to remember. Maybe it'll come to me. I finally remembered how Billy Thompson's youngest boy died."

"Yeah, how?" I opened my next file, flipped a page in my notebook, and wrote the name of the next defendant at the top.

"Suicide."

"That's too bad. Hey, if we're going fishing, I need to get back to work." My brain scrambled backward. "Did you say Billy Thompson's son died of suicide?"

"Yeah. A real sad case. His boy finally beat cocaine addiction, then a few months after rehab left a note on his pillow, drove to the river, and shot himself."

Air rushed from my lungs. *A son for a son.* I knew Thompson's son had died, but suicide? Was it possible he blamed Vernon for his death? Dad's journal confirmed he'd run into Billy Thompson. All the pieces fit.

I scrolled back through Vernon's cases. "Son's name was

Dylan?"

"Sounds right. I went to the funeral. The family took the death hard. And Billy lost his wife not long after."

"Wife died, too?"

"Yeah, cancer."

My brief phone call to Mr. Thompson, along with Dad's wouldn't-hurt-a-fly assessment, had thrown me off my game. I'd focused on Jed and his brief history with Grace, practically dismissed it as an item to check off, but not really urgent. I'd missed this connection. A child dying of suicide would be a potent loss—the kind of tragedy that could turn an otherwise reasonable man into a revenge seeking father.

I swiped through my "no" pile and yanked out notes on Dylan Thompson's case. "You remember who arrested Dylan?"

Dad shrugged. "Can't say as I do."

I located Dylan Thompson's file on Vernon's case log, scrolled through the pages, and found the arrest report. "Caleb made the arrest." I noted the file number and snapped a photo of the arrest report. "I'll be back."

"Where are you going?"

"To talk to Billy Thompson."

"Thought we were going fishing."

I looked over my shoulder. "Not for two more hours. And I'm going to need a pair of waders."

"Got an extra pair in the shed."

I found Colleen in the laundry room ironing. "You press sheets?"

She must've noticed the shock on my face because she took one look and laughed. "They sleep better."

"Isn't that a little like ironing pajamas?"

"Right." She slid the hot iron across a pale blue sheet I recognized from my bed. "I iron pajamas, too."

Not the time for this discussion. "I'm going out for a couple of hours."

Her iron hissed a spray of steam. "I have a roast in the oven for supper. Dinner will be ready by six."

"I should be back before four. We need to have a chat before you leave today."

Her hand paused. "Anything wrong?"

"No. Just some things have come up you need to know. We'll talk as soon as I get back."

She nodded and went back to her ironing.

Brenda pulled the afternoon shift and had taken up her watch on the front porch swing.

"Word of Dad's fingerprints on the bat has leaked."

Brenda frowned. "Honestly, I'm surprised it took this long."

"I have to go out for an hour or so. I've asked Dad not to leave the house without me, but you know it's possible he might forget our conversation."

"I'll keep an eye on him."

Satisfied I'd taken every available precaution, I ignored the nagging sense of unease that lived in my chest and plugged Thompson's address into my GPS.

CHAPTER TWENTY-SIX

ON ITS OWN, Billy Thompson living in the same neighborhood as Grace and Naomi Underwood didn't mean much but coupling the news with Thompson's son dying of suicide upped the ante. In my line of work, poking holes in coincidences was standard fare. And Jed Thompson and Grace Underwood dating, even for a short-time, had begun to feel less serendipitous.

My money was still on Billy. I couldn't afford taking a risk he might refuse to speak with me, so I arrived unannounced.

A man answered the door. He looked like an older Jed, so I took a chance. "Mr. Thompson, I'm Jackson Taylor. We spoke on the phone a few days ago." In all the years playing high school ball with Jed, I'd never noticed the father and son resemblance.

Thompson blinked, said nothing. Maybe he didn't recall our telephone conversation, or, perhaps he was surprised I'd drop by unannounced. I wedged the tip of my boot between the door and the frame in case he tried to shut me out. "I have a few additional questions. Shouldn't take more than a couple of minutes."

He tilted his head and looked me over. "You're Zachary Taylor's boy."

"Yes, sir."

"You favor him."

"I was just thinking the same about you and Jed."

He half-laughed, half-grunted. "Reckon I can give you a few minutes. Not like I'm busy."

I stepped through his door and scanned the foyer. The space so small there was only room for a small table shoved against the one wall. It was a shotgun style house with a long hallway opening into other rooms, and at the far end, a set of glass doors appeared to lead outside.

"Come on back to the kitchen. Just made a pitcher of tea. Weather's nice enough to sit on the porch."

Thompson led the way down the hall. Family photos lined the narrow corridor. I zeroed in on a large portrait of a smiling family of four. Based on Jed's age, I estimated the shot to be at least ten years old.

I pointed to one of his baseball photos. "Jed made All State that year, right?"

Thompson glanced at the picture, nodded, and kept walking.

I slowed and made a quick study of the photos. There were a handful of family shots, the kind taken by a professional photographer, and a couple of Jed playing baseball.

I'd estimate at least twenty of the wall pictures centered on a younger boy I recognized from Vernon's file as Dylan Thompson. His parents, like a lot of families who mourn the early loss of a child, had created a memorabilia shrine.

"How's your dad?" Mr. Thompson pulled my attention back to him.

"Dad's well, thanks. He retired a couple of months ago. He seems to be settling into the idea of having free time on his hands."

I mentally reviewed my profile of the killer. Whoever murdered Grace had a short fuse. Another trait gleaned from the recent message sent to the Bentons, he was neat. Precisely cut letters glued meticulously straight with no obvious guidelines. No glue smears. The letters bore no tattered edges or sloppy cuts. The author neat to the point of obsessive.

I surveyed my surroundings. I'd classify Thompson's kitchen as bachelor clean—a few dishes in the sink, crumbs next to the toaster, overall acceptable, but falling well short of obsessive.

Thompson busied himself with glasses and ice, dumped in sweetener, and poured. He handed me my tea and turned for the door. He'd left empty sweetener packs on the counter and hadn't refilled the empty ice tray. Billy Thompson didn't exhibit the characteristics of a Type A personality who'd spent hours tediously lining up cut-out letters and pasting them in perfectly straight lines.

I accepted the glass of tea. "Dad mentioned he ran into you recently."

Thompson's eyes squinted. After a few seconds, he gave a quick decisive head shake. "Must have me confused with someone else. I haven't seen Zachary in a good long while."

Denying an encounter with Dad must mean their meeting occurred without witnesses. "Perhaps I misunderstood."

"Believe the last time I saw the sheriff was at a fishing tournament."

"You do a lot of fishing?"

"Not so much lately. Lost interest when my wife died. She loved fly fishing." He opened the sliding glass door and we stepped onto a wood deck.

"I hear you tie impressive flies."

"Me? No, I never picked up the hobby. Dylan tried his hand at tying for a while."

On the deck, four wicker rockers faced a stand of pine trees separating the next house. Thompson sat, then as if remembering he had a guest, motioned me into a chair. "Have a seat."

I removed my phone and joined him. "You mind if I tape our conversation? It's easier than taking notes."

He shrugged. "I don't mind." I detected no hesitancy in his response.

I laid my cell on the banister. In order to run a positive identification match with the 911 call, I needed to register a baseline. The easiest way to accomplish the task was to ask a couple of nonthreatening questions. "How's Jed doing?"

Thompson began a slow rock. "A lot better now that he has the new job."

"New job?"

"Works on a man to lose his job after fourteen years." He sipped his tea, rocked a couple of rounds.

I searched my memory, came up empty. Jed and I weren't close and hadn't kept in touch after high school. I took a stab. "Didn't Jed go to work at the mill after graduation?"

Thompson nodded. "I got him on at the mill when he graduated. He worked his way up to supervisor."

"The mill closing has brought a lot of hard times to Loblolly."

"A month after Dylan died, Jed and I got laid off. Two months later, my wife passed." He sighed. "Jed and his ma were real close. He's had it rough."

Losing his job, his wife, and his son all within the span of a few months seemed a lot of family misery to bear. Tested the adage of when it rained, it poured.

"Does Jed still live in Loblolly?"

"Lives here with me. Works part-time as a security guard at the hospital. He should be home in a few minutes."

I had enough for a baseline, so I lined up my questions. "When we spoke on the phone, you mentioned knowing about the fire and murder at Ethan Benton's car lot."

"Jed's a volunteer firefighter. He discovered the body, or what was left of her. At the time, no one knew it was Grace Underwood."

Jed worked the fire—I filed that away for later. "You said you knew Grace?"

"Sure, I knew her." His slow rocking picked up speed. "Her family lives a couple of streets over. Our kids grew up together. Grace and Jed even went out a few times."

"How long did Grace and Jed date?"

"Not long. It was nothing serious. After Dylan and my wife died, Jed hit a rough patch. He had a tough battle with alcohol. I always figured it was the reason he and Grace didn't work out."

I sipped my tea, waited for more.

"But Jed's straightened himself out. He trained as a firefighter and hopes to get on full-time soon." Pride seeped into Thompson's voice. "He hasn't had a drop of liquor in over a year."

Had to be stressful to have both sons struggle with substance abuse. "I understand Dylan died of suicide."

Thompson's dark brown eyes faded into dull amber. "Broke our hearts losing our boy. My wife never recovered. I think it's the reason she refused treatment."

Dad mentioned Thompson's wife died of cancer.

"No matter how much Jed and I begged, after Dylan died, Maxie refused her treatments. She said if God thought it was her time to go, maybe Dylan needed her." His voice broke, and he turned away.

"I'm very sorry for your loss, Mr. Thompson."

On the drive over, I had played the 911 call several times, committing the voice inflections of the caller to memory. Occasionally, when Thompson lost himself in our conversation, his voice came close to matching, but his tone never really hit the mark.

I observed nothing in his mannerisms indicating nerves or any attempt to disguise his voice. No hint of underlying anger, or misguided blame. In fact, Thompson personified Dad's description of him, a gentle giant. Unless he was a Jekyll and Hyde, I didn't see Thompson as a cold-blooded killer who could bludgeon a woman to death.

I had enough on tape for an analyzer to either make a positive identification or rule out Billy Thompson as the 911 caller.

After this conversation, I had a strong suspicion the wrong Thompson was pinned in my crosshairs. Jed Thompson and Grace Underwood had a past. And, as a firefighter, Jed knew how to use accelerant to cause a blaze.

Because the sender used the term "*a son for a son*," I'd assumed a parent authored the letters to the Bentons. But perhaps the killer chose the term as camouflage.

I needed to touch base with Cramer and arrange for voice analysis of Billy's voice. In the meantime, I had to figure a way to get Jed's voice on tape. If he'd caught wind of Dad's fingerprints on the bat, it was likely he was already skittish. Seeing a strange car in his driveway might spook him.

I finished the rest of my tea in one swallow and stood. "I appreciate you talking with me."

Mr. Thompson lumbered to his feet. "You sure you don't want to wait around for Jed? He'd enjoy catching up."

"I'm tight on time, but I'll try and stop by soon."

He collected our glasses. "I'll show you out."

We stepped inside the house, and the front door opened, then closed. Jed walked down the hall towards us. He'd turned into a younger version of his father. Same hair color, same thick chest and muscled arms, same slightly off-centered nose. It wasn't difficult to see how Dad might confuse Jed with his father. But instead of the easy, slightly rumbled state of Billy's shirt, Jed's uniform appeared starched and neatly tucked into his pants.

I extended my hand. "It's been a while."

He stopped, took a step back. His expression turned

wary.

I kept my face blank and my hand extended, but I felt the jolt of truth.

Jed knew why I was here. Which meant he knew about Dad's fingerprints. Or, at least he knew the police had evidence Dad was involved. Had he remembered my father touching his bat?

A flood of emotions whizzed across his face. He suspected I was closing in on the truth. He blinked, blinked again, and his wary expression morphed into friendly. The smile came a few seconds later.

He grabbed my hand, his grin came close to cracking his face. "Jackson." He pumped my hand. "It's great to see you, man."

I glanced down at his meticulously groomed nails and shined shoes.

I had experience with criminals, recognized the obvious signs of guilt. The slight shifting from one foot to the other. The way their overzealous smiles didn't make it past their cheeks. The slight calculating squint, as if they were in search of a way to weasel their way into an upper hand.

But that wasn't the reason I knew Jed was the killer. Although an octave higher and embedded with a nervous rattle, I was certain Jed's voice would match the 911 call.

I forced easy and casual into my tone. "Your dad says you worked the fire at Ethan Benton's place."

He glanced at his dad. Nodded. "I did."

"Not sure if you know, but I'm representing Ethan."

"Yeah, heard you were in town." His gaze shifted from me back to his dad. He swallowed, shifted his stance.

"I'd like to ask you a few questions about the fire."

"The fire?" He swiped the back of his hand across his mouth. "Sure, but I'm only a volunteer. Alfred's the chief."

I stepped back to the kitchen table, removed my phone

from my pocket, and pulled out a chair.

After a second of hesitation, Jed and his father did the same.

"Mind if I tape our conversation? Like I explained to your dad, it's easier than taking notes." I pushed my phone to the center of the table.

Jed glanced down at the phone and immediately slumped in his chair. I might've bought his nonchalance except for his tendency to rub his palms over his thighs. And add sweating to the mix. It was as if his face had a million pinpricks, all releasing beads of sweat at once.

"Your dad mentioned you were the one who found Grace Underwood's body."

He shrugged. "Me and Tim Baker."

"Did you recognize the body as Grace?"

"No." He cleared his throat, gazed somewhere over my shoulder. "She was—" He shifted in his chair. "She wasn't recognizable." The skin on his forehead now as shiny as wet glass.

"Fire report states an accelerant was used."

"Camping fuel. Alfred said it was too common to trace."

"Not as common as propane these days."

He dabbed at his lips with his tongue, like a lizard testing his surroundings. Then he took a sudden interest in a scratch on the table.

"Your dad said you and Grace dated."

His head jerked. He cut his eyes towards his dad. "Only for a few weeks. Then she took up with Benton." An underlying anger slid into his tone at the mention of Ethan.

Bringing up Jed's relationship with Grace had been a risk, but his reaction confirmed I was on the right path. I had to play it cool, act as if he'd satisfied my questions.

"So nothing serious between you guys?"

"Nah, just a couple of dates."

"That's what I figured, but I had to follow up." I gave

him a smile and turned off my voice recorder.

I had enough audio to make a positive ID, no reason to rattle him further. I collected my phone. "Thanks for your time."

Jed popped out of his seat, and for a second he looked relieved. Then as if he had second thoughts, his entire body stiffened. Maybe he thought our conversation ended too abruptly.

Mr. Thompson shook my hand. "Give my regards to your dad."

"I'll be sure to do that."

"Jed." I nodded in his direction.

He didn't offer his hand. Instead, he stood five feet away, like a statue, fingers fisted, face set.

I followed Mr. Thompson to the front door, but all the way down the hall, I felt the heat of Jed's glare burning a hole into my back.

CHAPTER TWENTY-SEVEN

I BACKED OUT OF Billy Thompson's driveway, drove to the end of his street, and called Cramer. "I'm cashing in on your promise to help with Ethan's murder case."

"I'm listening."

"I need a voice match on a 911 call. And I need it yesterday."

"You have digital files?"

"Yes."

"Send them, and I'll make it happen today. But you know Georgia courts don't accept voice evidence, even if analyzed by a forensic linguist."

"Which leads to my second favor. I need to track a GMC Sierra 1500 using the vehicle's built-in GPS. Georgia tag number is BJT6893."

"Requires a warrant."

I popped my truck into gear and turned for home. "That's why I'm asking you instead of Caleb Benton. Thought you'd find a work-around."

"A work-around, huh?" By Cramer's tone you'd think my ask was above his pay grade.

"It's not beyond your scope. After your bust last night, you have the right ear of the State's attorney."

"Hell, I have him on speed dial, son."

"You're welcome."

Cramer laughed. "Okay, I'll weasel a warrant if the voice match verifies and you narrow the time scope to no more than twenty-four hours."

"Twenty-four hours works. Start the track at noon on September ninth."

A few seconds of soft tapping, then, "We're in luck. Cassandra's on today. She's our best linguist."

"The GBI has more than one forensic linguist?"

"Three."

Voice evidence might not be admissible in court, but it can verify if a case is headed in the right direction.

"Anything else?" Cramer asked.

"The forensic crew picked up an unidentified partial print on the murder weapon used to kill Grace Underwood." I heard more typing. "The man who owns the Sierra works as a security guard at the hospital in Blakeley. I'm thinking a hospital would require a security check that mandated fingerprinting."

"Got it. I'll wrap the hospital records in my warrant request."

I disconnected and called Caleb.

"Are you back from Atlanta?"

"Yes."

I made a left on River Road and picked up speed. "Can you meet me at my dad's?"

"Sorry, I can't. I'm at the precinct, and Hank's on his way. He seems real anxious to discuss my approval for security on Zachary. Might be a good idea for you to be in on that conversation."

The precinct was a twenty-minute drive. "Okay. I'll come to you. Do you have a man to put on Jed Thompson for a few hours?"

"Jed Thompson? The volunteer firefighter?"

"That's him."

Caleb blew a breath. "I don't know. Hank's already—"

"I just rattled Jed's cage. I'm afraid he may bolt. Tell Hank I'll explain everything when I get there. You need to put eyes on him before we lose him."

"You're on your way?"

"I am. And one more thing. Call your contact working Ethan's case and ask him to join us."

"You got something solid?" Relief slid through Caleb's voice.

"If my GBI contact comes through, you can collar Grace's real killer before sundown."

Going to the precinct would throw me behind, and Colleen left in less than an hour. I initiated my phone's digital assistant. "Call Dad."

Colleen answered.

"I'm running a little later than anticipated. Is Dad around?"

"He's napping in his recliner."

"How about Brenda?"

"She stepped outside to take a call."

"I have another favor. Sue Ellen's planning to stop by after her shift at the diner. Will you ask her to call me?"

"Sure."

"And would you mind staying until Sue Ellen arrives?"

"I don't mind. I'll put a dinner plate in the oven for you."

"Thanks, Colleen." With that weight off my shoulders, I headed into town. Worst case, I could ask Sue Ellen to explain to Colleen the rumors tearing through town about Dad's prints on the bat.

The Pine County Sheriff's Department provided the only law enforcement in the county. Loblolly being the sole municipality made it easy to combine the sheriff's office and city hall into one complex. The building, located two blocks south of Main Street, held a courthouse, the sheriff's department with four jail cells, and business offices for the city. There'd been talk of building a new law enforcement complex west of town, but Dad had said lack of funding nixed the deal.

I pulled into the back parking lot and jogged across the

blacktop. The municipal complex, an impressive building with a peaked roof and tall, slender windows, commandeered the entire block. Years ago, my mom and Sandra Benton worked tirelessly to list the property as a historical site. Then Mom and Sandra raised the money for a massive renovation.

I rode the elevator to the second floor. Sergeant Steve Nelson, an ex-linebacker for the University of Georgia, covered the front desk.

"Hey, Jackson." Nelson motioned me through the security detector. "Caleb said to send you to the bullpen. He and Hank are waiting."

Hank had been the acting sheriff since Dad retired. He'd been on the force for as long as I could remember. I'd grown up thinking of him as a pseudo-uncle. The idea it takes a village was ingrained into the fabric of my hometown. Returning had reminded me of what it meant to call a place home.

The bullpen consisted of six metal desks arranged police-style, front-to-front, so partners faced one another. The familiar smell of burnt coffee drifted from an open door to my left.

Hank and Caleb were in Dad's old corner office, made up of two glass walls, allowing the sheriff to view his bullpen. Three deputies—Miguel Sanchez, a longtime officer, and two younger officers I didn't recognize—were seated at three of the desks.

Miguel jumped to his feet. "Heard you were in town." He stuck out his hand. "About time you made an appearance."

We shook hands, and he nodded toward the office. "Hank's waiting."

Hank had his back turned, a phone to his ear, and his scuffed brown boots propped on the windowsill. His medium frame appeared heavier since I'd last seen him. His curly hair was grayer than the ginger red of his youth.

Caleb stood in front of Hank's desk and waved me in.

Hank ended his call. At first glance, his freckled-faced smile appeared welcoming, but the closer I got, the more his warm brown eyes read, *you're stomping on my last nerve, boy.* For an instant, I felt like the ten-year-old kid who'd hit a baseball into Mrs. Cochran's dining room window.

He swung out of his chair and grabbed me in a bear hug, just like he had after Mrs. Cochran gave me the verbal thrashing. Only now, at six-four, I stood at least six inches taller.

Hank slapped my back and said, "Good to see you."

"I'm hoping we can have a beer and catch up, but first, I need to bring you up to date on my case."

"Caleb tells me you agreed to represent Ethan."

"That's right."

"Says you have new evidence."

"I do."

Hank sat behind his desk, pointed to a vacant chair. "Have a seat."

I remained standing.

"I just got off the phone with Simon Cauthen," he said. "He's the new sheriff in Blakeley. Sheriff Cauthen sounds real anxious to hear what you've got."

"I'm waiting on a call from the GBI, but if I'm right, Jed Thompson's your killer."

Doubt swamped Hank's face, and he glanced at Caleb. "Yeah, I heard you had a bug up your butt about Jed."

Surprised at the negative response, I countered, "You know about the threatening letters the Bentons received?"

Hank shrugged. "Sure. We turned them over to the GBI for processing. Nothing's come of it so far. Looks like some kind of prank."

I tried counting to five, made it to three. "I don't think the letters are a prank. Caleb arrested Dylan Thompson on cocaine possession, and Vernon sentenced him to rehab. Now Dylan's dead."

To call Hank's expression skeptical would be like referring to the Atlantic Ocean as a pond.

Irritation snaked up my spine. "A son for a son." I didn't bother tempering my voice.

"Dylan died of suicide." The confusion in Caleb's voice matched his expression.

Hank's puffy eyes narrowed. "Go on."

"Jed and Grace Underwood dated a while back." My phone buzzed. I checked the screen. "Hang on. This is my GBI contact." I took the call. "Did the voices match?"

"They did," Cramer said. "And I wrangled a warrant for the Sierra. Unfortunately, the judge capped us at twelve hours."

"That's okay, start the track at nine PM."

"I should have something back to you within the hour."

I disconnected, turned to Hank and Caleb. "A GBI forensic linguist ran a voice match on the 911 call reporting the fire with the conversation I had today with Jed Thompson. The voices matched."

"Courts refuse voice evidence," Hank said.

"I realize. We used the voice match as probable cause and obtained a warrant to track the movement of Jed's truck for the night of the fire."

Miguel walked into the room. "Sorry to interrupt, but Sue Ellen's on the phone. She says Zachary's missing again."

Hank cut his eyes to me. "What do you mean, again?"

"Brenda's on surveillance, what's she say?" I asked.

Miguel glanced at Hank.

Hank rubbed the back of his neck. "I sent Brenda on a call."

"You pulled Brenda off Dad?"

Miguel ducked out of the room, and I found Caleb. "You put a man on Jed, right?"

The color drained from Caleb's face. "Hank—"

"Look, Jackson," Hank sputtered, "I only have three

men on patrol. It's not feasible to assign two officers to a case that's not ours."

I pointed at the glass wall. "What about those two deputies shooting bull in your pen?"

I was out of Hank's office door in two strides. My parting shot was unfair. The officers in the bullpen were probably finishing paperwork after their shift and working overtime without pay.

Hank's department served a population of 14,000 people, with fewer than fifty deputies. Half the number per capita of a larger city. Caleb stepped out on a limb when he assigned round-the-clock surveillance on Dad. But now, thanks to Hank, my effort to protect my father had disintegrated.

Maybe Dad had grown tired of waiting for me to return and slipped off to a favorite fishing spot. Off the top of my head, I could think of at least three within walking distance of his house.

Caleb caught up with me halfway to the elevator. "Hank pulled Brenda away because we got a call about a fatal traffic accident a half-mile from your dad's place.

I punched the elevator's down button and didn't bother with a reply.

"The caller claimed people were thrown from their vehicles and lying on the side of the road. Made sense to send Brenda, five minutes away, to deal with crowd control and wait for the ambulance."

How long did it take a damn elevator to ride two floors? I bypassed the elevator and took the stairs three at a time. Caleb stayed on my heels.

In the foyer, he grabbed my arm. "Wait. I need to tell you something."

I hesitated at the front door. "What?"

"Brenda just called in. There was no accident."

The realization the call had been a ploy doused the last of my anger. The call was a way to get Brenda away from Dad's house. "Send a copy of the call to GBI Agent Justin Cramer. Ask Cramer to run a voice match against Jed Thompson."

"Justin Cramer's your GBI contact? He's the agent who cut Ethan's deal?"

"Yeah? Small world. And call Brenda. There's a chance we may need her dogs again to track Dad."

I took off for my truck at a sprint. I skidded, turned back. "And put out an APB on Jed Thompson. I rattled him earlier. He knows I suspect he killed Grace." I ran full-out for my truck.

On the fifteen-minute drive home, I told myself Dad was fine. He only went fishing. He'd be back home when I arrived, threatening to skin me for causing an uproar.

But no matter how much I wanted to believe Dad was fly fishing on the river, the fiery eyes of Jed Thompson when I'd said goodbye wouldn't let me.

CHAPTER TWENTY-EIGHT

I FISHTAILED DOWN DAD'S gravel drive and came to a skidding stop three feet from the porch. Sue Ellen sailed from the front door and flew down the steps. "We've looked everywhere. His wallet and cell phone are on his dresser, and his truck is in the garage."

He wouldn't take his wallet fishing. And he rarely remembered to take his phone anywhere. "How long has he been missing?"

"Colleen says she checked on him about ten minutes before I arrived. He was napping in his chair."

"Was he in the house when you got here?"

"I don't know. I went straight to the kitchen with the pie. If he was here, he wasn't napping in his chair. I figured he was in the shed or his rose garden. I dropped off the pie and chatted with Colleen for a few minutes in the kitchen."

Sue Ellen followed me into the house. "Both doors in the shed are open."

"He keeps fishing gear in the shed." Waders, nets, an array of fly rods, his tackle.

"You think he'd go fishing this late?"

"Not ordinarily. But lately..." No need to explain further. Sue Ellen knew the change in Dad as well as I did.

Tears welled in her eyes, and she pressed fingers against her trembling lips.

"We'll find him." My assuring words as much for me

as for Sue Ellen.

I opened and shut the back door, verified the security chime we'd installed worked.

Colleen caught up with us in the kitchen. "I didn't hear the door chime," she said. "Mr. Taylor must've left the house when I put a basket of clothes away. I can't hear the door chime when I'm in the back bedroom." She tugged her bottom lip with her thumb and index finger.

I patted her shoulder. "It's okay, Colleen. Caleb's on the way, and he'll help me search."

"Jackson?" Caleb's voice traveled down the hall.

"Meet me in the shed," I yelled and kept walking.

Dad's storage shed, built to replicate his log cabin, was a twelve-by-twenty room with a concrete floor and open shelves. He stored his lawn equipment and rarely used sports and fishing paraphernalia inside. A few years back, he installed a roll-up door on the back wall to allow easy access for his riding lawnmower.

I stood in the overhead door opening and scanned the yard. If he left for the river by this door and walked straight into the forest, at this angle, no one in the house would've seen him leave. He probably got tired of waiting on me and went fishing. The thought settled my heart into a half-normal beat.

Caleb hurried in. "Brenda's rounding up her dogs. She'll be here inside of thirty minutes."

"I think Dad went fishing."

"Okay. But it'll be dark in thirty minutes."

"I know." I grabbed a floodlight and an old jacket hanging on a hook by the back door. "Can you stay here and wait on Brenda? I'll check out a couple of his fishing holes before we lose the last daylight."

I patted my back pocket, confirmed I had my phone. "Let me know when you head into the pines, and I'll text my location." I sprinted toward the river.

Fifty yards out, I stopped, backed up, and studied the ground. A small section of depressed land had turned muddy during the recent rains.

I slipped my phone from my pocket and called Caleb. "We've got fresh prints." I studied what appeared to be a man's work boot following another print of an all-weather shoe with a heavier tread—the kind of shoe Dad wore.

"Looks like two sets. From the shoe size and depth of the print, both appear to be male." Only one person I knew had a reason to pursue Dad into the woods this late in the day. "You put eyes on Jed Thompson?"

"He wasn't home. We issued an APB but so far, no hits. Jed's father said he left the house five minutes after you and didn't say where he was going."

I'd spent a fair amount of time on the firing range as a teen, back when I dreamed of following in Dad's career footsteps. I was proficient with a firearm, but I didn't personally carry a weapon. "I'm headed back."

After Dad took shots at me, I'd confiscated his Glock and locked it in the storage compartment of my truck. I made it back to my truck, located the Glock, and wasted precious time reloading six bullets into the clip.

I ran a fifty-yard-dash speed all the way to the river. At the bank, I pulled up, sucked in a few ragged breaths, and considered my options. One fishing hole was to the right, the other two were to my left. It was a toss-up which Dad would fish.

I headed left. If I hustled, I could cover the two spots to the north and be back to the middle before Brenda arrived with her dogs.

A prickle on the back of my neck stopped me from calling Dad's name. I couldn't identify my hesitancy other than instinct. I moved inside the tree line and traveled in stealth mode, holding out hope the two sets of footprints had a simple explanation.

The thought of Jed following Dad into the woods festered in my mind and kept my senses on high alert. A half-mile up the bank, built on a wide bend in the river, an old beaver's dam marked one of Dad's favorite fishing spots. By the time I made it to the bridge, the sun had set, and I realized I'd overshot the dam. I wasted fifteen minutes backtracking before locating the spot.

My phone buzzed a text.

12 hour GPS on the Sierra-BLT6893.

The message had an attached map with time stamps. I opened the file. Just as I suspected, the map verified Jed's vehicle arrived at Ethan's car lot forty minutes before he reported the fire.

I forwarded the message to Caleb, pocketed my phone, and searched for a clue that Dad recently stood on the bank—flattened grass, footprints in the damp soil at the water's edge. After two passes and no luck, I waded into the water, turned on the floodlight, and searched the bank.

Dusk quickly turned to night, and the sounds of croaking frogs, chirping crickets, a hoot owl's call, all seemed to cease at once. In the stillness, I listened for a rustle in the grass or a muted footstep. Nothing moved, and within a few seconds, the crickets started up again, followed by the croaking frogs.

I swept the floodlight across the brush one last time, drudged out of the river, and moved on. At this section of the river, the water ran swift, and walking the riverbank without a flashlight would be treacherous. Since Dad left during daylight, it was doubtful he'd packed a light.

Maneuvering back into the tree line, I continued north. A heavy layer of pine straw, coupled with a blanket of pine cones, turned the ground uneven and made walking difficult. If I kept up my sprinting speed, it'd be a miracle if I didn't turn an ankle.

I headed for a spot roughly a quarter mile north. A flat

rocky path led to a sizable rock island in the middle of the river. Dad considered the area a prime fishing hole. Wildlife also favored the spot and gathered by the river's edge in the early mornings and late afternoons. Over the years, I'd seen deer, fox, coyotes, bobcats, and once a brown bear with her cub.

A rumbling conversation filtered through the air, and I darted further into the forest using the trees as cover. I allowed my eyes to adjust to the dimmer light, but dark clouds overhead had delivered a black starless night. I could barely see two feet in front of my face, much less the ground.

Fumbling with my phone, I turned my back to the river and texted my location to Caleb. I slipped the phone in my back pocket and, without the moon or stars as a guide, crept forward following the voices.

My heel hit something slippery and slid. I swung my arms and somehow managed to grab the trunk of a tree before I face-planted.

"Where are you taking me?" Dad said. "If you're lost, we can call for help."

I went ice cold and overheated all at once. Dad might sound calm and unconcerned to anyone else, but I caught the nervous edge in his tone.

"I'm not lost. Just keep moving." I recognized the voice of Jed Thompson. Knowing the man who'd bludgeoned a helpless woman to death had followed Dad into the woods steeled my spine.

"It's late. I need to head home," Dad said.

"You're not going home, Sheriff." Unlike Dad, Thompson's calm tone held an eerie finality.

The steel in my spine grew teeth. I drew my gun, plastered my back against the bark of the nearest tree, blocking all sound but the voices growing closer.

A beam of light swept left to right, shining a path on the edge of the water. Squinting, I could barely make out the faint outline of two bodies. I inhaled a deep breath, held it, and took aim.

I slowly exhaled and lowered my weapon.

Dad and Jed were too far away to risk a shot. And I wanted Jed close enough to see my gun before demanding he step away from Dad. I eased up to the next tree. Leaves rustled to my right, and I froze. I slowly turned my head and eyed a buck five feet away.

The deer snorted.

Jed's head whipped in my direction.

CHAPTER TWENTY-NINE

THE BUCK SNORTED, and the beam of Jed's flashlight swept in my direction.

I huddled close to a pine, offering the smallest possible profile. Using the beam as a guide, I kept my gun aimed at Jed.

The buck snorted, flagged his tail, and sprinted further into the woods. After a few seconds Jed centered his light back on Dad.

Relief swelled in my chest. Dad had taken advantage of the diversion and sat on a downed tree limb. Did he feel my presence? Was he giving me a chance to intervene?

"Get up." Jed pulled on Dad's arm.

Dad's free hand slapped over his heart. "Can't." He drew a ragged breath. "Need a minute."

My momentary relief erupted into alarm. A heart attack? I flexed my knees and readied my legs to sprint forward. But my head screamed *Wait*. This could be a ploy.

Jed mumbled something I couldn't hear and moved closer to Dad. He switched off his light and my view went black.

I swung my spotlight up and braced my forearm against the tree. Too dangerous this far away to bathe them in light. But I had no choice. I needed to hear Dad speak, verify he was okay. Blood rushed through my head, and I forced myself to fine-tune my focus, concentrate only on their voices.

I stared into the dark. Jed wouldn't follow Dad into the woods without a weapon, but if I turned on my spotlight, it'd give me the few seconds I needed to cross the space between us.

But what if Jed used Dad as a hostage?

That kind of thinking would paralyze me. I pushed it aside. I had to get closer. Find my opportunity and strike.

"Without you, they can't prove I killed her. You're the only one who knows the bat is mine." Desperation rang through Jed's voice.

I slid to the next tree, then the next, each step gave more definition to the shadows. Dad still sat on what must be a downed limb. Jed treaded the ground in front of him like a lion stalking prey.

"Son, killing me won't keep your secret safe." Dad's voice sounded strong and calm. Not someone suffering a heart attack.

"With you out of the way—"

"Did you know Grace?" Dad asked. His timbre smooth and consoling.

My father was a talented and trained interrogator. He had the ability to slip information from people so gently they hardly knew the words crossed their lips.

"I *loved* her." Jed's voice broke. Was he crying?

I used their conversation to buffer the sound of my approach and eased forward. One step, stop, listened. Another step, stop, listen.

"Ethan's a cheat and a crook. Grace deserved better," Jed said. "You said as much the day you found me at his car lot."

"What day was that?" Dad sounded genuinely curious.

I risked another step.

"Ethan Benton didn't deserve a woman like Grace." Jed was inside his memory. It was as if he hadn't heard Dad's question.

I eased forward another six inches.

"There's bad coursing through everyone's veins," Dad said. "Doesn't matter. What matters is what a person does with the bad. They either control the bad, or the bad controls them."

"Grace would've come back to me if she hadn't gotten pregnant." Jed sat on the far end of the limb, his gun pointed at Dad.

"Grace was pregnant?"

"I saw her go inside the building and followed her. We argued, and she admitted she was pregnant." Jed still wallowed in his memory.

"Is that why you killed her?"

"I loved her so much."

"If you loved Grace, why'd you beat her to death?" Dad adopted an accusing tone. Switching tactics was a tricky technique and could elicit anger. Not a problem in a precinct setting, but here in the open without protection, not a smart move. Jed was younger and stronger and could easily overpower Dad.

Jed's back faced me, so I risked another step. The sound amplified in my ears, and I held my breath.

"I didn't mean to hurt her," Jed whined. "I just wanted her to listen. She wouldn't take my calls. Wouldn't talk to me."

Not the first time I'd heard a criminal playing the role of victim to explain uncontrollable anger.

"If you didn't mean to hurt Grace, why'd you have a bat in your hand?"

"I don't know—" Jed's voice broke again. He appeared to be slumped over in the shadows as if a boulder balanced on his bulky shoulders.

"Did you set the fire before or after you killed Grace?"

"After." Jed's tone now thin and strangled. "The camping fuel was in my trunk. I'd planned on burning Ethan's business the day you found me. Remember?"

"I remember." I couldn't tell if Dad was lying to keep Jed talking or if he remembered the incident.

"I didn't remember that you'd touched Dylan's bat until I heard the police considered you a suspect."

"The bat blocked your tackle box," Dad said. "You had to remove it to get the fishing tie you wanted to show me."

"The last one Dylan tied. You held the bat that day."

"You followed Grace into the building with a bat, and you must've worn gloves. You planned to hurt her."

"No. I just wanted to make her talk to me. That's all."

My heart couldn't keep up this pace for long without bursting.

"I wasn't looking at cars the day you found me at Ethan's car lot," Jed continued, "I was looking for Ethan."

"Because he and Grace were dating?"

"I couldn't stomach the thought of a Benton putting his grimy hands on Grace. Dylan's death killed my mom."

"Your mother died of cancer."

"She was never the same after Dylan came out of rehab. Blamed herself for his addiction."

"Why would she blame herself for your brother's cocaine addiction?"

"Mom opted out of chemo. She went to Texas and stayed with my aunt. My aunt had cancer years back and a holistic doctor cured her. Mom decided to go that route. It was after she left that Dylan was arrested. By the time she got home, Benton had stuck Dylan in rehab for six months."

"Rehab was an easier sentence than six years in a state prison."

"Something happened to Dylan in that clinic!"

"It's not reasonable to blame Judge Benton for a suicide death."

"It's his fault Dylan died. Dylan was a different kid after rehab. Sullen. Depressed. Nothing like the boy before he went into that clinic."

"You can't turn your brother into a walking angel. He liked to party. My deputy busted him for cocaine."

"What high school kid doesn't like to party? I should've kept a closer eye on him."

"You can't blame anyone for Dylan's death—not you, not your mom, and not Judge Benton."

"I'm telling you, before going into Whispering Pines Dylan was happy." Jed's voice turned low and threatening. "He wasn't a brooding teen with no friends. He was popular. He played All-State football and basketball, and baseball. He wasn't the kind of mixed-up kid to use a gun to end his life."

Dad offered no rebuttal.

After a few seconds, Jed heaved a long sigh. "After Dylan died, Mom lost any desire to live. She refused to take any more treatments. Wouldn't go to a doctor." He rested his elbows on his knees—the shadow of his gun dangling from his right hand.

I gauged the seconds Jed would need to rise and move behind Dad.

"It was Dylan's first offense," Jed said. "But instead of probation, Benton sentenced him to six months. He could've given him thirty days." His voice grew choppy and angry. "Even sixty days. But six months? Benton killed Dylan. And he killed my mom."

Jed's reasoning came out of left field, but I knew realism rarely reared its head in crimes of passion.

"Son, I know you're hurting. But your father's hurting, too. And you're the only family he has left." Dad's tone turned soft and comforting as if a madman's gun dangling thirty inches from his chest held no power.

"Dad is all I think about. That's why I came to find you. Everyone knows you've got Alzheimer's. Won't be long before you're a walking zombie. You won't remember anything."

The cruelty of Jed's statement sent a line of heat up my spine and into my head. I slid closer until the outline of their shadows grew clearer.

"Won't hold up. I didn't know Grace. And why would I frame Ethan Benton?"

Jed swung his gun toward the water. "The answers to those questions won't matter if you drown in the river. Everyone will assume you jumped. Assume you're guilty." Quick as a heart's flutter, he re-aimed the gun barrel at Dad's chest. "If you die, things will die down. People will believe you killed Grace. Everything will go back to normal."

"No one will believe I killed Grace."

"They will, if you drown yourself."

"I'm no stoolie." Dad sprung to his feet and took off. "I'm going home."

Dad was ten feet away by the time Jed lumbered to his feet. "I told you, you're not going home. You're never going home again."

"You'll have to shoot me then." Dad kept walking. "And a bullet in my back destroys any idea of suicide." Dad's voice grew more robust with each step.

My best chance at saving Dad was to jump behind him and block Jed from taking a shot. Come on, Dad. Just thirty more feet.

"Are you coward enough to shoot a man in the back?" Dad's tone came close to taunting.

"Stop, or I will. I swear I'll shoot." Jed half-sprinted after Dad.

Dad was ten feet away. I needed just a few more steps.

"Your choice," Dad said. "But know Jackson won't stop until you're behind bars for the rest of your life."

Jed slowed to a stop. His brief indecision widened his separation from Dad and gave me the opportunity I needed. Gun drawn, I switched on my floodlight and rushed forward.

Blocking Dad, I aimed at Jed's chest. "Drop your weapon."

Jed stumbled back. Used his hand to shield the beam of my light. The faint chorus of baying hounds flew above the trees.

"It's over, Jed. The dogs you hear are leading a search party. It's time to lay down your weapon."

He stared into the light, then his face crumpled and tears streamed over his cheeks. "Doesn't matter. My life is over. Benton stole it when he sentenced my brother to Whispering Pines. That place stole the life out of Dylan, and Dylan's death stole Mom's soul. Ethan stole Grace. I have nothing left."

"Your life isn't over." I extended my hand. "Give me your gun." I walked forward.

"Jackson, don't." Dad's voice no more than the faintest wind in my ear.

I set the floodlight on the ground, and walked forward.

Jed dropped his gun to his side. "I dreamed of marrying Grace." He stumbled back a step. "Why'd she do it, Jackson? Why would she give Ethan Benton the child that should've been mine?"

"Jed, look at me." I waited until his eyes met mine. "Give me your gun."

He glanced down at my outstretched hand, then met my gaze again. I was close enough to see his face, the indecision in his eyes.

"Give me the gun."

Something in his flat, direct stare resonated.

He raised his gun, and I reached forward.

Jed swept his hand up, pressed the barrel to his temple.

I shot forward. "No, Jed. Don't!"

"Tell Dad I'm sorry."

I dove, aimed for his arm. "Nooo!"

A gun blast cracked the air.

Jed's knees buckled, taking us both to the ground.

CHAPTER THIRTY

THE ACTING CORONER of Pine County, Dr. Lucas Simmons, pronounced Jed Thompson dead at two-ten AM Thursday morning.

Caleb offered to give Dad and me a ride home, but Hank pulled rank and insisted he'd do the honors. He took advantage of the twenty-minute drive to spew apologies for pulling Brenda off Dad's detail.

Dad and I finally tumbled into bed a little before four o'clock. I slept like a petrified log for the next twenty hours.

Then, Kendra called.

"You must've been sleeping." Her bright and cheery chirp hit my foggy brain with an irritating thud.

I rolled on my side, found my watch on the night-stand—eleven-fifty. Since the room was dark, I reasoned it was close to midnight. I switched on the lamp. "Can this call wait until morning?"

"This is too important to wait."

My brain still too fogged to respond. It was best to let Kendra ramble this late at night. She'd get to her point eventually.

"I have an offer for your half of the business.

"Another offer? You post an ad or something?"

"Of course not."

"Two offers in three days seems—"

"Don't be an ass. Besides, this one is better than the

last. You'd be a fool not to take it."

I placed my phone on speaker and pulled on a pair of sweats. "Email the offer, and I'll get back to you with my answer."

"When?"

"Tomorrow."

"Promise."

"Yes."

"Night."

With zero chance of going back to sleep, and my stomach as hollow as a beach ball, I went in search of food.

I found Dad sitting at the kitchen table drinking coffee and playing a game of Solitaire. He wore the plaid pajamas Mom bought us for our last family Christmas photo. His cuffs were frayed, and the once vivid green and red colors had washed to pale.

I realized, and not for the first time, mourning a loved one was a personal journey. My pair of Christmas plaid pajamas lay at the bottom of my dresser drawer, as bright as the day Mom gave them to me. The photo of the three of us in matching plaid—Mom hiding her bald head with an intricately tied scarf, and Dad and me sporting overly bright smiles—was carefully tucked under my pajamas. Some memories were too painful to see every day.

I let the memory wash over me, then packed it away with all my memories of Mom and said, "You keep drinking coffee, and you'll never get to sleep."

Dad waved away my warning. "Coffee doesn't keep me awake."

"Me, either." I poured a cup and joined him.

"I can't seem to sleep more than six hours straight." He placed the king of hearts on a stack of cards, then the ace of spades, and finished off the stack of hearts with the ace.

"Looks like Lady Luck's sitting on your shoulder."

"Some call it luck. I call it skill."

I snorted a laugh. "Deal a hand of Rummy, and we'll

see how skilled you are."

Dad shot me a winning smirk. "You up for a shellacking, boy?"

"Keep talking, old man." I opened the pantry, grabbed potato chips and chocolate chip cookies.

"Check the oven. Colleen left a shepherd's pie."

"God bless her." I removed the pie pan from the oven, plated a cold slice, and popped it in the microwave. Thirty seconds later, I savored steak, mushroom gravy, and whipped potatoes piled under a slightly soggy crust. "Have you tried this?" I asked, between bites.

"Went back for seconds about an hour ago, would've had thirds, but Sue Ellen's pecan pie was calling my name."

I scarfed the rest of my shepherd's pie, then foraged through the refrigerator for the pecan pie before carrying a slice and a fresh cup of coffee back to the table. I picked up my cards.

"Read 'em and weep," Dad cackled. From the gleam in his eye, he had a handful of face cards, or he wanted me to think he did. Rummy was serious business in our family. Unfortunately, reading Dad's face while playing cards was near impossible.

With a lot of effort, I managed to give him a run for his money in the first set, but by the time the sun rose, Dad had beat me three games out of five.

While he made a fresh pot of coffee, I looked over Kendra's email. "I have a decent offer for my half of Taylor and Vines." The proposal included a buyout offer of forty thousand for my interest in the office building, and two hundred eighty thousand for a fifty percent share of the business. Kendra was right; a profit of a hundred and twenty grand *was* too good to pass up.

The coffee finished brewing, and Dad poured two cups, sliding one in front of me before sitting. "You sure about leaving Atlanta?"

"I'm sure about moving home, but there's a snag. Mathew Finn's not interested in adding an associate. He says there's not enough business in Loblolly for more than one attorney."

"I suspect Mathew's got a point."

"I guess I'll make a few inquiries in Blakeley. Maybe the district attorney's got an opening."

"Blakeley's quite a step down from Atlanta."

I shrugged. "Options are limited. I'll make a nice profit on the sale of the law practice, and if I sell my house, I can afford to take a cut in pay."

Dad nodded, sipped his coffee. "You know, there's more than one way to practice law."

"Sorry?"

"With Hank retiring, Pine County needs a new sheriff."

"Caleb, or Brenda—"

Dad shook his head. "Both fine deputies but not sheriff material. Caleb needs more experience under his belt, and I talked to Brenda before I left. She's planning to put her twenty years in and retire."

"Governor has to have someone in mind." I'd always thought at some point I'd try for a judgeship, but a county sheriff—

"You know the law as well as anyone in the state."

Jesus. He was serious. I leaned back against my chair, sipped my coffee, and tried on the idea—ran it around. The thought of stepping into Dad's career shoes hadn't seriously crossed my mind since before I started law school. "I don't know if I'm cut out for it."

"I watched you work Ethan's case, and you're a natural detective. Logical and methodical—you have good instincts. More importantly, you trust your gut. Those are the traits of a good lawman."

I rose, cut the last two slices of pecan pie, and brought them back to the table. "Hank might not like being pushed out."

Dad forked a bite of his pie. "It was Hank's idea. He stopped by last night to apologize again for pulling Brenda off security detail. Says he's ready to turn in his badge and spend his days on the river fishing. He floated the idea of you taking over. Says you've got lawman in your blood. I agree."

I had to admit, I did enjoy investigative work. Ethan's wasn't the first murder case I'd solved. As a prosecutor, I'd dropped charges on multiple defendants based on the evidence I'd collected. When the detectives complained their hard work had been tossed aside, I gave them my theories and pointed them towards the guilty perps.

"So Hank would put in a good word?" I asked.

"Not that I think you need it, but yes, he would. Although it's Vernon and Sandra Benton who have the governor's ear. I imagine they're feeling a heap of gratitude right now."

"You and Hank wouldn't be behind the text from Sandra asking us to dinner tonight, would you?"

I took one look at Dad's face and had my answer.

He rubbed his chin. "You know, now that you mention it, I think Hank might've said something about talking to the senator."

I laughed. "I think I've been had."

I gave the okay for Cramer to release Ethan a day early. The next afternoon I paid him a visit.

He answered the door with a smile. He offered his hand, then spotted the black book I held, and stepped back. "Glad you stopped by. I want to thank you for everything."

I walked through the door.

He led me down the hall and into the library. "I just

poured a bourbon, you interested?"

I glanced at my watch. "Three-thirty in the afternoon is a little early for me. And this isn't a social call."

"You dropping off a bill?" He eyed the book in my hand, raised an eyebrow.

"Actually, I am." I slid an envelope out of the book. "Along with some news."

He tossed the bill on the bar, then carried his drink to a brown leather sofa and sat.

I remained standing. "Hank's retiring."

"About time."

"The governor offered me the position."

Ethan's eyes widened to small saucers. His surprise appeared genuine. "Really? Huh. And you're actually interested?"

"I am. In fact, I've accepted."

I wouldn't describe Ethan's expression as shock, but it was close. "Well, I'll be damned. You finally caved in to your old man after all."

I overlooked the jab and held up the black book. "You and I need to get a few things straight. Just because I don't believe in putting a man behind bars for a crime he didn't commit doesn't mean I won't bring charges against you if you step out of line. And make no mistake, I'm watching you."

We locked eyes, but after a few seconds, his gaze slid away. "You saying things are going to be different now that Jackson Taylor's back in Loblolly?" His tone didn't carry a full-on taunt, and I knew I'd gotten his attention.

"I'd say that about sums it up." I held up the black book. "Don't make the mistake of thinking we're friends."

He nodded.

I tucked the book under my arm. "I'll see myself out."

I found Dad in the rose garden snipping his Dolly Parton buds. I suspected he had plans to see Sue Ellen tonight. He looked up, smiled. "Hank called, said it's official." He stuck out his hand. "I'm real proud of you, son."

I gripped his hand and pulled him into a hug. "Thanks, Dad."

We stood beaming at one another for a few seconds. "I only have one condition before being sworn into office."

"What's that?"

"You have to agree to come back to work and show me the ropes."

He waved me off and stuck the rose in his hand in a blue bucket. Focusing his attention on a white rose bush, he began dead-heading. "You don't need me to show you the ropes, you've got Hank."

"Hank wasn't the sheriff for the last twenty years."

He stopped snipping, turned, and faced me. "Jackson, my memory is failing me more every day."

"Maybe so, but you still know more about Loblolly and the people in this county than anyone I know. I'm asking that you help me for as long as you're able. We'll share the office."

"There can only be one sheriff, son."

"Then you can be my assistant. Or a deputy, or a volunteer. Heck, you can be whatever you want, as long as you agree to show me the ropes."

He snipped a few more dead roses. "I'll agree to volunteer for a few months."

Relief seeped through my heart. "I'll take it." I stuck out my hand and forced his shake.

A man's word is his bond, he'd said to me more times than I could count.

He grabbed his bucket of blooms and started for the back door. "You hungry?"

"Starving." I hurried to catch up.

"How about a sandwich?"

I slung my arm over his shoulder. "You got any bologna?"

DON'T MISS THE NEXT MYSTERY SUSPENSE THRILLER FROM VERONICA MIXON

Bringing down a crooked judge
is the definition of danger!

Purchase **To Trap a Thief** today:
https://amzn.to/3SgsXr8

\

ACKNOWLEDGMENTS

Once again, I extend my heartfelt thanks to my ARC team. I truly could not publish my books without you! Thanks to Marie, Pam, Winette, Danielle, Denise, Katy, Connie, and a special thanks to Katelyn, Jennifer and Ann, the three women brave enough to read first drafts. I adore you all!

Veronica Mixon

Captivating suspense with an air of mystery and small town intrigue...

ABOUT THE AUTHOR

Join My Email List For Updates On My Books!
www.veronicamixon.com

VERONICA MIXON IS an Amazon chart-topper who writes suspense and contemporary book club fiction. She has authored eight books, all set in the South, except for one international thriller.

A career in marketing, twenty years of world travel, and a large and boisterous southern family supply her with ample material for the fiction novels she loves to write. She lives on the Georgia coast with her husband and two-year-old Australian Labradoodle, Fiddler.

You can find a catalog ofVeronica's work on her Amazon author page or her website at: *www.veronicamixon.com*

Manufactured by Amazon.ca
Bolton, ON

35368273R00155